GROWING LIGHT

Who wanted George Ashby dead? Who didn't? Anne Munro is thrilled to land a job at Growing Light, a New Age software company in rural California. But the company's lax atmosphere veils an unconventional cast who have only one thing in common: they hate George Ashby, their control-freak leader. Ashby soon gives Anne reason to hate him, too. After the discovery of his corpse, she must prove that wielding a knife is not a skill she left off her résumé — and clear her name by finding the real culprit.

MARTA RANDALL

GROWING LIGHT

Complete and Unabridged

LINFORD
Leicester

First published in Great Britain

First Linford Edition
published 2020

A catalogue record for this book is available
from the British Library.

ISBN 978–1–4448–4376–7

Published by
F. A. Thorpe (Publishing)
Anstey, Leicestershire

Set by Words & Graphics Ltd.
Anstey, Leicestershire
Printed and bound in Great Britain by
T. J. International Ltd., Padstow, Cornwall

This book is printed on acid-free paper

Dedication:
This one's for Caitlin

Acknowledgments

Unlike the State of California, Lake Harris County, including its topography, geology, and history, exists only in the author's imagination. Likewise, all the characters in this book and most of its institutions (living, dead, or undetermined) are entirely fictional and do not represent anyone or anything existing in the real world (living, dead, or undetermined).

Computers, however, do exist, and the author wishes to specifically thank Robert Bergstresser, computer maven extraordinaire, for his help with the digital details and other useful suggestions. I also want to thank Pat Ellington, of Ellington & Thompson Antiques, and Jamie Hildreth, EMT, for their invaluable assistance. Any mistakes here are entirely my own, and made despite, and not because of, their excellent advice.

The author also wishes to thank the

members of the Third Saturday Gourmet Fiction Society, who tire not, neither are they are mute.

Prologue

Memo time, George Ashby thought with satisfaction, and tapped on his computer keyboard. Outside his door, the building was silent, his staff having long since departed for the night. George stretched while the computer screen flashed a variety of colors and finally cleared to a pale amber, with a deep green cursor pulsing in a corner. He had chosen the color scheme himself and was so pleased that he insisted everyone in the company use it. It had to be good for them, after all — soothing amber, on which words appeared in the deep green color of life.

Let's see, Carein first tonight, he thought. Thursday nights were always reserved for memos to the staff and updates in personnel files, and were perhaps his favorite time of the week.

'Good progress with self-actualization, but watch need to overcompensate for lack of nurturant outlets,' he typed. 'And tell Max to get to work on time, he's obstructing the process.'

He read this over and, satisfied, called up another file. He always printed out the memos before he left on Thursday night, so that each employee would find them on the message wall on Friday mornings. *TGIF indeed*, George thought. *Work is life*.

'Mike — forget it. Insisting this way is non-accomplishing and obstructive. Shut up.'

George saved this one too, and typed a brief note to Jimi in engineering; a line to Cynthia reminding her to re-order replacements for the aura sensors; a demand that Brian in marketing order new copies of the installation manual. This wasn't really Brian's responsibility and the note would make him furious, but he just had to learn, George thought, that in this company, George was the boss.

He cleared his screen, thought a moment, then turned away from the computer to grab pen and paper.

'My precious Audrey,' he wrote, grinning. 'It's over. I think you have learned enough now to go on to greater self-esteem and potentiation by yourself. Sunday night at my place, we'll go out and celebrate your graduation into the real world.' He paused for a moment, then added, 'Bring your diaphragm.'

He scrawled his initials, then sealed the paper into an envelope. Of course, all the memos were properly sealed before they went up on the memo wall. Privacy, as he told his staff over and over again, was a thin line away from self-centered negativeness, although it did involve issues of respect and esteem that could not be overlooked. A difficult position to take, he knew, but he had never been one to shy away from difficult positions.

Like the Audrey thing, for example. It was definitely time to end it. The girl was sweet and certainly compliant, but it was time for George to move on. Still, he might be able to get some last good out of the arrangement. Grinning even more broadly, he turned back to the computer and started another memo.

'Max! Come pick up extra system, my house, Sunday 8 p.m. No excuses!'

He looked at that, then underlined and bolded the word 'excuses'. Finally, satisfied, George Ashby sent the whole batch to the printer. Mike would be in bright and early the next morning, and would find and seal the memos for him. He stretched his arms up and rocked his head between them, working out the kinks. Mike had left a clipping for him on the message wall this morning, about how the recession would be over soon and computer software would really take off. *What recession?* George thought. Sure, jobs were hard to come by, but it only meant that his staff had to display the loyalty and trust that made for true inner growth. The upcoming 1990s, George knew, were going to be a great, great decade.

Pleased with himself, George Ashby turned off his system, clicked off the lights, and bicycled home.

1

Anne Munro stood in the cluttered reception room, clutching her packet of writing samples and resisting the urge to smooth back her hair. *Confidence*, she told herself. *You're the best they've ever seen. Oh dear and merciful powers that be, please let me get this job.*

A partition divided the reception room front to back. From its other side, she heard a young woman giggling into the phone. Anne tried not to eavesdrop, but the young woman's voice was so loud that ignoring her was impossible.

'I mean, he's all, it's a semi-formal affair and I'm all, you mean he's gotta wear a tie or something and he's all, yes, we expect that since Mr. Ashby is accepting this award that — oh, yeah, it's like in his desk or something.'

Anne shook her head and slid one finger along the bottom of the samples packet, assuring herself that it was all in one piece. A few farm trucks rumbled along the road outside, and she thought about the gas station in Melville, a couple of miles back. With luck, she'd have enough gas left to reach it, once this interview was over. And with more luck, the two dollars in her purse would buy enough fuel to get her home. She sent up another brief but forceful prayer as a plump blond man in bluejeans stuck his head into the reception room.

'Ms. Munro?' He thrust his hand at her. 'Mike Thompson, vice president. George Ashby will see you now.' He eyed Anne's business suit with disapproval.

'Fine,' Anne said, shaking the proffered hand.

Mike Thompson led the way from the cluttered room down a narrow and equally cluttered hallway. 'You're here for the technical editing job,' he said over his shoulder, side-stepping a pile of brown boxes.

Anne nodded, then said, 'Yes, I am.'

Thompson didn't respond. Anne followed him along another corridor whose walls seemed to double as a message board. Bright red tape divided the walls into squares, each square bearing a name and hung with colored self-stick notes. As they passed one square, Thompson's hand arched along the wall, collecting his own messages.

He pulled open a door and stood aside. 'Here we are. Mr. Ashby, here's Anne Munro. She came.'

'Huh? Oh, great, come on in,' said a muffled voice. 'I'll be right with you.'

Anne took a breath, put on a smile, stepped inside, and stopped.

The room was empty. Not of boxes, books, and teetering stacks of paper, piled atop surfaces and in corners, but certainly empty of George Ashby. A computer screen glowed from a stand behind the desk, pulsing with a moving array of color which reminded Anne of the lava lamps so popular during her college years. A mural of forest glades and star fields competed with more self-stick notes, a yellowed software flow chart, and a bookshelf heaped with magazines and computer manuals. A partially open door in the far wall exuded steam, the smell of soap, and a voice which said, 'Have a seat.'

'There's a chair over by the desk,' Thompson said, wedging himself into the room. Anne followed a narrow aisle between boxes and paper piles. At the end she found the promised chair and sat in it. Thompson stepped over another series of piles and, pushing a mass of papers aside, perched on the edge of the desk and stared at Anne's suit again. She held the writing samples against her jacket.

'Is something wrong?' she said.

'We at Growing Light aren't into formality,' Thompson said. 'We believe that starched clothes lead to starched thoughts. Mr. Ashby said that.'

'I see,' Anne said.

'We believe,' Thompson said, still inspecting her suit, 'in the free and unstructured flow of ideas.'

'We certainly do,' a voice behind Anne announced. She rose as a man whipped into the room, hand outstretched.

'George Ashby,' he said, pumping her hand. 'Glad you made it.' Still in possession of her hand, he moved around the desk and held onto her a moment longer, staring into her face, before releasing her fingers and sitting. His dark graying hair, knotted at his nape, framed a generous bald spot, but mustache and goatee were both coal black. His eyes were a pale blue, and stuck out.

'Your résumé — Mike, where's her résumé?'

Thompson shrugged. 'I gave them all to you.'

Ashby glanced at the clutter on his desk top, then planted both elbows in the heaped papers and leaned forward.

'Well, it was interesting, very interesting. What can you tell us about yourself?'

Anne blinked. 'Well, I have a degree from San Francisco — '

'In what?' Ashby said.

'History. But I've had quite a bit of experience as an editor. I think most of it is in the résumé.'

'I find,' Ashby said, 'that résumés don't cover what we really need to know, Ms. Munro. We have a very unusual business here. Do you know about us?'

'I'm afraid I don't know much — '

'Don't be afraid,' Ashby said. His smile revealed very white, very even teeth. 'But go on.'

'It's simply a figure of speech,' Anne replied. 'You produce a software package, but that's all I — '

'Growing Light is much, much more than that,' Ashby declared, finally breaking eye contact. 'Growing Light is an integrated hardware and software package, of course, but we also believe that Growing Light is a way of treating people, a way of working that is very different from the — ' his hands chopped an imaginary staircase from the air, 'from the structured, hierarchical modes you find elsewhere. We're a team here, Ms. Munro, a very special team.' The imaginary staircase, erased with a flick of the fingers, was replaced by an imaginary balloon. 'In many ways, we're trying to re-define what 'working' means.' George Ashby sat back, staring at her again.

'That's very interesting,' she said after a moment. 'I understand you're looking for a technical editor?'

'*And*, Ms. Munro — ' He stuck a

forefinger in the air. ' — a member of our team.' The forefinger carved a circle. He paused expectantly.

'I see,' Anne said.

'We have written material,' Thompson said. Anne glanced at him, but he was staring at Ashby. 'Manuals, guides, brochures, very interconnected and integral to — '

'But I *don't* believe in job descriptions,' Ashby said, interrupting him. Thompson pressed his lips together. 'I think,' Ashby continued, 'that people work best when they find the things that expand their consciousness, that let them . . . ' His arms opened to the universe. ' . . . grow. Intention is all, Ms. Munro. Without it, nothing else matters.' He leaned back. 'Mr. Thompson was hired as a site technician, but he wanted to do management work, and now he's the vice president in charge of our daily operations. And he does an excellent job.'

'Mr. Ashby gave me a chance to believe in myself,' Thompson said solemnly, 'and I ran with it. I would never have come so far if he hadn't made space for me.'

'Mike — that is, Mr. Thompson — has been doing all our technical writing,' Ashby said. 'But of course, his talents take him in more useful directions. Don't they, Mike?'

Thompson shrugged. 'We are growing very quickly,' he told Anne. 'We need someone with the desire to keep up with us.'

'I see,' Anne said. 'I'm sure you noticed, from my résumé, that I haven't held a paid position as a tech editor. But I've done quite a bit of volunteer and freelance editing work. I have samples, if you'd like to see them.'

'Excellent,' Ashby said. Anne lifted the writing samples across to him. He took the package and dropped it on the desk, causing another paper quake. Thompson went around the desk to look over his shoulder.

'Excellent, excellent,' Ashby muttered, flipping quickly through the pages.

'Mr. Ashby is a speed reader,' Thompson said without looking at her. Anne smiled.

'Very impressive,' Ashby said. 'Mike?'

He offered the binder. Thompson took it and returned to the edge of the desk, where he held the binder in his lap and resumed staring at Anne's suit. She quelled the urge to stare back at his paunch.

'You mentioned manuals and brochures,' she said.

Ashby smiled. 'Everything,' he said. 'We produce hardware and software manuals, user documentation, installation guides, in-house manuals, a newsletter, update reports . . . ' His hands carved a turret of papers in the air. 'It's teamwork, you understand, but we need someone to mentor the process, to shape a cohesive sound, a special feel that says immediately, 'This is Growing Light.''

'I understand,' Anne said. 'Many companies have style formats — '

'No, not a format,' Ashby said. 'I don't believe in rigidity, Ms. Munro.' More chopped stairs, which fattened into circles as his hands invoked ideas. 'I want this to flow from who we are, an organic, natural process that's part of — part of our own definition of ourselves. Yes. I want a feel, a touch, a sense of who we are and what we mean.' The hands, momentarily still, bracketed a triumphant smile. Thompson, however, just scowled.

'And,' Ashby continued, 'I want that sense to be part of everything we produce here, from the manuals all the way to team memos. I need a team worker who can develop that. Can you do that, Ms. Munro?'

'I believe that I — '

'But the important question, Ms. Munro . . . ' Ashby leaned so far forward that he almost rested atop his desk. 'The most important question *is*, Ms. Munro, do you really *need* this job?'

Anne leaned away from him and stared back, wondering if George Ashby had heard a single word she'd said. California was still mired in recession, and Anne had to juggle mortgage payments, Danny's school clothes and child care costs, the grocery bills, the ancient pump in the well house, the drip in the kitchen roof, insurance bills, taxes . . . She took a deep breath and nodded.

'Yes, Mr. Ashby. I really need a job.'

Thompson snorted. 'What are your salary requirements?' he asked.

Anne looked at him. 'Well, in San Francisco a technical editor makes a fair amount. Of course, I know that salaries are lower here. But I am experienced, and,' she said with manufactured confidence, 'I am very good at what I do. Certainly it would depend on benefits.'

'Flex time,' Thompson recited. 'Profit sharing. Medical and dental benefits. A week of paid vacation to start.'

'And you set your own schedule,' Ashby said. 'We don't believe in rigid timetables, as long as you put in forty hours a week. People with children appreciate that.'

'I can see why,' Anne said. 'I do have a young son.'

'Our benefit package includes child care,' Thompson said. 'People seem to like that.'

'Good. Is that full medical and dental coverage?'

'Absolutely,' Ashby said. 'We pay your premiums, and you can use the benefit plan to cover your dependents.'

'That sounds fine,' Anne said. 'In that case, I think about thirty thousand a year would be adequate.'

Ashby and Thompson looked at each other: Thompson triumphant, Ashby satisfied, Thompson surprised, Ashby smug, then Thompson's face went blank. Ashby rose.

'Well, good talking to you. We'll discuss you with our personnel committee. Mr. Thompson, find someone to give Ms. Munro a tour, would you? Ms. Munro, thank you very much. We'll get back to you.'

Anne shook his hand, trying to ignore the cold lump in her stomach. She followed Mike Thompson into the corridor.

'He's in a hurry,' Thompson said. 'He's going to accept a major award.' This time his stare was very serious, and directed at her face. 'The world is beginning to acknowledge his vision.'

Before Anne could reply, Thompson had stuck his head into the next room. 'Ms. Baker! Do you have a minute?'

'No,' an irascible voice replied, followed by an irascible face. 'What now?' Ms.

Baker wore leather pants, a sweatshirt with Albert Einstein's face across its front, and a number of improbable colors in her hair.

'This is Anne Munro. Show her around.' Without waiting for a reply, Thompson went back into George Ashby's office and shut the door. The door re-opened immediately. 'And make sure she gets to run Growing Light,' he said.

'Yeah, sure, okay,' Ms. Baker said to the closing door. She turned to survey Anne, hands on hips. 'You been hired?'

'No,' Anne said. 'I just interviewed.'

Ms. Baker laughed. 'Quite an experience, isn't it? I'm Cynthia Baker.'

'Anne Munro,' Anne said, shaking her hand. 'Are you management too?'

'We're all management here,' Cynthia said. 'I'm the senior site technician. You know, when the customers can't figure it out, I do it for them. Come on, we'll start at the back and work our way to the front. And when that's done, I'll sit you down with Growing Light.'

2

The tour took less than fifteen minutes. The company occupied two huge spaces, divided into a maze of hallways and cubicles by seven-foot-high movable partitions. The only separate rooms seemed to be along the northern wall, where Ashby and Thompson had their offices.

One cubicle, larger than the others, functioned as a computer hardware laboratory; 'Research and Development', Cynthia called it. A very tall man hunched over an exposed circuit board, and a younger man with a blond braid and nervous eyes poked at a computer keyboard. Another space, divided by file cabinets, contained what Cynthia described as 'marketing and site technicians, that's me.' The shipping clerk had a commodious room to himself. And everywhere, computer screens glowed, either pulsing with lava-lamp colors or jumping with brightly colored icons.

The tour ended in the staff lunch

room, where Cynthia offered a cup of coffee.

'Or tea — are you the herbal tea type?'

'Coffee would be great,' Anne said. Here, finally, a large window looked out over the rolling northern California countryside. Anne cradled the coffee cup between her palms and stared, appreciating as always the sweep of green hills dotted with rounded native oaks, the shapes of cows in a distant pasture, the higher hills to the east that walled away the rest of the state.

She and her husband had moved north almost three years earlier, after Jeff's Aunt Caroline died and left them her home in tiny Lake Harris County, north of Marin and south of San Antonio Creek. They drove up for the funeral and fell in love with the quiet farmlands and rolling hills of the county; Santa Bolsas, the major city and county seat, numbered less than twelve thousand citizens, and farm tractors still, by county law, held right of way over any other vehicle. Even Highway 101, the north coast's main arterial, skirted the county by a good two miles, and the citizens were known for sneaking out to the highway periodically and ripping down any signs that even hinted at the county's presence. But modems, fax machines, and overnight delivery kept Jeff in touch with his clients, and San Francisco was barely two hours way.

For fifteen months it seemed like paradise, until the auto accident on the Cotati grade that had left her a widow alone with a small son, a mortgage, and no income. Life without Jeff had been difficult, but over the months she had learned to make it by herself, to create a home and a life for herself and Danny. Throughout it all, the countryside infused her with a sense of peace and permanence and strength, and she leaned briefly on some of that strength now before turning her back to the window and smiling at Cynthia Baker.

'Everyone seems very busy,' she said. 'I hope the tour didn't interfere.'

'No way,' Cynthia replied. 'Everyone who even drives down the road gets a tour. We're used to it. What job are you applying for?'

'Technical editor,' Anne said.

'Jeez, no wonder Thompson looked like he ate a lemon,' Cynthia said. 'Well, God knows we need an editor — everyone knows it, except Mike. They hire you?'

'I don't know,' Anne said. 'Mr. Ashby said he'd take it to the personnel committee.'

Cynthia made a face. 'That's George and Mike. Talk about a fifty-fifty split.' She smiled, a wide, friendly grin. 'Well hell, that's one thing about working here. You never get bored. What's your background?'

Anne started to explain when a telephone on the long table squawked.

'Ms. Baker? Are you in there?'

'Yeah,' Cynthia shouted at the machine.

'There's a call from Boz Wilson, he's all, 'I still can't get behind the rain sensor hookups.' Could you talk to him? He's really, like, off the wall or something, and I just can't, you know, communicate with him.'

Cynthia rolled her eyes. 'Jeez, Audrey, all right. Put him through to my desk, okay?'

A brief pause ensued.

'You're supposed to call me Ms. Lincoln, remember?' the telephone said reproachfully. 'Mr. Ashby said that we have to share our self-esteem and use last names so everyone will feel respected and . . . '

'Crap,' Cynthia Baker said. 'Listen, buzz Karen and ask her to come show Ms. Munro the software, will you?' The phone didn't reply. 'Ms. Lincoln,' Cynthia added.

'Of course,' the phone said.

'And put Wilson through to my desk. Please. Ms. Lincoln.'

'I'd be happy to,' the phone said, and clicked off.

Cynthia rolled her eyes. Sunlight painted green and purple highlights in her hair.

'Last names?' Anne said.

'Crap,' Cynthia said again, and stalked out of the room.

Anne took another sip of her coffee. The wall clock, decorated with glow-in-the-dark stars, read three-fifteen: she still had plenty of time before she had to pick up Danny at daycare. A mural of redwood trees and ferns, decked with a few tattered self-stick notes, flowed around the clock, and in the quiet Anne heard a soft murmuring which sounded very much like surf. Surf? Growing Light's office was at least ten miles from the Pacific. After a moment, she realized the sound came from yet another computer, on a desk in a corner. She rounded the desk and found the ever-popular lava lamp display but no prompt, or message, or any other indication of what to do about it.

'Ms. Mallow?'

'Munro,' Anne said, looking toward the door. The woman had graying hair in a knot, soft and flowing clothes, laugh lines around the eyes. Framing each cheek was a cluster of antique sterling buttons, suspended on individual sterling chains and refitted as earrings.

'Oh! Sorry, that's what I heard. I'm Carein Forest. That's spelled C A R E I N, get it, care in? I'm supposed to show you the system, are you thinking of buying it?'

'No,' Anne said. 'I'm here for a job interview.'

'Oh.' Carein stopped. 'Whose job are you taking?'

'I beg your pardon?' Anne said. 'I'm a technical editor. I thought you didn't have one . . . '

'Well, that's all right then,' Carein said, and smiled. 'That's something Mike, uh, Mr. Thompson did; I guess he could use a little help. Here, sit down and let me share Growing Light with you.'

The next half hour went by in a blur of amazement. The lava lamp, it turned out, was a stand-by screen, used whenever the program was either inactive or processing behind the scene. Clicking the computer's mouse brought up Growing Light's main menu.

'It's really simple to use,' Carein said enthusiastically. 'See, what it does is help you run your plantation — I mean, a farm or a garden, just about anything that you want to grow, really. It ties the software in with all these neat sensors; you can see the wires heading right out the window, right there. See? The sensors measure temperature, and humidity, and rainfall, and hours of sunshine, and you can have lots of them, like say if you have a place where you get ten hours of sunlight one place and only about two somewhere else, it can keep all of that straight for you. So you set up the computer and the sensors, and then you do the setup menu, here, see?'

The user interface had obviously been written by an icon-iphiliac. The setup menu stepped through factors from latitude (a circle with horizontal lines) and longitude (another circle with vertical lines), through altitude (an arrow rising from the ocean), distance from large bodies of water (an arrow pointing away from a wave), the last ten years' weather patterns . . .

'We can provide a database tailored to your particular area,' Carein assured her. 'It only costs a little extra. And once you've got all the stuff about the land in, then you tell the system all about yourself.' She moved the mouse cursor to a happy face, and clicked on the grin. 'Here, when's your birthday?'

'Early May,' Anne said.

'Great, you're a Taurus. So, you just float the mouse over here . . . ' Carein paused. 'Some people talk about dragging the mouse, but we just don't like the feeling of that, too, you know, well . . . ' She shook her head sadly, as though the proper disapproving word simply wouldn't come.

'Negative?' Anne suggested.

'Hey, that's pretty good.' Carein glanced at her with admiration. 'I'm not really great with words and all that, I mean, not like writing and stuff. Well, it goes like this.' The mouse cursor slid around astrological symbols and clicked on a bull. The screen lava-lamped into a new set of icons. 'What's your rising sign?' Carein said.

It took Anne a second to realize what she wanted, and another second to realize that she had no idea.

'I don't really have a lot of time,' Anne said.

'No problem,' Carein assured her, floating the mouse out of the setup screens. 'But we also have a module where you just enter your birthdate and time, and it'll pull in all your astrological data for you. Isn't that neat?' She floated the mouse toward an icon of a seed.

Anne watched as Carein pattered and floated her way through vegetable or flower options. Growing Light provided a compatibility list keyed to the area, weather patterns, sunlight and temperature range, and Anne's astrological sign, with suggestions for planting times and a series of icon-decked boxes to fill in as she completed the planting. Carein announced that if the program knew Anne's rising sign, it would suggest not only types of vegetables, but specific hybrids.

'It even tells you when to water, and how much,' Carein assured her. 'And right now George — I mean, Mr. Ashby — is working on this wonderful module to share your biorhythms with the system, so that you and your garden are perfectly attuned all the time. We're already tuned in with the phases of the moon, of course. And,' she added breathlessly, 'we're working with a guy in Berkeley to add a module tying in all your past lives, too.

Won't that be great!'

'Amazing,' Anne said. 'Uh, do you sell a lot of these?'

'Thousands,' Carein said. 'Mr. Stein, our marketing person? He's even talking about an east coast office. I just think it's so great that this sort of system, and consciousness, you know, is finally really getting shared all over the country. I've known George, I mean Mr. Ashby, for, oh, since the sixties, you know, and I always had faith in him. I just knew he'd change the world. And he is! Or, at least, the way people grow stuff. And that's really the key to everything!' She looked at the doorway and glowed. 'It's just so great, Mr. Thompson, isn't it?'

'It's revolutionary,' Thompson agreed, as George Ashby pushed him aside. He had added a hand-painted tie to his sports shirt and tan work pants, and carried her writing samples under his arm.

'Ms. Munro, I think we're all agreed,' he said, offering his hand. 'Can you start on Monday?'

'Monday?' Anne repeated. 'Start work?'

'Sure, we think you'd fit right in with

our team. I've got to run, Mike will fill you in on things. Oh, here.' He dumped the writing samples on the table. 'See you Monday,' he said, and rushed out the door.

'Welcome to Growing Light,' Mike Thompson said, shaking her hand and staring at her jacket.

'Thanks,' Anne said. 'Uh, the salary — '

'It's all been worked out. Just show up on Monday and we'll find you a desk. Eight o'clock, Ms. Munro?'

'Eight o'clock,' she echoed, as visions of poverty receded. 'Thank you, Mr. Thompson. Thank you very much.'

'Ohhh!' Carein said. The cascades of her sterling button earrings twinkled as she bobbed her head. 'You're going to be so happy here, I can just tell!'

3

Ed Beckson was trimming the hedge along the lane when Anne pulled into her driveway. Danny caught sight of him and started to tug at his seatbelt.

'Gonna see Ed,' he announced, but by the time she pulled the key out of the ignition, Ed was already tramping through the clutter of low pines and roses that separated their property. When Jeff and Anne had moved in after Aunt Caroline died, the Becksons had shown them a distant friendliness. Lake Harris County, the neighbors let it be known, did not welcome strangers, but the Munros were treated well because Aunt Caroline had, after all, been born in the county, and that made Anne and Jeff almost, but not quite, natives. When Jeff died, however, the Becksons had taken Anne under their wing. By turns compassionate, stern, gentle, and meddling, Ed and Millie Beckson had brought Anne through the worst of her grief, and fully into the community. On nights when she couldn't sleep, she thought about that with gratitude, and mourned that Jeff had never been part of it.

Now she untangled Danny from the harness and opened the door, letting in the crisp December wind. Danny made a beeline for the old man. Ed set down a brown paper bag and scooped the boy up, swinging him high into the air. Danny shrieked with happiness.

'Afternoon, Annie,' Ed said. Danny grabbed him around the neck and delivered a full-bore, five-year-old hug.

'Danny, don't strangle him. Ed, they hired me! I'm going to start on Monday.' Anne clutched her writing samples to her chest and beamed.

Ed smiled back. 'That editing job? That's great, Annie. Oh, here, before I forget. Millie says you should have these.' He pinned Danny with one arm and reached for the brown paper bag. 'Want me to bring 'em up for you? It's steaks.'

'Ed!' Danny said urgently. 'Wanna go fishing?'

'Steaks?' Anne repeated. 'That's very

generous, Ed, but why?'

'Carl went and told Millie what you and Danny here had for dinner last night,' Ed said. 'Now, I don't like sticking my nose in neighbors' business, but Millie says you've got to feed the boy better than that — '

'Ed!' Danny insisted.

'But he likes macaroni and cheese,' Anne protested. 'With hot dogs. And salad.'

'Millie said bring 'em over, I brought 'em over. Carl workin' out okay, back there?'

'I suppose,' Anne said with exasperation, taking the bag. 'When he's not ratting on me to his aunt.'

'*Ed!*' Danny howled. 'Let's go fishing!'

'Maybe this weekend, son.' Ed peeled Danny off his neck. 'If it's okay with your momma.'

'If it's okay with the weather, you mean,' Anne said. Ed nodded and tramped back through the roses, and Danny waved before following Anne up the graveled driveway.

Danny held the screen door while she juggled papers and bag and keys, then darted in before her. The aroma of fresh biscuits and thick stew filled the air, and for a moment she stood frozen in the doorway, overwhelmed by such a sudden wave of longing for Jeff that she lost her breath. *He's not here anymore*, she told herself angrily, slammed the door, and marched into the kitchen.

Carl Neilsen, Ed's nephew and tenant of Anne's back cottage, stood in front of Anne's stove, wearing one of Anne's cotton aprons, and wielding one of Anne's cooking spoons over Anne's middle-size cast-iron kettle. Anne glared.

'Did your stove break?' she demanded.

Carl attempted to look nonchalant. 'No. Just thought I'd fix you and the boy some dinner.'

'Oh. So that we don't starve on a diet of macaroni and cheese?'

Carl put the spoon down warily. 'You talked to Aunt Millie,' he guessed.

'No, *you* talked to Aunt Millie. Millie talked to Ed. And now I have you in my kitchen and every soul in the area knows what I do and don't cook for dinner.' She dumped her papers and the bag on the kitchen table.

'It wasn't my idea,' Carl said. 'Aunt Millie just about marched me in here — '

'Well, what made you think you ought to — '

' — shame on me if I let a widow lady starve — '

'*What?*'

' — you think this is *my* idea?' Carl concluded.

'Uh, Mommy?' Danny said, tugging at her skirt.

'What is it, pickle?'

'Can I watch *Sesame Street*, please? Are you mad at Carl? Can I have some macaroni 'n' cheese? Please?'

She opened her mouth, then looked at Carl. Carl shrugged.

'I tried to tell her,' he said. 'Honest. She's a very determined woman, my Aunt Millie.'

Anne rolled her eyes, then smiled. 'She made Ed bring over some steaks,' she said. 'I'll set the table, okay?' She put the steaks in the freezer.

'Sure. Dinner's on in ten minutes.'

Carl went back to the stew. Anne peeled Danny out of his jacket and turned on the television, leaving the boy happily communing with Oscar the Grouch and Telly Monster while she quickly changed into jeans and a sweatshirt, and went back to the kitchen. Carl had just pulled a pan of biscuits from the oven and was expertly pitching them into a cloth-lined basket.

'Got the leak fixed in the pumphouse,' he said. 'I put the receipt for the washers on the counter.'

'Good.' She lifted two bowls from the shelf, then added another. 'You're going to eat with us,' she said.

Carl frowned. 'I don't know if Aunt Millie would consider that proper.'

'If she's going to insist that you cook, she'll just have to accept the results,' Anne said, and finished setting the table.

Carl had moved into the small building in back of the main house a year ago, when Anne decided that she had to find a tenant for the place. Ed and Millie had tried to talk her out of it, worried, as Millie put it, about a young widow alone with a little boy and some stranger on the property. Sometimes it seemed, Anne thought with annoyance, that Millie's favorite word was 'widow'.

The small building had been a work-shop originally, then probably a storage room, and Aunt Caroline had used it as a den and garden shed. Anne and Jeff had gutted the building, insulated it, and installed a small bathroom and kitchen, planning to use the building as Jeff's consulting office. After Jeff died, Anne hid herself in the work, as if completing the plans that she and her husband had made would somehow excuse or explain his death, even if it couldn't restore him to her.

Anne wasn't eager to have anyone living out back, but money was scarce and renting out the back building was the obvious solution. Jeff's life insurance had paid off most of the mortgage, but the bank refused to renegotiate the remainder of the loan.

'We're sorry, Mrs. Munro,' the woman in Santa Rosa told her, smiling around an impressive number of very white teeth. 'We'd love to help you out. We are very concerned with the well-being of our clients, you know. But you don't have any sources of income, so we couldn't possibly give you a mortgage on that basis. I'm sure you understand.'

'What I understand,' Anne had told the woman tartly, 'is that because I have no job, you are saddling me with a mortgage payment that I can't possibly meet because I have no job, and since I don't have a job you won't renegotiate it down to something that I could manage; and if I did have a job I wouldn't need to renegotiate the damned mortgage to begin with.'

The woman's teeth momentarily disappeared, but returned quickly. 'I'm so glad you understand. Well, if there's anything else we can do to help you,' the woman said, rising, 'please give us a call. After all, we're here to serve.'

Anne fumed about that for days, but there was no solution. Jeff's parents survived on a fixed income that seemed to buy less and less each year, and her own parents were dead.

Selling Jeff's practice brought in enough to invest, but the interest was not enough to live on.

'Sell the house and rent instead,' one advisor told her. 'You'll never keep up with repairs by yourself anyway.'

'Hold on to it,' her tax accountant insisted. 'If you sell, you can't afford to buy another place. Besides, that house is your only real asset.'

But the most important argument was Danny, who had taken his father's sudden death with anguished bewilderment. Holding on to the house, and the country neighborhood with its long, quiet lanes and friendly people, was part of keeping Danny's world together. Anne shopped at the thrift stores, bought sweaters and turned down the heat, silently thanked God for Danny's taste for macaroni and cheese, and decided to rent out the back building.

Ed and Millie were aghast. They warned and grumbled and complained, then introduced Carl as a prospective tenant. His mother was Ed's sister Ginny; he worked at Evvie's Café on Main Street in Santa Bolsas, just down the road. He'd been to college, and he could keep an eye on the place, help fix things up: doing all the husbandly kinds of things, Anne thought, that Millie wasn't convinced Anne could do on her own.

But she had to admit that the arrangement worked out well. Carl's job kept him out of the house from five in the morning until mid-afternoon, and he spent the rest of the time puttering around the place, fixing leaky faucets, tending the small coop of chickens, and working in the garden or on his collapsing pickup truck. In return, she charged him a lower rent than normal, but even the little bit helped, especially when she added up the money she wasn't spending on plumbers and carpenters. This, however, was the first time he'd offered cooking services. Anne wasn't sure she'd allow it to continue, but the stew was delicious, and Danny declared it good and dug into it.

'How'd the interview go?' Carl asked, passing the biscuits.

Anne grinned. 'I got the job. I start on Monday.'

'Terrific. Look like a good place to work?'

'I think so. They make a software and hardware thing to manage gardens — maybe even farms, I'm not sure yet. They're all very, well, New Age, you know what I mean?'

Carl shrugged. 'What is it, get in tune with the whales sort of thing?'

'I suppose — I don't really know,

either, but I'm sure to find out. The company is called Growing Light.'

'Oh,' Carl said. 'I've heard that name before.' He frowned. 'It'll come back to me, sometime.' He offered a biscuit to Danny. 'What do they do?'

Anne explained the Growing Light system, or as much of it as she could remember, while Carl's eyebrows rose.

'Does it really do all that stuff?' he said when she finished.

Anne shrugged. 'I suppose so. They told me they've sold thousands of these things.'

'Oh yeah?' Carl said. 'And the government says this ain't a recession, too. Wait'll Uncle Ed hears about irrigating by past lives!'

'Oh, Lord, don't tell him,' Anne said. 'He'll tell Millie, and there'll be hell to pay.'

'Hey,' Danny demanded, emerging from his dinner. 'Don't you want to know about my day? Huh?'

They spent the next ten minutes talking about the intricacies of kindergarten and what Mrs. Prizwalski said in daycare when Jackie painted Auralia's face with glue and then Penny stuck feathers and buttons into the glue, and what Auralia's mother said to Jackie's mother and what Jackie's mother said back, and what Mrs. Prizwalski muttered when she locked the glue away and what did that word mean, anyway, huh?

By the time they finished eating, Carl couldn't suppress his yawns. Anne said she'd clean up herself, thanked him for dinner, and sent him out. He paused at the back door.

'I remember where I heard that name, Growing Light,' he said sleepily. 'A few folk get together every Tuesday morning for breakfast at the café I think they used to work there. Can't remember anything else, though.'

'That's interesting,' Anne said, distracted by a teetering armload of dirty dishes.

'Got the impression they didn't like it much,' Carl continued. 'Well, nobody likes an ex-boss, know what I mean? If I hear anything else, I'll let you know, okay?'

'Yes, fine,' Anne muttered, and waved goodbye with her elbow. 'Oh, Carl, thanks again.'

'Don't thank me,' he said. 'Thank Aunt Millie.'

Anne deposited the dishes in the sink, rinsed them, and went to spend the next hour with Danny, before it was time for bed.

4

Anne always enjoyed driving through the Lake Harris countryside, especially in the morning when winter sunlight washed through the native oaks and alien eucalyptus. Low gray clouds filled the sky, promising rain. California wildflowers had emerged from their summer sleep, dotting the roadways with gold and lavender and red, and sheep grazed along the hilltops. A few sleepy commuters drove east on the Santa Bolsas-Melville Road, heading through the narrow pass and across the county line into Sonoma County and the junction with Highway 101 south of Petaluma. The junction was marked only by a sign a quarter mile north that proclaimed the end of the highway, and another one a quarter mile south assuring motorists that the highway had miraculously sprung into existence again; the junction itself was the intersection of a two-lane blacktop with the whizzing four lanes of 101, and terrified Anne every time she negotiated it.

Once on the highway, commuters faced the long, clogged drive down through Marin County to San Francisco. Passing them on her way west to Melville and Growing Light, Anne felt smug. She had spent the weekend calculating, and assured herself that although the pay scale in Lake Harris County might be lower than elsewhere, the money she'd save on commuting alone would help. Not to mention the money she'd save on clothes, considering how people dressed at Growing Light. Certainly the pay was better than what she had made at her last job before the move to Lake Harris County, clerking at Alicia's antique shop in Berkeley. She smiled, remembering the tiny shop spangled with sparkling crystal and the smooth shine of porcelain.

A tractor chugged down the lane ahead of her. She slowed for it, and when it moved over to let her pass, she waved. The man in the tractor tilted his baseball cap amiably.

Hand-made signs outside the small

town of Inez assured her that the Inez 4-H Club welcomed her to their village. Originally the town had been called Santa Inez, and its easterly neighbor Las Bolsas, but an early federal postmaster had confused the two and refused to rectify the error. As a result, Inez became desanctified and her larger neighbor became, absurdly, Saint Bags.

A mile or two further on, the road narrowed even more and started to climb the hills that bracketed Lake Harris County to the west. Dairy cows watched her curiously as she downshifted for the climb toward Melville.

Downtown Melville, what there was of it, was already awake. At the intersection of Melville and Bloomfield, people lined up for breakfast at a small, plant-decked café; a little further on, two people clung to power poles, stringing a banner across the road. FREE THE LAKE HARRIS THREE, the banner read. Anne grinned, remembering the three activists from the Poultry Rights League who had been arrested for sneaking into the poultry exhibit at the County Fair and freeing the

Inez 4-H Club's exhibit of prize Leg-horns. The resulting chaos was intense, as 4-H members chased their fowl through the cow and sheep exhibits and between the carnival booths — Danny had loved it. But a dozen chickens had died, and the kids had been in tears. Anne wasn't surprised to see the banner here in Melville. The town, perched on the western hills near the county border, had always had a reputation for strangeness.

Downtown Melville dropped behind her, and a few minutes later she pulled into the lot behind Growing Light's small building, frowned, and checked the dashboard clock. Seven fifty-five on Monday morning, and save for a dust-covered Volvo, hers was the only car in the lot. She parked beside the Volvo, double-checked the time on her wristwatch, then got out of the car just as George Ashby pedaled into the lot, almost grazing her. She jumped out of the way, clutching her blue canvas tote.

'Excellent morning,' George called, riding in circles around the lot. 'Isn't it?'

'Yes,' Anne called back.

'Nothing like a bike ride to get the blood going,' he continued. 'Great exercise, gets you in touch with yourself again, really fine. You need to drive that car?'

'It's twenty-five miles,' Anne said, surprised. 'Uphill.'

'Oh, right.' Ashby came to a halt before her. 'You live in Santa Bolsas, don't you?' He made it sound like an accusation.

'Outside Santa Bolsas,' Anne said.

Ashby waved this away. 'Mike lives out by the reservoir, and he rides. Every day.'

'Indeed,' Anne said, and hoped she got the inflection right.

Ashby wheeled to the door, unlocked it, and rode inside. 'Come on,' he yelled. As she entered the building, three cars pulled into the lot in quick succession.

'Turn on the lights, will you?' Ashby called, already out of sight. Anne peered at the walls, almost tripping over Ashby's abandoned bicycle.

'I'm sorry, I can't seem to — '

'Here.' He appeared beside her, flipped on a bank of switches hidden in a mural of redwood trees, and disappeared again.

47

'I think Carein found you a desk,' he yelled, his voice getting fainter. 'She'll show you where it is.' A door clicked shut just as Mike Thompson, panting and damp, pushed his own bike through the front door. He wore Spandex shorts that did little to improve his hefty appearance, and a sweat-soaked T-shirt bearing a slogan in favor of world peace.

'He's already in the shower, isn't he?' Thompson muttered. 'There goes the hot water.' He leaned his bike against the wall and stared at her. 'You. Talk to Carein.' Then he collapsed into a chair, eyes closed. A crescent of white belly showed between his T-shirt and his Spandex shorts.

'Are you all right?' Anne said, but Thompson didn't reply. The front door opened again.

'I made the coffee all last week,' a young woman said darkly. 'I mean, like, every day, and I don't even drink the stuff, and that's not, I mean, *fair*, you know? I think people who drink the coffee ought to make the coffee.'

'Jeez, Audrey, nobody asked you to,'

Cynthia Baker said. Her hair this morning was mostly purple with a streak of yellow down the middle. 'What's eating you, anyway?'

'Nothing,' Audrey said. 'Just none of your business. And you're supposed to call me *Ms*. Lincoln.' With that, she marched behind a partition.

'Uh, Cynthia, is Mr. Thompson —' Anne said.

'Oh, hey, good morning,' Cynthia said. 'First day on the job, always a real treat. Carein's got it set up for you.'

'That's *Ms*. Forest,' Audrey Lincoln said. She came back into the room. Flip blond hair, sullen green eyes, freckles, and this time, a strained smile. Cynthia rolled her eyes and disappeared.

'Hi, I'm Audrey Lincoln. And you're, uh, I mean Ms. Forest told me your name and I've just, you know, it's totally slipped my mind!' She shook Anne's hand. She looked, Anne thought, like a petulant high school cheerleader.

'Anne Munro,' Anne said. 'Listen, is Mr. Thompson — '

'Who's making the coffee?' a new voice

demanded. 'All last week it was dish-water, can't anyone make a decent pot of coffee in this place?'

'I'm like sick and tired of making it and everybody's always, this is awful and I don't even drink the stuff,' Audrey Lincoln said furiously. 'So you can like make it yourself!' She retreated behind her partition again.

'Gee, wow, Audrey, thanks for sharing,' the man said, then thrust his hand at Anne. 'I'm Brian Stein, marketing. And you are — '

'Anne Munro,' Anne said. 'I was just hired.'

'Great, just call me Brian.' Red hair, business suit, firm handshake. 'Come on, Anne, I'll get you a cup. Carein won't be in for a while.'

'Last names!' Audrey protested from behind her partition.

'Yeah, yeah, yeah.' He took Anne's elbow and steered her down the hallway. She craned back over her shoulder.

'But is Mr. Thompson — '

'Mike'll be okay as soon as George is out of the shower,' Brian Stein said.

'Happens every morning, you'll get used to it. What the hell's eating Audrey? I guess we'll find out soon enough. Come on, if I don't get to the coffee pot first, it'll be piss poor all day.'

They negotiated a series of corridors, none of which looked familiar, and entered the lunch room. Brian pounced on the coffee maker.

'You're the new tech editor,' he said as he worked. 'I gotta say, we sure as hell need someone literate around here, but I don't envy you.'

Anne turned from the window, where low clouds had turned the view of hills and trees into a soft mist. 'Why not?' she said.

'You looked at the stuff yet? No, of course not. Mike wrote it all, or most of it, and George decided it needs fixing. For once he's right, even if Mike can't see it.' Brian poured coffee beans into a grinder. 'What's he want you to do, exactly?' He pushed down on the grinder's top.

Anne waited until the grinder stopped shrieking. 'I believe he wants me to

51

develop a company style,' she said as Brian poured grounds into a filter.

'Thank God,' Brian said. 'Listen, you just can't succeed in today's market without professionalism. There's just too much competition out there, and unless you can convince the public that your company is solid, that it's here to stay, you don't stand a chance, period. I mean, look,' he said, pouring water into the coffee maker. 'The public's looking for value, for a responsive company, one that's going to be there to take care of them. Especially with computers. The field's littered with orphan hardware and software, and people are getting cautious. You can't blame them, can you?'

'I suppose not,' Anne said. Brian turned on the coffee maker, and it groaned and started trickling brown liquid into the pot.

'Look, a part of all that, you know, marketing the stuff, is the literature. It's gotta look professional, and stable, and informative. And I hope to God that's what Ashby wants you to do for us.'

'I believe so,' Anne said uncertainly. 'He said something about a style that — '

Brian peered at her. 'You ever done tech editing before?' he said.

'Of course,' Anne retorted. 'And I've also managed small businesses. I know how important it is to be professional.'

'Great.' Brian grinned and punched at her shoulder. 'We gotta have more professionalism around here.' His voice dropped and Anne had to lean closer to hear him. 'I mean, hell, George hires the damnedest people, total incompetents most of them. But between you and me and Cynthia, we've got a fighting chance. Keep this boat afloat, you know?' His voice rose again. 'It's a great opportunity, there's nothing like it. I mean, the market's wide open for this stuff.'

'Well, I'm eager to get to work,' Anne said. 'I even brought my reference library.' She patted her tote, feeling the lumpiness of her purse inside, and the comforting solidity of her books.

'Great.' Brian slid the pot from the coffee maker, emptied it into his own cup, and slid it back into place. 'Cups in that cabinet there. Listen. I've got to go, phone calls, all that. Carein'll fix you up,

53

you know, desk and forms and everything. See you!' And with that, he and
his coffee disappeared into the maze of
hallways.

Anne glanced at her wristwatch: eight
twenty-five already. She wondered just
when Carein would appear, and decided
to wait in the reception area. She looked
at the coffee pot, then ventured into the
corridors.

Three turns later, George Ashby found
her. He clamped a damp hand on her
shoulder and said, 'Let's get some breakfast.'

Anne pulled away. 'I still need to see
Carein . . . I don't even know where my
desk is.'

'Come on,' Ashby said. '*Ms.* Forest won't
be in for another half hour. You drive.'

And so, twelve minutes later, Anne
tucked her canvas tote under her feet and
looked across a Formica table at George
Ashby, who was busy perusing a menu.

'You sure you won't have anything?' he
said.

'Just coffee,' Anne replied. Ashby ordered
a tofu omelette and cup of herbal tea, and

shook his head at her.

'Coffee's not good for you,' he said. 'Caffeine is a poison.' He snapped forward. 'Do you smoke?'

'Smoke? No.'

'Your car smells of cigarette smoke,' he said, blue eyes stern.

Anne squashed the urge to get angry. 'My husband used to smoke,' she said.

'Ah!' Ashby sat back. 'He gave it up. Good.'

'He died,' Anne said. 'Not good.'

Ashby leaned forward again avidly. 'Cancer?'

'Car crash,' Anne snapped. 'Do you mind changing the subject?'

'No need to feel defensive. It's important to get behind your emotions, especially now. Did you love him?'

Anne pressed her lips together as the waitress brought the coffee and tea.

'Mr. Ashby,' she said quietly, 'I loved my husband very much, and I miss him very much. But I think questions like this are insulting and invasive.'

Ashby stared at her. 'Call me George.'

'Not *Mr.* Ashby?'

'We do that at Growing Light to show

respect,' he said, still staring. 'I'm not looking for respect here, Anne. I'm looking for something deeper, something closer to your soul. Work,' he said, 'should be an integral part of life, just like family. I want everyone at Growing Light to feel that they can talk to me, at any time, about anything. I don't feel like a boss, Anne, not the kind of boss you find in most companies. So you don't have to treat me like one, you know, keeping your distance, all that. Remember that you're part of our team now, Anne — a team that's re-creating what 'working' means.'

He sat back as the waitress settled his breakfast in front of him, slid the check under his plate, and went away.

'My wife left me,' he said, and forked omelette into his mouth. 'I think she just couldn't get behind what Growing Light is trying to do.' He chewed sadly. 'I still miss her.'

'I'm sorry,' Anne said.

'Why?' Ashby darted forward again. 'You weren't there, it wasn't your fault.'

'It's an expression,' she said, annoyed. 'Of sympathy.'

'But it's false. Sorry means you think you're to blame. I certainly don't blame my wife, even though she's wrong. If I'm sorry about anything, it's that she's missing this wonderful chance to be part of the future. But that's not my fault and it's not your fault, so don't be sorry.'

Anne almost said 'sorry' again, and instead hid behind her cup. She missed Jeff fiercely. For the first few months, Jeff had been with her every moment, his loss a wound too large to hide or heal. She hadn't been able to care how she appeared to others; then, slowly, she learned to connect to the world again, but only by repressing all thoughts of Jeff until she could flee home, close the doors, and release the locks on her mind. This last year, finally, she seemed more able to live in her own body, to get through most of her days and some of her nights without the constant knowledge of Jeff's absence.

Now this thin, intense man had re-opened the wound. She sipped at her coffee, distancing herself from the familiar mix of pain and anger. She put the cup down and took a final, calming breath.

'So how did you start Growing Light?' she said, hoping that this would be a safe topic.

Ashby grinned. 'A stroke of genius,' he said. 'That's what a magazine called it. You can look at it when we get back. Have you ever worked for a large company?' He waved, not waiting for her answer. 'It's grim, life-threatening. There's no room for personal growth, no place for real people to explore themselves. I couldn't stand it. I mean, these places outlaw innovation, they just kill people. I know.'

Anne, remembering her three-year stint as a corporate drone, nodded. 'How long did you work for — '

'So I thought a lot about how it ought to work. People have so many talents, you can't lock them into one rigid system and expect them to do their best. They need to be free, to explore potential, and if you give them a chance to do that, then the company has to thrive. It's all based on respect, Ms. Munro — respect and truth and independence, working together to create something that benefits everyone.' He lifted his last forkful of omelette. 'It's that simple — and that creative.' He ate triumphantly.

'Interesting,' Anne said. 'What about the system, the hardware and software?'

'Ancient history,' Ashby said. 'Never look back.' He pushed his chair back, stood, and dropped money on the table. 'Let's get going, it's late.'

Anne scrambled for her tote and followed him out of the café.

5

It was close to ten o'clock by the time they left, and Ashby promptly rolled the car window down and breathed deeply. A misty gray drizzle invaded the car and sparkled in Ashby's suspiciously black goatee. Anne sniffed, not smelling any cigarette smoke, and thought briefly about asking Ashby to close the window. In the parking lot, she parked between a red Asian econobox and somebody's rusty Volkswagen.

In the reception room, Carein stood talking with Audrey Lincoln. Carein's sterling button earrings were missing; instead, she wore a fabric necklace to which were sewn small silver teacups and spoons. The fabric matched her batik headband.

'Oh, Mr. Ashby.' Audrey put up her hand. 'Mrs. Ashby, I mean Ms., well, Lena's here, she wants to see you, I put her in your office; I hope that's okay.'

Without responding, Ashby disappeared into the maze. Audrey looked at Carein.

'Was that okay? I mean, I couldn't just leave her, you know, right here, not after last time, right? I mean, she's all, 'Where is that bas — ' well, I can't say it, but it's not very, you know, self-actualizing.'

'I'm sure it's fine,' Carein said. She chewed at her lower lip. 'Audrey, are you sure he hasn't called this morning? No message on the machine?'

Audrey snapped, 'Yeah, I'm sure, okay?'

'Yes, of course.' Carein attempted a smile. 'Well, if he does call, I really need to talk to him, okay? Will you let me know if he calls? If I'm not at my desk — I mean, right away?'

'Sure,' Audrey Lincoln said, and headed around her partition. Carein shook herself quickly and smiled at Anne.

'Ms. Munro, I'm so glad you're here. Let's go find your desk, right?'

Anne nodded and followed Carein down the corridor.

'That's a nice necklace,' Anne said. 'I've never seen one like it.'

'Oh, yeah, thanks,' Carein said. She turned around, lifting the neckpiece for Anne's inspection. 'I made it, I mean, I collect antiques. You know, special ones, stuff women used. It's so important not to lose that, you know, our history. Anyway, I just knew these would make a great collar, and it's like wearing past lives, you know?'

'Uh, yeah,' Anne said.

Carein smiled. 'I just knew you'd like it, I felt it in your aura,' she said, and scurried on through the maze.

'I think you're going to like this.' Carein ushered Anne into a closet-sized room. 'Mr. Thompson wanted to give you a desk in the engineering room, but I just know that you need some quiet to be creative, you know? And here you're right across from the mail room, and right down the hall from the lunch room. And look, you even have your own door!'

'That's, uh, great,' Anne said, squeezing around the side of the desk. A computer, in component pieces, lay scattered across its surface; the monitor teetered on an old typing chair. Anne put the monitor atop the system box and sat down.

'Cynthia — I mean, Ms. Baker can help you get behind setting up the system,'

Carein said. 'But if you can get those forms done first, it would be really excellent. Just bring them to me when you're done, my space is right near the front door. Oh, don't take your jacket off — heater's broken again. Bye!'

Anne sat back and closed her eyes for a moment, then reached into the canvas tote and took out a framed photograph of Danny. She looked at it for a moment, moved computer parts out of the way and put the photo in the middle of the desk.

'It'll be all right, pickle,' she whispered to Danny's smile, and started in on the forms.

A few minutes later, Brian Stein squeezed himself into the room and shook his head at the door. Red curls bounced on his forehead.

'Don't close that,' he said. 'They given you the manuals yet?'

Anne put her pen down. 'No. I need to fill out these forms, then I thought I'd set up the system and — '

'Come on,' Brian said. 'This will only take a minute. I think they're in engineering.'

Anne followed him out. 'Maybe you

could answer a question for me,' she said.

'Sure.'

'This probably sounds funny, but — who's my supervisor? I got the impression that Mr. Thompson does most of the writing, but nobody told me who — '

'Quiet,' Brian hissed, grabbing her arm. He glanced through a darkened doorway, then rushed her inside. Anne saw postage charts, meters, scales, and flattened piles of cardboard boxes. She snatched her arm back and frowned at him.

'Listen,' Brian whispered. 'Here's the way it works. George and Mike say there aren't any hierarchies around here, so you don't have a supervisor, okay? Someone gives you work to do, you do it, you give it back. But better give George a copy, no matter what. I mean, manuals, memos, anything; George always gets a copy. But no supervisors, understand? He hates that word.'

Anne shook her head. 'Then who decides if I'm any good or not? Who's responsible?'

'Everybody's responsible,' Brian whispered back. 'That's the point. And look, there's another thing.' His voice dropped even lower. 'Mike doesn't want you here. Hiring you was George's decision, and Mike hates it.'

'But I thought Thompson had too much to do . . . '

'Yeah, but that's not the point. Power's the point, and don't let anyone tell you otherwise.' He pulled back. 'Come on, we can't stay in here.'

He surveyed the corridor, then sauntered out.

'And, whatever you do, don't close your door,' he muttered. 'Makes George crazy. Mike too. Watch yourself.'

The man's paranoid, Anne thought, following him into the corridor that housed engineering. Agitated voices spilled over the top of the partition; Brian stopped and put his hand up, and Anne paused beside him.

'Well of course he'd call you,' a woman said. 'You're, I mean, you work together. If he wasn't going to be in, you're the one he would call.'

'Carein, calm down,' a man replied. 'He called me Sunday morning and said he'd be getting the extra system from George's house that evening.' The voice paused. 'He sounded real up, real confident. I told him to be careful, you know how George was on his case last week, and he said things were going fine.'

'He was supposed to come by for dinner Sunday night,' Carein said. 'He never showed up. He should have called me, he always calls.'

'I'm sorry. Listen, if he calls I'll let you know, okay?'

Brian, looking fascinated, said loudly, 'Knock-knock!' Then he walked around the partition, beckoning Anne to follow.

Carein, standing beside a tall man, looked worried. 'Brian! Have you talked to Max today?'

'Heavens, no,' Brian said. 'What would we have to talk about? Is he missing?'

Carein glared at him and pushed him aside, then paused.

'I still need those forms,' she said to Anne, and marched away.

Brian's eyebrows rose. 'My, my, the little mother is agitated this morning,' he said. 'Jimi, this is Anne Munro, she's our new technical editor. I want to give her the manuals. Anne, this is Jimi Hendrix Johannsen, our chief engineer.'

'Hi,' Jimi said, extending his hand. Anne shook it. Jimi Hendrix Johannsen was extremely tall, extremely blond, and extremely myopic.

'Jimi *Hendrix*?' Anne said.

'Yes, well, I usually don't use the middle part,' Jimi said, but he didn't seem offended. 'The manuals? Which version? I've only got hardware and installation. You know, the shipping versions, and the revised versions, and the ones with engineering notes.'

'Wait,' Anne said. 'How many versions are there?'

Four, Jimi told her, not counting the ones partially annotated by previous engineers, or the software manuals: which, he implied, were the province of another department and about which he didn't particularly care. After some discussion, he provided her with copies of the hardware manual and the installation guide, plus versions with engineering notes, told her to call him if she needed anything further, and turned back to the circuit board on his bench.

'See what I mean?' Brian said cryptically, leading her back to her cubicle and leaving her there.

The desk was full, so in the Growing Light tradition, Anne dumped the manuals on the floor in the corner and went back to her forms.

★ ★ ★

By eleven forty-five she had completed the forms, found a shelf for her reference books and arranged them neatly, and taken half an hour to put the computer together. She adjusted the monitor, tucked her tote bag under her desk, and gathering the forms, went in search of Carein. The partitioned office by the front door turned out to be a small space surrounded by file cabinets and holding two desks, three chairs, four telephones, two computers, and Audrey Lincoln, who looked like she'd been crying. She glanced at Anne, quickly wiped her cheeks, and said, 'Yes?'

'These are for Carein,' Anne held out the forms. 'Is this where she works?'

Audrey sighed. 'Carein left. I'll take them.' Anne put the forms in her outstretched hand, and Audrey sighed again before, with a visible effort, she smiled brightly. 'Technical Editor. Okay.' She looked up. 'I'm bookkeeping and reception. And billing. And all that. I'm sorry about your husband.' The bright smile faded. 'Losing people is tough.'

'Yes, it is,' Anne said. 'How did you know?'

'Mr. Ashby.' Audrey glanced at her watch. 'Is it lunchtime already? You bring your lunch? No? There's a deli down the road. Come on, I'll show you.' She draped a handwoven purse over her shoulder, put on her smile again, and led the way through the maze.

'I need to get my purse,' Anne said.

'Let's sign out first.' Audrey stopped at the message wall, picking up a clipboard. 'You didn't sign in this morning.' She frowned. 'You're supposed to sign in. And pick up your messages. Every morning.'

'I am?' Anne said. 'Nobody told me that.'

'I put a section up for you this morning, after Carein left. See, here it is.' She gestured at a small taped-off square near the floor and sniffed. 'Besides, how am I, you know, supposed to figure the hours if you don't sign in?' she continued. 'You're supposed to sign in when you get to work. Then you sign out whenever you leave the office, I mean the whole office, not just your space. And you write down what you're signing out for. And you're supposed to sign in when you get back. And sign out when you leave, like at night. And pick up your messages. I mean, Mr. Ashby, he's always, communication is very important, and if you don't pick up your messages, then you're obstructing the process.'

'But — '

'I mean, I know you lost your husband and all that, but that's like no excuse for — '

'I beg your pardon,' Anne said. 'Nobody told me about signing in. I'll be delighted to do it now. I didn't pick up messages because nobody told me where they would be. And my husband's death has nothing to do with it.'

Audrey just stared at her. 'Denial,' she said.

'Oh, jeez.' Cynthia Baker whipped around a corner, slid between Audrey and Anne, and took the clipboard.

'Audrey, that's enough,' she said. 'Come on, Anne, lunch's on me. Here, you're not even on the list yet.' She wrote Anne's name on the bottom line, scribbled beside it and beside her own name, and handed the clipboard back to Audrey.

'Good Lord,' she said, and tapped Anne's message square with her foot. 'Do you expect Anne to break her back every time she checks her messages?' she demanded.

'That's *Ms*. Munro,' Audrey protested. 'So like, I'll fix it, okay?'

'Aw, jeez, Audrey,' Cynthia said, and all but dragged Anne down the hall.

'That's *Ms*. Lincoln,' Audrey shouted. Cynthia let the door slam closed behind them.

'You okay?' Cynthia said, glancing at her. 'No, you're not okay. Let's walk to the deli — you don't need your purse, come on, I've got it covered.'

They cleared the parking lot, and Anne pulled away. Cynthia grabbed her arm and shook her head.

'Not yet,' she said. 'Just keep walking, the deli's a block away. Come on, you'll be okay.'

'It's all right,' Anne said. She pulled her arm back and marched down the tree-lined sidewalk. The thin, half-hearted drizzle had let up; across the road, beyond where the pavement swooped into an overgrown ditch, a couple of cows raised their heads to watch them, then returned to their lunch.

'Okay,' Anne said at last. 'Did Carein set me up, or what?'

'No,' Cynthia said. 'Carein's a flake, but she's not nasty. She just forgot because she's worried about Max. He's a sweet kid, but not too stable. Carein sort of adopted him, and now she's upset 'cause he didn't show up.' Cynthia shook her head. 'Jeez, kid probably needed a few days of peace and quiet, and nobody mothering him to death. Look, when we get back, I'll take you through everything, okay? The phones, message wall — anybody showed you where the bathroom is?'

Anne slowed down, and smiled faintly. 'No, not even that.'

'Figures,' Cynthia said. 'And Audrey . . . jeez. Listen, keep track of your hours, I mean by yourself, and double-check your pay. Audrey, well, she's a sweet kid, but she's not real good with numbers.'

Anne stopped. The Growing Light offices were out of sight behind them. 'Not good at numbers? Isn't she the bookkeeper?'

Cynthia nodded. 'Yeah. She needed a job and she said she really wants to expand her life experience to include finances, so George let her be the bookkeeper. I know,' she said, raising her hands. 'It doesn't make sense. So what does? Just ride with it, it'll be okay. Come on, we've gotta keep walking.'

A chilly gust beat down the street. Anne shivered and zipped her jacket closed as she walked.

'I don't know,' she said. 'Look, I really need this job — I've got a kid to support.

But all this . . . '

'Yeah. But once you've figured out the system, it's not that hard. And the benefits are pretty good, especially the health stuff. Did you have health insurance — before?'

Anne shook her head. Her health insurance had expired when Jeff died.

'That's tough,' Cynthia said, and paused. 'Look, I don't want to pry, but — you still got a lot of doctor bills? From your husband, I mean?'

Anne frowned. 'No.'

'I heard it really adds up,' Cynthia said apologetically. 'You know, chemo and radiation and all that.'

'Cynthia, what are you talking about?'

Cynthia looked embarrassed. 'Well, you know, cancer.'

Anne just stared at her.

'Look, if you don't want to talk about it, that's okay.'

'Jeff died in a car crash,' Anne said. 'They don't do chemo and radiation for car crashes.'

Cynthia looked confused. 'But George said . . . ' she said, and stopped. 'Oh, jeez.'

'What?'

Cynthia Baker turned in a little circle, cursing. 'That son of a bitch did it again! Look, Anne, I'm sorry. George told everyone that your husband was a drug addict — '

'*What?*'

'Nicotine. George says smokers are drug addicts. He said your husband died of lung cancer. He said you told him at breakfast.'

'That,' Anne said furiously, 'is a damned lie.' She turned and marched back up the street.

'Where are you going?' Cynthia called after her.

'Where the hell do you think?' Anne yelled back.

Mike Thompson caught her as she stormed in the front door.

'Ms. Munro, we need to talk,' he said.

Anne tried to step around him. 'Later. I want to talk to *Mr.* Ashby.'

Thompson pivoted, blocking the corridor. 'He's busy right now. You can talk to him when we're done, then I'll get him into my office for you. Now, please.'

Not replying, Anne feinted toward his other side, but Thompson was surprisingly quick.

'Ms. Munro, I don't want to say this in the corridor,' he said. 'Please.'

Audrey Lincoln stuck her head around her partition to watch. Anne stopped dodging.

'All right,' she said. She shoved her fists into her jacket pockets and followed Thompson into the maze.

'Listen,' he said, once they reached his office. 'We don't know much about you, but I know Mr. Ashby explained about our team, about how we all have to work together here.'

'At length,' Anne said.

'Well, I'm afraid we have some questions about you,' Thompson said. 'I mean, we don't feel that anger and bitterness help advance Growing Light or our team, or Mr. Ashby's vision of the workplace of the future. We base our company on cooperation and openness and a free and fair exchange of information and concept, so that everyone, no matter what their job, has a right to feel like a valued part of

Growing Light, and — '

'Look,' Anne said. 'I need to talk to *Mr*. Ashby, so just tell me what you want to say.'

'Very well,' Thompson said. 'I'm afraid that we've already had a complaint about you. There's some question whether you're really the right player for the game.' He crossed his arms and stared at her.

Anne laughed angrily. 'You must be joking. I was the first person here this morning, and wasn't even shown a desk until after ten o'clock, and then nobody told me about signing in or signing out, or the message board, and then I hear this stupid, vicious rumor about my husband and — '

'Well,' Thompson interrupted, 'you'll have to accept the truth about it, Ms. Munro. Denial is not healthy.'

'What?' Anne shouted. 'George Ashby lied about my husband's death, said Jeff was a *drug addict*, and if I object I'm in denial?' She took a deep, steadying breath. 'Mr. Thompson, I want to speak to George Ashby and I want to do it *now*. Where is he?'

'In his office,' Thompson said. 'Next door.' He nodded toward a door in the side wall. 'But I should warn you, Ms. Munro, that he does not take kindly to — '

'Neither do I,' Anne said, and opened the door into a damp bathroom. She paused, surprised, then saw the door at the other side and marched through it. Thompson, breathing heavily, followed her.

Thin light from the curtained window and the pulsing glow of the computer screen lit an otherwise dark room. Anne glanced at the haphazard boxes and teetering piles of paper.

'Mr. Ashby,' she called. When no one answered, she turned toward Thompson. He took a quick step backwards.

'Okay, where is he?' Anne demanded.

Thompson spread his hands. 'Mr. Ashby is the president, Ms. Munro. He doesn't have to tell me where he is every minute.'

'Then I'll find him!' Anne headed for the outer door. She stepped around one pile of boxes, turned to avoid another pile, and found George Ashby.

Growing Light's president lay face down on the carpet, one hand tucked beneath him and the other stretched toward the computer. Someone had planted an ornate carving knife in his back, its handle an upright female figure. *Silver*, Anne thought in shock. *And certainly antique.*

'Oh. My. God,' Mike Thompson said behind her, and passed out.

6

Ten minutes later, Lake Harris County deputy sheriffs swarmed over the building, and within half an hour the Growing Light staff was collected and herded into the lunch room, with a deputy standing guard. Anne perched at a corner of the table, cradling a cup of coffee, and watched while two officers outside solemnly encircled the building and parking lot with yellow police barrier tape. The cold drizzle had started again. The coffee in her cup shivered.

'God, you're shaking like a leaf,' someone said. Anne looked up as Cynthia took off her jacket and draped it over Anne's shoulders. 'Hell of a first day on a new job, isn't it?'

Anne carefully put the cup down.

'I keep . . . ' Her voice caught. 'I keep seeing him, with that knife — and then I keep seeing Jeff, afterwards . . . ' She gestured helplessly.

'It's okay,' Cynthia said, sitting and

wrapping her arm around Anne's shoulders. 'Have you seen the paramedic?'

Anne shook her head. 'I'll be all right.'

'Sure you will.' Cynthia grimaced. 'Jeez, I never thought someone would knife the bastard, you know?'

'Maybe poison,' Brian said, agreeing. 'Or electrocution by his own computer. More fitting, don't you think?'

Audrey sobbed louder. 'That's — you're — how can — Oh!' Jimi Hendrix Johannsen patted her shoulder awkwardly.

'Sounds like you wish you did it,' Thompson said where he lay on the table, still recovering from his faint.

'Bull,' Brian said. 'I was at my desk all morning, and so was Cynthia, so we're both clean. Where were you, Mike?'

Thompson snorted and turned his head away.

'I was on the phones all the time,' Audrey said, so alarmed that her sobbing stopped. 'I've got, like, the messages, you know, with times on them and everything. I mean, nobody would suspect me, would they?' She started sobbing again. 'I mean, would they?'

Outside, a county car pulled up and people carrying cases and cameras piled out. They high-stepped over the yellow tape and disappeared around the corner of the building.

'Anybody seen Pete?' Brian asked.

Jimi said, 'God's sake, Brian, you don't suspect Pete, do you? He worships George.'

Brian simply arched his eyebrows and smiled.

'Who's Pete?' Anne said.

'Shipping clerk,' Cynthia replied. 'George probably sent him on some errand.'

Silence, punctuated by Audrey's sobs.

'Has anyone let Lena know?' Cynthia asked.

Everyone in the room looked at her.

'Well, she's still his wife . . . Someone ought to call her, at least.'

'Oh, she knows,' Audrey said. 'I mean, it had to be her, didn't it? She killed him!' Audrey dissolved into tears again.

'Oh, no.' Thompson, still prone, shook his head. 'Not Lena.' But when Brian tried to press him for details, Thompson pushed his lips together. 'Not before I talk to the police,' he said to the ceiling.

'Where's Carein?' Jimi said.

Now everyone looked at him.

'Well, she was here this morning,' Jimi said.

'I don't know,' Audrey sobbed. 'She made a few phone calls and got all uptight and left. And I had to do all her work and I was all alone in there all morning. It's just not right.'

'She went to look for Max,' Cynthia said. 'Everyone knows she was worried.'

'He was supposed to have dinner with her last night,' Jimi said. 'He didn't show up, and he didn't call. And remember how George was down on him all last week?'

'Ah,' Brian said. 'And where, pray tell, is Max?'

For some reason, this caused Audrey to cry louder.

A minor commotion erupted outside. Everyone crowded the window to watch as Carein, clambering out of a battered Toyota, tried frantically to get into the building. One of the deputies took her arm. Carein, in perfect 1960s fashion, went limp.

'Wow,' Audrey said, forgetting to sob.

Two deputies, looking confused, supported Carein into the building. Shortly thereafter, she was ushered into the room. She stared around, her batik headband damp against her disheveled gray hair.

'George is dead?' she said blankly, and Audrey started to cry again.

★ ★ ★

Brian finally arranged to send out for pizzas. They hadn't arrived by the time a second deputy appeared at the door and stood whispering with the first one. The first one nodded at Anne, and she stood as the second one said, 'Ms. Munro? Could you come with me, please?'

'Hah,' Mike Thompson said with satisfaction.

Ignoring him, Anne followed the deputy into the corridor. Someone had stretched more yellow barrier tape along it; the deputy followed the tape through the maze. The hallway outside George's office was cluttered with official-looking people who moved aside to let her enter. The knife was gone from George's back but they hadn't covered him yet, and she looked away.

'Lieutenant Van Damme, it's Anne Munro,' the deputy said.

'Munro,' a compact man repeated. 'Munro?'

'She found the body,' the deputy said.

'Oh, Munro. Correct.' The man extended his hand. 'I'm Gene Van Damme, sheriff's department.'

Anne simply nodded and shook his hand. Lieutenant Van Damme had red hair and a sprinkling of freckles that made him look, Anne thought, much younger than he probably was.

'Good.' He dropped her hand. 'Could you, ah, show me how you found the body? *You* found the body? Correct?'

Anne nodded. 'Mr. Thompson was with me, but I came in first.'

'Okay. Now, you came in from . . . '

'There,' Anne said, pointing. 'The bathroom door.'

Lieutenant Van Damme raised his eyebrows. 'The bathroom door. And Mr. — ah, Thompson was with you?'

She felt her cheeks warm. 'We were in his office. I wanted to see Mr. Ashby, and

Mr. Thompson pointed to that door. The bathroom connects the rooms. So that's where I went.'

★ ★ ★

She spread her hands. 'Today's my first day here and I don't know my way around very well.'

'I see.' Van Damme took her arm. 'If you please — around here.' He guided her through another narrow alley toward the bathroom door. For some reason, Anne had expected that she'd be asked to step over George, and found herself shivering.

'So, you came in through the bathroom, and Mr. Thompson was with you.' Van Damme led her into the bathroom and closed the door. 'Could you show me?'

'Yes.' Anne stepped in front of him and put her hand on the knob. 'It was misty in here, as though someone had just taken a shower,' she told him. 'I opened the door and came in, and didn't see anyone.'

'Ah, okay,' Van Damme said, following

her into Ashby's office. 'And then?'

'I think I said something about finding Mr. Ashby, and went toward the other door, like this.' Anne walked around one pillar of boxes, sidestepped another, and stopped, frowning.

'That's strange,' she said.

'What is?' Van Damme crowded beside her.

'Did somebody move him?' Anne said. 'I'm almost sure his hand, that one, was pointed that way, toward the computer. Not this way, toward the bathroom.'

Van Damme looked at her. 'You sure? Sometimes, you know, the angle is different, or, ah, maybe the shock. Are you sure?'

'I think so,' Anne said. She stared, thinking. 'No, I'm positive.'

'Okay, we'll check into it,' Van Damme said, and the deputy nodded, scribbling a note on her pad. 'Okay, you found the body. And then . . . '

'Mr. Thompson fainted,' Anne said. 'I came around to the desk and picked up the phone.' Van Damme trailed her as she illustrated. 'But I didn't know how to get an outside line, I mean, nobody's showed me how, yet. So I went back through Mr. Thompson's office.'

She turned, but Van Damme held up his hand. 'You can just tell me,' he said.

'I ran to the engineering office and told Jimi Johannsen. He called 911.'

The deputy nodded, still busy scribbling.

'And Mr. Thompson?' Van Damme said.

'I just left him there,' Anne said. 'I didn't think he was in danger. Jimi came back with me, and he checked Mr. Ashby while I checked Mr. Thompson. Jimi said Mr. Ashby was certainly dead, and Mr. Thompson seemed all right, except that he had fainted, of course. Then Jimi said we should make sure that nothing was disturbed, and I agreed, so we stood guard at the doors.' She paused for a breath. 'He stood by the bathroom door.'

'I see.' Van Damme stepped back to look at the body again. 'And did you notice Ashby's hand then?'

Anne thought for a moment, then shook her head.

'Okay. You ever see the knife before?' He held up a large transparent plastic bag. 'Take a look, Ms. Munro. It may be important. But don't remove it from the bag.'

Her stomach felt queasy, but she bit her lip and peered at the knife. Blood covered the blade. The handle was silver underneath a tarnish of age. The figure wore medieval court dress and a small coronet; a cartouche against her midriff held symbols almost obscured by age and dirt.

'That's interesting,' Anne murmured. She looked up. 'Do you have a magnifying glass?'

Van Damme looked at her. 'Why?'

'This cartouche, here on her midriff — there's something on it. I'd like a better look.'

'Landry,' Van Damme said, and a moment later a hand passed over Anne's shoulder, holding a magnifying glass. She took it and bent closer, her initial queasiness forgotten.

'Hard to tell,' she said. 'This looks like a, a rose? And this could be, wait, I'm not sure.' She raised the glass. Under the tarnish, a calm, rounded face surrounded by a circular headdress; the eyes, bracketing a firm, long nose, gazed modestly downward. Anne frowned.

'That face looks familiar,' she murmured. 'And the cartouche — that's the Tudor rose, definitely. And letters, below it? H and C, I think. Yes, intertwined. Henry Tudor then, and she's Catherine of Aragon.' Anne looked across the knife at Van Damme. 'But what was Catherine of Aragon doing sticking out of George Ashby's back?'

Van Damme raised his eyebrows. 'Maybe you could tell me,' he said. 'You've seen this knife before?'

'No,' Anne said. 'I used to work for a friend, an antiques dealer.'

Van Damme just looked at her.

'I was a history major,' Anne said. The nauseous feeling returned, and with it a definite tightness in her chest. Surely this man couldn't believe . . .

'I specialized in it, late medieval, mostly the fourteenth through sixteenth century, royal marriages, all that. I just, well, recognized the symbols, and her face, I'm pretty sure but you know, I'm not an expert or anything . . . '

Van Damme looked at her in silence for a minute, then held out his hand. She handed him the magnifying glass, and he handed it back to Landry.

'No,' she said. 'I've never seen this before.' Her knees felt weak, and she held on to a box to steady herself.

'Lieutenant?' Officer Landry said. 'The coroner's here.'

'Good. We'll get out of his way.' He gestured, and Anne followed Van Damme and Landry out of the room, down the hall, and into Thompson's office.

She told them about the interview on Friday and the events of the morning. Van Damme asked a few more questions about her background and Jeff's death, then rose from behind the desk and stretched, and Landry closed her notebook.

'You'll have to stay until Sheriff Jackson gets here,' Van Damme said. 'Landry will take you back to the, ah, lunch room. Oh, and Ms. Munro?'

'Yes?'

'Thanks for your help.'

Anne nodded and followed Officer Landry out of the room.

7

'Here, I saved you some pizza,' Cynthia whispered. 'You okay?'

'I guess so.' Anne took the pizza and stared at it without enthusiasm, wondering if her stomach would keep it down. In a corner near the door, Carein rocked slowly, eyes closed, muttering under her breath. A collection of self-stick notes on the wall seemed to halo her batik headband. Audrey Lincoln sat beside her, holding her hand and trying to keep up with the muttering.

'Her mantra for serenity,' Cynthia said with no trace of sarcasm. 'They took Audrey after you, then the rest of us. Jimi and Mike Thompson aren't back yet.'

'And they won't let us use the phone,' Brian announced at normal volume. Carein winced, but kept her eyes closed.

'They ain't supposed to,' said a young blond man, turning from the window. He was short, thick, and sported a scraggly mustache and an excessively macho black leather jacket. 'You guys are *suspects*, get it? They think one of you did it. Me, I was off in Novato, I'm clean.'

'Don't be ridiculous,' Brian replied. 'You could have sneaked back.'

The young man didn't seem angry. 'But I got no motive,' he explained. 'I tell you one thing, I get my hands on who did it, the cops ain't gonna have a chance to string him up, 'cause I'm gonna do it first.'

'Violence is *not* the answer,' Carein said, and went back to her mantra. She looked very pale.

'Pete Dixon,' Cynthia told Anne. 'He's shipping. Pete, this is Anne Munro. Today's her first day on the job.'

'Tough break,' Pete said, nodding at her. 'Dontcha worry though, we'll get him. Or her.'

Brian humphed and came over to Anne. He sat on the table beside her, glanced around, and stage-whispered, 'You tell them about being mad at George?'

'Of course,' Anne said. 'It wasn't a

94

secret.' She looked at the pizza again, then put it down. 'I was going to quit,' she said.

'Bad move,' Brian decided, and walked away.

'To quit, or to tell them?' Anne said.

Cynthia shrugged. 'You start adding up all the people who've been mad at George, you're gonna end up with a long list. You better eat that, Anne. No telling how long they're going to keep us here.'

'Me, I ate in Novato,' Pete said. 'I got the receipt and everything. George always pays me when I gotta eat on the road.'

'Well, don't rub it in,' Brian said. 'He certainly didn't reimburse anybody else's business meals.'

Pete gestured that away. 'George was always straight with me, you know? Whoever done him, they're gonna regret it. Gonna be real sorry,' he added with relish, and turned back toward the window.

'That's gross,' Audrey said suddenly. 'I mean, you know, you sound like you're *happy* that George was, you know, like it's some sort of game, and . . . '

She started sobbing again. Carein looked upward, then put her arm around Audrey's shoulders and clucked at her.

'Hey, look,' Pete said. 'Sheriff Jackson's here.'

Everyone crowded the window. Outside, reporters and photographers clustered around a black-and-white, Sam Jackson's famous Stetson visible over their shoulders. The group moved across the yellow police tape toward the front of the building, leaving the tape in tatters behind them. Two deputies started stringing it up again.

After that, things seemed to happen very quickly. A deputy escorted Jimi Hendrix Johannsen into the room, followed by another with Mike Thompson. The deputies stayed by the door, arms crossed, staring at the ceiling. Thompson glanced triumphantly around the room and appropriated a chair.

'Well?' Brian demanded.

Jimi shook his head. 'Nothing much. I just, you know, told them where I was, and what I did. That's all.'

'Hah,' Mike Thompson said. 'The sheriff's here. Things ought to start moving now.'

'That's why folk elected me,' Sam

Jackson spoke from the door. He had his Stetson firmly in place and his hands rested on his wide leather belt. 'You can go home. And stay there, hear me? I don't want anyone going anywhere until we're done.' He glowered around the room. 'Shouldn't take too long. Which one of you is Anne Munro?'

'I am,' Anne said, standing.

'Okay. You stay.'

Cynthia said: 'Why Anne?'

The sheriff looked at Cynthia's purple and yellow hair. 'I know your type, young lady, and I don't like it. You know what's best for you, you'll stay out of it. The rest of you, scat.'

'Not me,' Mike Thompson said. 'I mean, I was his partner, vice president, I've gotta be here.'

'Hell, man, I ain't goin' nowhere,' Pete Dixon said, putting his shoulders back. 'I'm gonna help you find the bastard that did him.'

Behind the deputies, a thin frizzle-haired woman pushed her way into the room, elbowed Jackson aside, and grinned at the staff.

'If I ever called any of you twerps gutless, I take it back,' she said happily. 'God damn! Who did it, huh? I want to shake your hand!'

There was a moment of stunned silence, then Brian laughed.

'Really, Lena, if you're trying to wring a confession out of anyone — '

'Now just hold it,' Sam Jackson said. 'Wringing confessions is my job, it's what the good folk of this county elected me to do, and I'll damned well do it. Just who the hell are you?'

Lena put her shoulders back and beamed. 'I, Sheriff, am Lena Ashby, the almost ex-wife of the recently deceased. How do you do?' She pumped his hand and dropped it. 'Now, then, according to my watch it's three forty-five, and I'm sure we still have business to conduct, don't we? So if you'll all get back to your desks, we can get on with it.' She grinned again.

Thompson crossed his arms above his bulky midriff. 'Since when did you take over around here?'

'That, Mr. Thompson, is a question the

corner can answer better than I can,' Lena said sweetly. 'Growing Light was mine to begin with, and it's finally mine again. Community property, and George wasn't the type to leave a will, was he?'

Thompson's face purpled. '*Ms.* Ashby, I am George's partner in Growing Light, I invested in this business, and George promised me — '

'Well I just hope you have it on paper, snookums,' Lena Ashby said. 'It's so hard to litigate hot air, isn't it? In the meantime,' she said, turning away from him, 'everybody's busy busy busy, right?'

'Now just a god damned minute,' Jackson said. 'There's been a murder here — '

'I know,' Lena crowed.

'If I say that everyone can go home,' Thompson announced, 'then that's it.'

'And if I say they can't — ' Lena started.

'Shut up!' Jackson roared. 'You two take it outside. The rest of you, scat. Anne Munro, you stay. *Is that perfectly clear?*'

Lena, unimpressed, stared at him a moment. 'Perfectly, Sheriff,' she said with heavy politeness. She turned toward the staff. 'If the law says you go, you go. But I want everyone back at work tomorrow morning at eight sharp. If it's all right with the sheriff, that is.'

Jackson looked at her suspiciously and nodded, and one by one the staff of Growing Light left the room, leaving Anne alone with three deputies and the sheriff of Lake Harris County.

★   ★   ★

The air in Mike Thompson's office smelled stale and dangerous, and it made Anne's throat ache.

'Please,' she said again. 'I have to pick up my little boy at child care. At least let me call someone; he'll be all alone.'

'Sheriff, let her make the call,' Van Damme said. 'It's not going to hurt anything.'

Jackson shrugged and Van Damme gestured toward the phone. Anne picked up the receiver and paused.

'I don't know how to dial out,' she said, and for some reason this almost made her cry.

'Here.' Van Damme took the receiver away and unclipped a portable phone from his belt. 'What's the number?'

'Damn it,' Jackson said.

'I'll pay for it, Sam,' Van Damme replied, and punched in Carl Neilsen's number as Anne recited it, then handed her the phone.

'My tenant,' she whispered to the lieutenant, and when Carl answered she asked him to pick up Danny, told him she didn't know when she'd be home but she'd try to call, and to tell Danny not to worry.

'No, I'm fine, really,' she said in answer to his alarmed questions. 'Just a . . . a delay at work. I'll tell you about it tonight. Okay? Thanks, Carl. Yeah. Goodbye.'

She handed the phone back to Van Damme and reached for her glass of water.

They had been at it for almost an hour, she and Jackson and Van Damme, with Landry patiently taking notes. She had waived the right to a lawyer, knowing her innocence, but now she regretted it. Her initial confusion had given way to anger, and by now even that had worn down to a sullen, stubborn indignation that threatened to become tears. She gulped the water and looked up wearily as Jackson came back across the room.

'Look, Ms. Munro,' he said, 'we got witnesses that say you were mad at Ashby.'

'It wasn't a secret,' Anne said for what seemed like the millionth time. 'He told a lie, a nasty lie, about my husband. I was angry. Cynthia knew, and I think Audrey did, and Mike Thompson. But I wasn't angry enough to kill him. I just wanted to quit.'

'Uh huh,' Jackson said.

'Look,' Anne said. 'I talked to Audrey and she told me some garbage about denial and Jeff's death. Then Cynthia told me what Ashby said. Then I went back inside and talked to Mike Thompson, and then Thompson and I went into Ashby's office *together* and found him dead. He was probably dead before I even heard what he'd been saying about Jeff.' She turned toward Van Damme. 'So why would I want to kill him *before* I was mad at him?'

The lieutenant shrugged, but Jackson tapped his note pad. 'According to witnesses, Ms. Munro, you had breakfast with the victim. Maybe he said it then. Or,' he continued, holding up a hand to silence her, 'or maybe he didn't. He got back here, talked to his wife, then he came out of his office, made sure everyone knew about your husband, and then went back in his office, and somebody killed him.' He sat back. 'So maybe somebody told you *before* lunch.'

'Nobody told me,' Anne said.

'Uh huh,' Jackson said again. 'We can check that out. And besides,' he said, forestalling her objection, 'what was in your bag?'

'My tote bag?' Anne repeated. 'What's that got to do with anything?'

Jackson produced her canvas tote and waved it. 'Big bag, Ms. Munro, and not much in it.' He shook her purse onto the desk. 'Why'd you need such a big bag?'

'To carry my books,' she said. 'My reference library. I thought I'd need them, so I brought them in.'

'Yeah, they're by her desk, Sam,' Van Damme said. 'Five of them, they've all got her name in them.'

Jackson thought about this. 'Maybe she brought them in on Friday.'

'I wasn't working here on Friday!'

'Okay, maybe not,' he conceded. 'It's still a big bag, Ms. Munro. Big enough for these books of yours, and your purse, and maybe even that knife.'

Anne gripped hard to her temper. 'I never saw that knife before today. I told you that.'

'But you *recognized* it!' Jackson said.

Anne took a deep, steadying breath. 'I graduated from San Francisco State eleven years ago,' she said. 'With a degree in history. I worked for Alicia's Antiques in Berkeley until three years ago. She's a friend of mine. She specializes in silver and crystal. I gave you her phone number. I figured out who's on the knife. That doesn't mean I know the knife, and it doesn't mean I used it!'

'You had a chance,' Jackson said. 'You had a motive.' He leaned forward. 'That

104

knife came from Ashby's place, Ms. Munro. We got an informant who says so.'

'I don't even know where he lives,' Anne said with desperation.

'Yeah?' Jackson said. He reached into her tote and pulled out a piece of paper, neatly folded in two. 'Recognize this, Ms. Munro?'

'No,' Anne said.

Jackson opened the paper and spread it over the desk. 'You don't, huh? Here's this piece of paper in your tote that we found beneath your desk, so it's gotta be yours, right? I mean, who'd go stickin' pieces of paper in somebody else's purse? Especially, Ms. Munro, especially pieces of paper with George Ashby's address on 'em.' He sat back with satisfaction. 'Well?'

Anne craned her neck to look at the note. 'That's not even my handwriting,' she said indignantly.

'We'll see about that. Besides, we've got inside information, Ms. Munro.'

'What inside information?' Anne demanded.

'We happen to know,' Jackson said with satisfaction, 'that the victim was planning to fire you. There'd been a complaint already, and this your first day on the job.'

Anne took another deep breath. 'Look, Sheriff, whoever said that probably planted that note, too. Somebody's trying to set me up.'

'Now who would want to do that?' Jackson said. 'Your first day on the job, you don't know anybody here, nobody knows much about you. That seems pretty farfetched to me.'

Anne closed her eyes for a moment. 'Are you going to arrest me?'

'Not right now,' Jackson said.

'Then may I go home, please?'

'Sam, might as well,' Van Damme said. Jackson looked annoyed, then nodded.

'Don't you try to bolt,' he warned. 'You know what I mean.'

'Yes, I know. May I have my purse?'

Jackson hesitated, and Van Damme said, 'Sam, you've been through it. She needs her keys and license, at least.'

'Let her take it,' Jackson said. 'But I'm keeping the tote, Ms. Munro. Understand?'

'Yes.' Anne took her purse, stood up, and steadied herself with a hand on the desk. Van Damme held her arm and helped her out of the office.

'Can you, ah, drive okay?' he said, and Anne started to cry, not caring whether his question was sincere or not. He led her into the misty evening. She fumbled in her purse for a tissue, blew her nose, and controlled herself.

'Yes, I'm all right. But why me?' she said. 'All I wanted was a job; I hardly knew the man. I got angry, I know about history and antiques . . . Why me?'

Van Damme shook his head and sighed. Anne opened her car door, and he leaned on the roof for a moment, looking at her.

'It's an elected position,' he said. 'Sheriff, I mean. All you gotta do is run.'

Then he closed the car door and, waving, turned back toward Growing Light.

8

'*Mercy*,' Millie Beckson said with emphasis. 'That place is a madhouse.'

Anne nodded wearily. She, the Becksons, and Carl Neilsen sat at Anne's kitchen table; Danny, stuffed to the ears with macaroni and cheese, had gone to bed an hour ago.

'But don't you worry, Annie,' Millie continued. 'That boy Jackson has been a sore disappointment to me. I campaigned for him, you know. He had this slogan, 'Let's Keep Lake Harris Quiet.' Seems he means to do that by tossin' everyone in jail and lettin' God sort 'em out.'

'That's just what I need,' Anne said, and felt like crying.

'Take it easy, honey.' Millie reached across the table to pat Anne's shoulder. 'We'll just have to find the killer ourselves. Sam Jackson's got a one-track mind, and that track's not too wide, either. He couldn't investigate his way out of a chicken house in broad daylight. Carl, you're gonna give Annie a hand.'

'Beg pardon?' Carl said.

'Of course you are.' Millie pushed herself away from the table and stood. 'This poor child's got herself mixed up with a bunch of crazies, and heaven knows there's no one else gonna help her. Now, you two write down a list of suspects, then Annie and Carl can start figuring out which one of them did it. Then we get 'em to confess, and turn 'em over to that idiot Jackson. Just like Jessica Fletcher and Cordelia Gray and Miss Marple.' She regarded them with satisfaction. 'Ed, let's get home to bed. Tomorrow comes early, you know. Carl, you do right by this girl, hear me?'

And with that, Millie Beckson exited the house, trailing Ed behind her. Anne stared after her with amazement.

'Best get some paper,' Carl said unhappily. 'Mind if I make another pot of coffee?'

'Carl, you can't possibly be serious,' Anne said. 'You have to be at work at five in the morning, and it's almost eleven already. I'm sure Millie was trying to do her best, but — '

Carl, on his way to the coffee maker, shook his head. 'Maybe you don't understand about my aunt Millie yet. I'll just call in sick tomorrow morning. You find some paper and a couple of pencils, okay?'

'Carl, don't be foolish.'

'I'm not,' he said.

'Yes, you are,' she replied. 'Listen, remember telling me about some Tuesday morning group that meet at Evvie's?'

Carl nodded.

'Tomorrow's Tuesday, so we'll start with them, first thing in the morning. What time do they get there?'

'Six-thirty,' Carl said. 'Are you sure that — '

'Yes.' She took the coffee pot from him and pushed him toward the back door. 'I'll start on a list of names for Millie, you get some sleep, and I'll meet you at Evvie's tomorrow morning. All right?'

Yawning mightily, Carl stumbled toward the small house. Anne watched until he was inside, then closed the door.

She tiptoed into Danny's room, tucked his legs back under the blankets, and sat beside him for a moment. His thick, dark eyelashes cut a crescent through the freckles on his cheeks. *I am not*, she thought with quick ferocity, *going to lose him; not going to let anyone take me away from my son. If I have to fight, then I'll damned well fight*.

She kissed Danny's warm forehead and carefully closed his door. In her bedroom, she dug through her closet, found one of Jeff's old hooded sweatshirts, and dragged it on over her shirt. Then, properly armed, she sat at her desk in the dining room, found a pad of lined paper, and sharpened a pencil.

She started to write SUSPECTS and decided that it sounded melodramatic. Instead, she lined in three columns, headed NAME, OPPORTUNITY, MOTIVE. She skipped a line and wrote MIKE THOMPSON. He had to be her accuser, she thought. Why? To cover something up, of course. His office was next door to George's; he could have gone in through the bathroom, done it, gone back, and no one the wiser. She paused, remembering the heavy mist in the bathroom when she'd first gone through it.

Gone in, done it, and cleaned himself off, she amended. And he had made it clear that he thought he'd inherit the company.

Could he have planted the note in her tote bag? Somebody had, probably while she was out with Cynthia. Or perhaps even earlier, when Brian took her to the engineering office. She thought for a moment. No, she'd taken the books out of her bag after that, and surely she would have found the note then.

What about George's hand? she thought. Pointing toward a clue that would lead to his killer? No, she decided. That was just too hokey.

Jackson said the knife had come from George's house. Either George had brought it to the office himself, which seemed unlikely, or whoever killed him must have had access to his house. Who could that have been? Max, maybe? Both Carein and Jimi had said that Max was supposed to pick up a computer from George's house that Sunday night. And Max was certainly missing. He had never shown up at Carein's for dinner that night, and didn't call in on Monday. And someone had mentioned that George had given Max a hard time last week. Anne frowned. Max was so mysterious that she didn't even know his last name. Oh, hell, she thought, and wrote his name below Thompson's.

Carein had been gone much of the morning. Could she have slipped in without anyone knowing it? Or killed George before she left? Carein hadn't explained her alibi, at least not in Anne's hearing. And why would Carein want to kill George? True, she was worried about Max, and Max had supposedly been to George's house the day before, then disappeared. Was that enough? Anne doubted it. Besides, Carein didn't seem the type to kill anybody — or anything, for that matter. But Anne wrote Carein's name under Max's, and put question marks in the next two columns.

Lena Ashby, she thought, remembering that when she and George had returned after breakfast, Audrey said something about putting Lena in George's office. Was that sufficient opportunity? Lena had seemed indecently happy about the murder. A clever killer could act that way, hoping to disarm suspicion. And as far as motive went, if George could create so many enemies during an eight-hour work day, think of what twenty-four hours a day of him would lead to. Lena's name followed Carein's on the list.

Cynthia? Brian? They said they had been together all morning. Neither of them liked George, and she supposed they could have murdered him jointly, but it simply didn't seem right. And Audrey Lincoln had a pile of phone messages with time notations. That should clear her, too, unless the messages were faked.

How about Jimi Hendrix Johannsen? Anyone with a name like that, she thought, ought to be capable of anything, right?

She paused. Thompson, if he hadn't been lying, said that someone had complained of her. Certainly it wouldn't have been Carein, or Cynthia, or Brian, or Jimi — and that left only Audrey. Anne frowned, trying to remember what she had said to the young woman before Cynthia interrupted them. Something about not having been shown the sign-in sheet. Surely that wasn't enough to lead to a complaint, was it? She shook her head and continued.

'Pete what's-his-face,' she muttered, writing. 'The shipping clerk who worships George. Why not?'

She sat back, looked at the list, and sighed.

'Except for the police, that's every single person I met today — and a couple I only heard about!'

I just don't know enough, she thought. *I don't know any of them. I don't even know who George really was. How can you figure out who murdered someone if you don't know why?* She sighed with exhaustion. Let the cops worry about it. She would just quit the job, and let Van Damme and Jackson deal with it.

Whoever killed George Ashby, she thought, would be delighted if Anne Munro took the blame for it. If Millie Beckson was right, Sheriff Jackson wasn't going to be much help. Van Damme seemed competent, but Jackson, after all, was his boss.

So Anne couldn't quit. If she had to

track down a murderer, she'd have to learn more about these people, and she couldn't possibly do it from the outside. She'd have to try being Miss Marple and V.I. Warshawski and J.P. Fletcher all rolled into one, and the sudden image of what this might look like made her smile.

Then, feeling marginally better, she turned off the lights and went to bed.

9

'Good thing I didn't call in sick,' Carl said from behind the counter. He had fresh syrup stains on his apron and looked harassed. 'Evvie's got the flu, so it's just me this morning. Hiya, kid,' he said to Danny. 'Want some breakfast?'

'Yeah!' Danny swarmed up the counter stool and perched on top. The trucker on the neighboring stool raised his eyebrows.

A subdued morning clatter filled the small café, laced with the rustle of news-paper pages; the smell of coffee and bacon overlaid the lemony smell of disinfectant. A row of booths lined the far wall; sparkl-ing Formica tables filled the space between the booths and the counter.

'I'll keep an eye on him,' Carl said. 'It won't get real busy for another half hour. They're over in the corner booth, under the Pepsi sign.'

Anne nodded and kissed Danny's fore-head. 'Hey, pickle, I'm going to talk to some people right over there, okay? If you'll stay here, Carl will make you some blueberry pancakes.'

'Yeah,' Danny repeated. 'And some bacon, and some milk, and some — what's that?' He poked a finger at the trucker's plate.

'Hash browns,' the trucker said. 'Want some?'

Danny hesitated. 'My mom says not to take food from strangers,' he said sadly.

'It's all right, Dan,' Carl said. 'This is Mr. Gleason; he drives for the creamery. So now he's not a stranger, okay?'

'Okay,' Anne and Danny said together, and Danny dug into Mr. Gleason's hash browns. Anne clutched her notebook and turned toward the corner booth.

Four people, two women and two men, leaned toward each other, talking animatedly. They looked perfectly normal, Anne thought as she walked toward them.

'Excuse me,' she said, and waited until they all looked at her. 'I know you don't know me, but my name's Anne Munro, and I, well, I started work yesterday at Growing Light — '

'Good Lord!' The younger man, with thinning hair and dark glasses, sat back suddenly. 'Were you there when he was killed? When they found him?' He pointed at the front page of the *Lake Harris Intelligencer*, which occupied pride of place in the center of the table. A photo of George Ashby grinned up at her under the headline, 'Local Businessman Murdered'. Mike Thompson, also grinning, stood beside George.

'Well, actually, I found him,' Anne said.

'Wow,' said one of the women, whose abundance of blond hair showed streaks of gray. 'That's far out. Hey, scoot down, make her some room. What's your name again?'

'Now hold on, Grace.' The older man, with dark Latino good looks and silvering hair at his temples, held up a hand. 'Let's not be so hasty. Let's find out why the lady wants to talk to us. Well?' he said to Anne.

'Oh, Toby, don't be such a downer,' Grace said, but the handsome man just shook his head.

Anne gestured with her notebook. 'I

heard that you all used to work there.'

'Who told you that?' the younger man demanded.

'Just a friend,' Anne said. 'Someone who eats here. When I said I'd got the job, he said he'd heard you talking about Growing Light. And now that George Ashby's dead — '

'You think one of us did it,' Grace said. 'Oh, that's so wild! I mean, we didn't, I don't think any of us did, but wow, if we could have — '

'Grace, hush,' the other woman said.

The handsome man regarded Anne somberly. 'Ms. Munro, I'm Toby Sanchez. This is Hank Fowler, Grace Lathrop, and Angie Grimaldi. Do you think one of us did it?'

Anne shook her head. 'I don't know. I only know that I didn't, and someone believes that I did.'

At that, Grace elbowed the woman beside her and made room for Anne at the corner of the bench.

'Sister, if you did it, more power to you,' she said. 'Here, have a cup of coffee.'

'And if you didn't,' said Angie, 'for God

sake, tell us all about it. The paper only said that somebody stabbed the bastard and the sheriff thinks he's got a lead.'

'Great.' Anne sighed, sitting and taking the offered cup. 'That's probably me.'

'Naw,' Grace said. 'You started work there yesterday? No way, you'd have to get in line.'

Anne sipped the coffee. 'In line? Can you tell me about it?'

'Sure,' Hank said. He took off his dark glasses. 'But you go first.'

So Anne told them about the first day on the job, starting with getting to work in the morning. When she reached the part about her desk, they laughed and nodded; when she reached the part about Jeff's death, Grace shook her head.

'He does it to everyone,' she said. 'He says it's to check on people's stability, but that's just bull. He told everyone I was an ex-dope freak. Can you believe it, me, an ex-dope freak? That's why he fired me, too, said that I was too uptight, and if I went back on dope again, I'd be better off. *Back* on dope! Gimme a break! The bastard used to sneak down to the parking lot to split a doobie with me!'

They paused while Carl came over to take their orders.

'I'm amazed someone didn't sue him,' Hank said when Carl had left. 'I have a masters in computer science from Princeton, I've written three operating systems for God's sake, and he told everyone I took a job with him so he could be my computer guru. Guru! That man wouldn't know a decent piece of code if it screamed at him.'

'Yeah,' Toby said. 'He told everyone that I was forced out of my previous job for sexism. Lies, of course, unsubstantiated lies, but the damage was done. It's all too easy for other people to believe the worst of you, especially when your employer is the source of the gossip.'

'Couldn't you do anything?' Anne said.

Toby Sanchez shrugged. 'He stood up at a staff meeting and said that my previous employer gave me a fine reference. Which proved nothing, of course.' He smiled. 'I outlasted the average, at least. I mean, the AGA average.'

'The AGA average?' Anne said.

'After George Ashby,' Toby said. 'Before George took over, we were a pretty stable bunch. Then he was in and Lena was out, and the AGA was about nine and a half months, average length of employment at Growing Light. Lena hired me and Angie here, but George hired Hank and Grace.'

'Don't rub it in,' Hank said. 'He hired Thompson first, then Carein. They're still around, right? And Pete Dixon, the shipping clerk, he's been around for a while. But for everyone else, it's in one door and out the other.'

'I had been there two and half years,' Toby said. 'Then Thompson called me in and said — '

'You're not the right player,' the other three chorused, 'for the game.'

'My God,' Anne said. 'That's what Thompson said to me yesterday, and that was my first day on the job.'

'First time's always just a threat.' Grace said. 'Third time is when they're gunning for you. But that's not George's image, you know. So he hired Thompson as his — what's that word you used, Toby?'

'Pistolero,' Toby said. 'You know, the muscle man, the guy with the gun.'

'George's image is bullshit,' Hank said. 'The man's a coward, pure and simple. Was a coward.'

Anne sipped her coffee. 'You said, After George Ashby. Lena had the company first?'

Absolutely, they said, and told her about Lena bringing George in as her office manager. 'That's the first time he tried to fire me,' Toby said, 'but Lena stopped him.'

Then, according to Angie, he tried sleeping his way through the female staff. The ones who objected were accused of being hysterics, and the ones who didn't soon found their bedroom secrets spread throughout the company. Most of the original women quit, Angie among them. A lot of the men followed. And George hired their replacements.

'Like me,' Grace said. ''Course, he had no way of knowing that I'm a tough cookie. So pretty soon he thinks he's got the staff all sewn up, convinced us that Lena was outdated, or incompetent, or something. I didn't buy it, and I told her so. And wow, did they have a fight over that!'

It pretty much killed the marriage, according to the members of the Tuesday Morning Breakfast Club. George moved out and filed for divorce, and to the amazement of the few remaining original employees, the judge awarded him the company in a preliminary decree. Within a month, all of Lena's original staff had gone.

There ensued a moment of somber quiet, during which Carl brought their breakfasts.

'Well,' Hank said, 'did they close the whole place down, or what? Who owns it now?'

'I don't know,' Anne said. 'Last I heard, Mike Thompson and Lena Ashby were going at it full blast.'

'Mike Thompson!' Hank said, hooting. 'That poisonous little toad.'

'That poisonous little toad,' Anne said, 'probably told Sheriff Jackson that I'm the one who killed Ashby.'

'Sister,' Grace said, 'I may be a

burned-out old hippie, and the rest of us are no great deal, but if you need our help, you got it.'

The others nodded and Anne smiled and dug into her breakfast, comforted by their words — even if, she thought, one of them might possibly have stuck Catherine of Aragon into George Ashby's back.

10

Anne left Danny at kindergarten and drove the twenty miles from home to Growing Light. The clouds had cleared and a pale winter sky arched over the green hills and soft valleys. Fat sheep, shaggy in their winter coats, browsed along a hillside beside the banks of the Harris River, swollen now with winter rains.

A few miles beyond Inez, the road left the valley and started its snaking climb up the Coast Range to Melville. Along the hill crest, the ruins of Francis Hopkins Harris' utopian community soaked in the sun. Anne smiled at it. Harris had come West in the 1840s, bought what was now Lake Harris County from General Mariano Vallejo, and proceeded to found a colony amid the quiet hills and valleys. Within a decade, two hundred disciples tended vineyards and livestock and, according to a traveler's report, indulged in mystic rituals during which Harris was paraded around the ranch on a gilded farm cart while his followers whirled like dervishes and sang, in the traveler's words, 'in a language which may be known to God, Who knows all, but is undoubtedly unknown to His lesser creations, of whom Mr. Francis Harris is most certainly a member.' The traveler went on to imply, with Victorian delicacy, that the rituals ended in manifestations of free love.

In order to irrigate his fields, Harris had his followers dam Coronation Creek at a small valley above Inez. Two good wet winters created a lake, which Harris proclaimed to be a work of God, in that God, he said, had led Harris to the valley and shown him the dam in a dream. Divine inception, however, did not stop him from naming the lake after himself. The Victorian traveler, having toured the dam, was less enthusiastic, and proved right when, ten years later, the dam broke one wet February day and inundated the first town of Inez. Up until that time, the farmers and the visionaries had observed a polite truce, but Harris made the mistake of proclaiming the flood an act of divine retribution against the pumpkin farmers and small ranchers of the valley. Soon after, plagued by a declining congregation and increasing lawsuits, Frances Hopkins Harris decamped for southern California, leaving behind a small winery, an impressive amount of debt, an undetermined number of children, and his name affixed to the smallest of California's counties.

Since his time, the county had preserved its blend of farmers and ranchers on the one hand, and mystics, visionaries, and seekers after truth on the other. Certainly George Ashby, his wife, and his partner seemed to fit the traditional mix. Of the things she had been told over breakfast, Anne wondered how much was true, how much was speculation, and how much of it was known to the current staff of Growing Light.

She bumped over a cattle guard and downshifted to start the climb up the hill. Growing Light's offices, she thought, must be very near the site of Harris's first ranch house, the one he later abandoned to dwell, according to that same traveler, 'together with his acolytes, sharing bed, board, and, it is said, each and every other thing to which man is entitled.' The new buildings had been shaped like an arrow, the point aimed at the original ranch where Harris had first received the vision upon which, he claimed, he had founded his church. All his structures, he proclaimed, must ever point toward the truth.

Just, she thought, as George Ashby's hand had pointed at his computer. She didn't for a moment believe that George had, in his dying moment, deliberately pointed at the computer as a clue, but despite Van Damme's skepticism, she was positive that Ashby's hand had been moved. If so, it could only have been by someone who didn't want Ashby's computer noticed. As far as she knew, only Mike Thompson had been alone in the room after the murder and was the only one who had the chance to move Ashby's hand. It made sense, she thought, especially if Thompson knew that something in George's computer might implicate Thompson himself. All she had to do, she thought, was get her hands on that computer. Somehow.

It was seven-fifty when she arrived, but unlike yesterday, three cars sat in the parking lot in addition to the abandoned Volvo. Lena Ashby stood at the open front door, arms crossed, like a teacher awaiting the arrival of her students. A few feet away, Mike Thompson leaned against the hood of a green Honda, arms also crossed. The two glared at each other. Pete Dixon slouched against a bright red, all-terrain, full-size pick-up decorated with a chrome roll-bar and yellow-jacketed rally lights. Pete, too, glared at Lena Ashby with such concentration that even his silly mustache looked belligerent. Anne took a steadying breath and parked next to Thompson's car.

'Good morning,' she said, getting out. Thompson ignored her. Pete transferred his glare to her, then back to Lena. After a second she walked to the front door. The yellow police tape had been removed.

'Who are you?' Lena demanded.

'Anne Munro. I'm the technical editor.'

'Oh, yeah, right,' Lena said, and

grinned. Today she wore her frizzy hair pulled into a frizzy bun, and she had donned the Growing Light uniform of blue jeans and sweatshirt — hers had a picture of a black-hatted witch on it, over the word 'Mother'.

'Well, just go on in,' Lena continued. 'They took George away and his room's all sealed shut, but everything else is ready to work. Breakfast meeting in ten minutes, make sure you're there.'

Anne nodded and found her way to the message wall and sign-in sheet. To her surprise, her message square had been moved from its position near the floor to a thin rectangle fitted in beside a door frame. She shrugged; there were no messages there anyway. She signed in, then stood for a moment, tapping the pencil against the clipboard. If the police had sealed George's office, then no one had been able to get into his computer and tamper with his files. By the same token, though, it might be impossible for her to get into his system.

She looked around and, deciding that she was alone, walked around the corner and stood for a moment beside George's office. The yellow tape seemed untouched. What about through Thompson's office? she wondered. Then she heard voices from the reception office, and walked away.

What she needed, she decided, was help — but from whom? She reached her own closet-like office, tucked her purse away, and, in the interest of looking busy, picked one of the manuals from the floor and centered it on her desk. Everyone in the company was on her list of suspects, and she could imagine what Millie would say if the person she picked as an ally turned out to be the murderer. For the first time in her life, she wished that either she was a hot shot computer expert — what the media called a 'hacker' — or that she knew one.

Voices, footsteps, and scraping noises sounded outside, and Brian stuck his head in. 'Mandatory breakfast meeting,' he said. 'Just when I should be on the phone to the east coast. Come on, and bring your chair.'

'My chair?' Anne repeated. 'I don't know if I can even get it out of here.'

'Sure you can,' Brian said, then looked over his shoulder. 'I'm just giving her a hand, so hold it a minute, okay?'

He squeezed in beside Anne, picked up her wheeled typing chair, and swung it over the desk. 'There,' he said with satisfaction, and grabbed his own chair. Behind him, Jimi and Cynthia stood impatiently, each hauling a seat. Anne waited for them to pass by, and Cynthia paused to let her into line. This morning, her hair was green with black stripes. Anne made a decision.

'Cynthia, could you give me a hand after the meeting?' she said. 'I'm not sure I've got my computer set up right.'

'Sure,' Cynthia said. 'There's not a lot to it, but I'll take a look. How're you doing, after yesterday?'

'All right, I guess,' Anne said. Everyone came to a halt as chairs were maneuvered through the lunchroom door. 'How about you?'

'No problem. I was with somebody every minute yesterday. Airtight alibi, so Jackson's not messing with me. Pig.'

A tub filled with ice and bottles of fruit

juice sat on the lunchroom table, beside a large basket overflowing with muffins. Brian groaned.

'Oh no, not Mother Mary's All Organic,' he said. 'I almost chipped a tooth on one of those.'

'They're good for you,' Mike Thompson said. He had staked out a position at the far end of the table.

'Balls,' Lena said, coming in from the hallway. She carried two huge pink pastry boxes. 'Doughnuts,' she announced, and someone sent up a subdued cheer. Mike Thompson glowered at her, and she glowered back. Anne appropriated a cup of coffee and a coconut doughnut, and pushed her chair into a corner, out of the line of fire. Lena took a bottle of juice and a jelly doughnut, and glanced around the room.

'Where's Audrey?' she said as Carein entered.

'She's not feeling well this morning,' Carein replied. She looked as though she'd spent the night crying and didn't wear any jewelry at all, homemade, antique or otherwise. She put a large jug on the table; pale brown liquid sloshed within. 'And who can blame her? I mean, the auras around here are just awful, tension and fear and everything. I called Reverend Hankins, you know, the aura cleaner, and he's coming this afternoon.'

'Hold it,' Lena said. 'You called who? To do what?'

'Reverend Hankins,' Carein repeated, producing a stack of paper cups. 'To clean our auras, get us centered again, on the right astral plane. I put up memos about it last night, before I left.'

Anne raised her eyebrows and looked at Jimi, who waved a message slip at her.

'Now just a minute,' Lena began.

'That's fine,' Mike said. 'A good move. Growing Light will even pay for it.'

'I will not,' Lena said.

'I didn't mean you,' Mike said, and smiled grimly.

'Please,' Carein said. 'This is just, I mean absolutely exactly what I mean. Reverend Hankins will clear this all for us, but he can't come until three, so I just, you know, knew we'd need this, so I made it last night.' She began pouring.

'Moon tea?' Jimi said, guessing.

'Of course,' Carein said. 'It's chamomile, mostly — comforting, you know. And much less harsh than sun tea, more in tune with your spiritual plane. Here you go.'

Anne looked dubiously into her cup as Mike Thompson said. 'I hardly think that Moon Tea is going to fix — '

'It's fine,' Lena said, overriding him. 'All the help we can get, right? Who else is missing?'

'Max,' Pete said helpfully. 'Anybody hear from Max?'

Everyone looked at Carein, who paled and shook her head. 'I haven't seen him since Sunday morning,' she said. 'I tried calling everyone and driving around, and I just can't, I can't . . . ' She stopped and, closing her eyes, took a deep breath. Everyone waited.

'There,' she said, opening her eyes. 'I'm centered now.'

'Okay,' Lena said. 'Audrey and Max are absent, but everyone else is here, so let's get down to it.' She looked around the table, and Anne followed her glance.

Brian looked sadly into his cup; Cynthia ignored hers; Jimi sipped and grimaced. Pete scowled at the tabletop, and Mike glowered alternately at Lena and at Anne. Anne raised her chin and sipped at the tea. It tasted cool and bland.

'Okay,' Lena continued. 'Yesterday was quite an event, but it's behind us now, and I think what we need to do is get back to work. After all, this is an ongoing company and there's work to be done, thank God.'

'Goddess,' Carein muttered.

'Whatever,' Lena said. 'As you know, I haven't been involved with Growing Light's daily operations for some time now, so I think the best way to start our new life together is for everyone to spend a few minutes this morning, at your desks, writing me a job description.'

'Hell, no!' Mike Thompson said, coming to his feet. 'George Ashby had a vision for this company and we're going to stick with it, no matter what. Just because George isn't with us, it doesn't mean that we're going to destroy everything he stood for — '

'George Ashby stood for grabbing all he could get and screwing as many people as he could while doing it,' Lena stated. 'And don't pretend otherwise, you little — '

'Stop!' Carein yelled. Mike and Lena, surprised, turned toward her.

'Just stop,' she said, more quietly. 'There's been a terrible shock, just a horrible psychic blow, and all this yelling doesn't help. We need to stabilize things, we need to get centered. Then we can go on. Okay?'

'We, like, need to meditate, right?' Pete Dixon said. 'Here, gimme your hands.' He latched on to Cynthia and Brian, and snapped his eyes closed. 'Come on, you guys, George would've wanted it.'

Lena opened her mouth, but Brian shook his head at her. 'A minute of silence, what could it hurt?' he said, and closed his own eyes. Lena mouthed a curse, reached behind her, and grabbed Anne's hand. Jimi reached for the other one.

And so, for a moment, the staff lunchroom filled with quiet breathing and the asthmatic hiss of the coffee maker. Anne closed her eyes. *Dear God, get me out of this in one piece*, she thought. *Amen*.

Jimi's large hand felt a little clammy.

'There,' Carein said eventually. 'Much, much more peaceful.'

Anne glanced around. Everyone still looked like hell, but the atmosphere, she had to admit, was slightly less poisonous.

'Now then,' Carein continued. 'Where were we?'

'Job descriptions,' Lena said. 'I need to know what everyone does around here.'

'Bullshit,' Mike said. 'Job descriptions are hierarchical bullshit foisted on workers by an uptight repressive system.'

'That's just the kind of thinking,' Lena said, 'that's led this company to lose money nine months out of the past twelve.'

'But we haven't lost money,' Carein said. 'We all saw the figures last September, and we were doing just fine.'

'Well, those aren't the figures he showed my lawyer,' Lena said. 'Who's the bookkeeper around here? Well?'

'Audrey,' Brian said. 'Who isn't here.'

'My, my, my,' Lena said, leaning back. 'Not feeling well, huh? Carein, when we're done you call her and get her in

140

here ASAP, got it?'

Carein opened her mouth, then closed it and nodded.

'This is nuts,' Mike said. 'We don't need bookkeepers, what we need to know is who killed George, that's what we need to know. I want everyone, and I mean everyone — ' He looked pointedly at Anne. ' — to tell us exactly where you were every minute of yesterday morning. You, Ms. Munro, can start.'

'Jeez,' Cynthia said, 'give it a break, Mike. We already know. You think the gossip mill around here is that sloppy? We knew all that yesterday.'

She gestured with her doughnut and proceeded to recite everybody's whereabouts, while around the table, people nodded as she came to their names. Pete was in Novato and had a receipt from Jack in the Box with the date and the time, eleven forty-five. George, she speculated, must have died between ten-thirty, after Lena left his office and he saw Audrey and told her about Jeff's death, and noon, when Anne and Mike found him. Mike looked icily at Lena, but nodded. So, Cynthia said, there was no way Pete could have been around when George bought it. Cynthia herself was at her desk from nine-thirty until a quarter to twelve: Brian, who shared the space, had been right across from her the whole time. Audrey was answering phones from eight until ten-fifty, when she went to the bathroom, and from a little after eleven until noon, when Anne saw her. Jimi was in Engineering: Carein saw him there, then Brian and Anne did. Carein came in around nine-thirty, left around ten fifteen, and didn't get back till about one; she had spent the time driving around Melville and down to Inez, looking for Max. Anne had breakfast with George, talked with Carein, saw Brian, was at her own desk until almost noon, then was with Audrey and Cynthia.

'And we haven't heard from Max,' Cynthia said, 'but Max couldn't hurt a fly. Have I left anyone out?' she concluded. 'Oh, yes, of course. Where were you, Mr. Thompson?'

Thompson stared. 'I talked to Sheriff Jackson,' he said. 'I don't have to talk to you. Besides, Ms. Munro had George's address in her tote bag.'

'How did you know about that?' Anne demanded.

'The sheriff told me,' Thompson said. 'Looks like you've got some explaining to do.'

'Looks to me,' Anne retorted, 'like somebody's trying to set me up. Maybe you, Mr. Thompson.'

'That,' Thompson said, 'is simply ridiculous. And I'm sure the sheriff thinks so too.'

Cynthia raised her eyebrows. 'The sheriff, Mr. Thompson, doesn't seem to think at all.'

Lena rapped on the table. 'People, we're wasting time here. I want those job descriptions, everyone. On my desk by noon. I'm working in Audrey's area until the sheriff lets me into George's office. Anything else?'

'Yeah,' Pete said. He spread a piece of paper on the table. 'We got that new shipment of sensors coming into Oakland tomorrow, somebody's gotta go get them.'

Cynthia made her eyes round. 'Gee,

Pete,' she said. 'I thought that was your job.'

'I got important stuff to do,' Pete Dixon said. 'I'm helpin' the sheriff catch the guy that done George.'

'Really.' Brian leaned forward. 'Does Jackson know about this yet?'

'You listen up, you New York bastard,' Pete said.

'Stop!' Carein shouted again. 'This is *not* helping.'

'Bastard?' Brian mouthed, eyes wide.

'Jeez,' Cynthia said. 'Someone's got to get the sensors. Boz Wilson has been on the phone every day demanding his replacements. Does it matter who does it?'

'Why don't you just have them delivered?' Anne said.

'Because we don't work that way,' Mike Thompson said. 'In fact, Ms. Munro, you can go get them. You haven't done any work around here so far anyway.'

'Totally unfair,' Cynthia said. 'She only started work yesterday, what do you expect?'

Thompson's eyes narrowed. 'Yeah. Interesting first day. Well, Ms. Munro,

Pete will give you directions and the paperwork. You can do it tomorrow morning.' He smiled. Pete, copying him, pulled his lips tight against his teeth.

'All right,' Anne said, keeping a lid on her anger. 'Do I get to use the company car?'

'We don't believe in company cars,' Thompson informed her. 'Your own car will do just fine.'

'Yeah,' Brian stage-whispered. 'But don't expect to be paid for gas or bridge tolls, unless your name is Dixon.'

'Please,' Carein said before Pete could yell again.

'Besides,' Pete said, 'I'm not the shipping clerk anymore. I'm Mr. Thompson's personal assistant. He said so.'

'He did what?' Lena said. 'And just what gives you the right, Mr. Thompson, to tell my employees what to do?'

Mike smirked. 'My lawyers, Ms. Ashby, have a signed agreement between George and myself, giving me a full partnership and, Ms. Ashby, control of the company in the event of his death. Growing Light is *mine.*'

'The hell you say,' Lena said. 'George may have gotten management of Growing Light, but I still own half of it and I've got right of first refusal on the rest. So I'll believe it's so when a judge tells me it's so — but it sure would be a great motive to murder someone, wouldn't it, Mr. Thompson?'

'Oh yeah?' Thompson replied. 'And what about that little argument you had with George at the awards dinner last Friday night, hmm? You think nobody knows about that? Well I'll remind you, Ms. Ashby, that I was there for it, and Sheriff Jackson was very interested when I told him about it. And we got a law says a criminal can't profit from her crime, Ms. Ashby. So don't go threatening me.'

Jimi Hendrix Johannsen, with a look of absolute disgust, uncoiled himself and loomed over the table. 'Oh, shut up, all of you,' he said, and, in the ensuing amazed silence, stalked out of the room.

'Jimi?' Brian said. 'Was that our quiet Jimi?'

'This meeting,' Carein said, 'is over.'

'Ah-men.' Cynthia grabbed her chair

146

and dragged it out of the room. The rest left in very short order.

Anne hauled her chair back into her closet, muscled it over her desk, and collapsed into it, eyes closed. A minute later, Pete Dixon banged on the door.

'Here's the stuff,' he said, dropping a file on her desk. He stared down at her; his imitation of Dirty Harry would have worked if he hadn't stuck his lower lip out so far. 'Just don't get any ideas about skipping town,' he growled.

'Pete,' she said, 'does that make any sense at all? Why would I kill George Ashby?'

'I don't know that yet,' Pete said. 'But I'll find out. You just remember that.' He nodded, pivoted, and disappeared down the hall.

Anne closed her eyes again, took a deep breath, and turned on her computer. No matter what she tried, though, the screen stayed stubbornly blank. Anne cursed under her breath. Cynthia would give her a hand with it. In the meantime, she went back to the message wall.

Her skinny rectangle was still empty.

Anne thought a moment, then bent down to the area where yesterday Audrey had originally taped out Anne's square. The tape and Anne's name were both gone, but sticking to the wall was a folded note. Anne peeled it off and opened it.

'Rev. Hankins, Tuesday 3 p.m., aura cleaner. Don't be late.'

Anne started to crumple the note, then smoothed it out and tucked it into her pocket. Odd that Carein should have put it in the old location.

Just then Cynthia came down the corridor and grinned.

'Just the woman I wanted to help,' the technician said, and led Anne back to her closet.

11

'It works like this,' Cynthia said, bending around Anne to tap the keyboard. 'Think of it like having three disk drives — your regular floppy, here, and the computer's hard drive. So your floppy drive is drive A and your hard disk drive is drive C, like always. You don't have a drive B — none of us do — so the network is the third drive, drive D. In order to use it, you have to make sure that the network cable is connected, then cold-boot into it. You know, turn the whole system off, then on again. And if you want to access anything on your own hard drive, your Drive C, you have to exit the network, disconnect the cable, and cold-boot again.'

'But I did connect the network cable,' Anne said. 'And all I get is this blank screen.'

'Of course,' Cynthia said. 'First you have to log on, you know, sign on to the network. To do that, you just type

LOGON. Go on, type it in, but don't press Enter.'

Anne typed the word and raised her hands from the keyboard. 'Okay, now what?'

'Now you type in your password. And your password is your last name, plus a G and an L. I set it up Monday morning. Go ahead and try it. It won't echo on the screen because it's supposed to be secret, but it should work.'

Anne carefully typed in her last name, a G, and an L, and pressed Enter. The screen lit up, leaving her facing a single quotation centered on the screen:

Good Morning!
Only the Egoless Team
Ever Reaches the Mountain.

Anne blinked. 'What the hell does that mean?' she said.

'Damned if I know,' Cynthia said. 'George wrote them all. Story is that some ex-employee asked him to explain one and George fired him for being stupid. Just press Enter and it'll go away.'

Anne did so, and the screen began blinking so rapidly Anne couldn't read it.

'Glitch in the system,' Cynthia said. 'George wrote the program for color monitors only, but he was too cheap to buy them for everyone, so if you've got a mono, you're up the creek. It's just a stupid intro screen, nothing useful. Press Enter again.'

This time Anne faced a menu:

The Growing Light Digital Family
1 Growing Light
2 Growing Light Demo
3 Staff Communications
4 Utilities
5 Passage

'Passage?' Anne said.

'Yeah. George didn't like 'Escape' and Carein thought 'Exit' sounded too negative. It just means, get me the hell out of here.'

'Oh, great,' Anne said. 'So where's word processing? How do I use this thing to write something?'

'That's staff communications. Press 3.'

'No mouse?'

Cynthia grimaced. 'It takes a decent programmer,' she said, 'to make a mouse work.'

'Oh.' Anne pressed 3. The screen cleared and presented a new menu:

Staff Communications

1Compose

2Retrieve

3Print

4Passage

'I guess that's pretty straightforward,' Anne said. She hesitated, then added, 'Listen, Cynthia, I wanted to ask your help about something. Something else, I mean, but I've got to get this job description done and I guess you do, too.'

'Naw,' Cynthia said. 'I've had one for months, I just didn't advertise it. I mean, jeez, I'm not gonna be here forever, nobody ever is. And I want some record to show the next place I work. Here, look.'

Cynthia tapped the number 2 and typed 'cd.. \baker' after a prompt line that read, 'Team Member:'. The screen cleared to show a directory listing.

'Hold it,' Anne said. 'You mean anyone can access anyone else's stuff, as long as it's on the network?'

Cynthia, busy tapping the down arrow to move through a list of files, nodded.

'Yep. You want something private, you keep it on floppy and don't go through the network. There.'

She pressed Enter when the highlighted bar was over a file called, innocuously enough, 'SKILLIST.DOC'. It took a moment to load, then filled the screen with a listing of skills, assignments, and responsibilities. Cynthia added a blank line on the top, typed 'Job Description — Senior Site Technician — Cynthia Baker,' then sent the file to the printer.

'There,' she said with satisfaction.

She saved the document, returned to the staff communications screen, created a new subdirectory for Anne, and opened an editing window.

'Your turn,' she said, moving away from the computer. 'I've got some free time now, but you've gotta get your description done . . .'

'Give me five minutes,' Anne said, putting her fingers on the keyboard.

Job Description
Technical Editor
Anne Munro

Review all manuals, hardware & software

Review all sales material, letters, brochures, etc.

Develop overall company style

Rewrite all company materials as needed.

'There,' she said, saving the file and sending it off to the printer. 'Cynthia, you mean that if I wanted, I could get into George's subdirectory and change things? Just sitting here at my own computer?'

'No way.' Cynthia stood. 'Come on, let's get the printouts and give them to Lena. Then maybe you and I should take an early lunch.'

★   ★   ★

Ten minutes later, bundled into down jackets, the two women walked down the hill toward the deli. The crisp, clear weather hadn't broken, although the weather reports optimistically predicted rain in the evening.

The Growing Light offices dropped out of sight behind a stand of trees, and

Cynthia slowed her pace.

'Okay, we're clear,' she said. 'Listen, you ever want a private talk, you do it walking. There's no privacy back there and none at the deli, either, 'cause everybody eats there.' She scuffled through a pile of dried leaves, sending them flying. 'So what's up?'

Anne shoved her fists deeper into her pockets and toed some of the dead leaves. Then, making up her mind, she told Cynthia about Jackson's belief that Anne herself was a prime suspect, and told her about George's hand.

'I'm positive it was pointing at the computer when I found him,' she said in conclusion. 'And it wasn't when I was back in there with Lieutenant Van Damme.'

'And not when you went back with Jimi,' Cynthia said thoughtfully.

'I just can't remember.'

'Maybe Jimi moved it when he checked George?'

'No. He was on George's other side; he couldn't have reached it. And, Cynthia, I'm sure it's important. I think there's something in George's computer files,

155

something that someone doesn't want anyone to know.' She shook her head. 'But if anyone can access the files . . . '

'No, they can't.' A stand of dense evergreens loomed over the road; they walked into the shade while Cynthia explained that while everyone else's work directories were open, George kept his own on his private hard disk.

'I see it every Saturday night,' Cynthia said, 'when I come in to back up the network. George made sure that I knew to come into his office, boot up his system separately, and back up his hard disk onto floppies. Took forever too. We have a tape backup for the network, but the bastard was too cheap to buy a decent backup system for his own disk.'

Anne stopped walking. 'You mean, you have a copy of George's files? Where you can get hold of it?'

'Sure, it's in the safe with the tapes for the network.'

Anne put her hand on Cynthia's sleeve. 'Cynthia, do you think — I mean, look, I know it's a lot to ask, and you don't really have anything at stake in this, but

. . . could you get me a copy of the disks? I'm positive there's something in them, something that can help show Jackson that I didn't do it.'

Cynthia frowned. 'Jackson's not the only one,' she said. Anne pulled her hand away. 'No, not me,' Cynthia continued. 'I'm sure you didn't do him. You're not the type, and he hadn't even started jerking you around yet. But Thompson — jeez, you'd think he has something to hide.'

'Yes,' said Anne. 'I do. I think he's convinced Pete Dixon, too. Pete's beginning to scare me.'

'He ought to. There's more to Pete than you'd think.' Cynthia looked at Anne, considering. 'Okay, tell you what. Jackson's already taken George's computer, so there's no way that anyone can get to his hard disk now. I'll try to get a copy of the back-up disks. I think I can get Carein or Audrey to let me into the safe. But if I do, I want to be in on all of this, okay? I mean, you're so new here, you don't even know what to look for. I can help, but we've got to go partners on this, all the way.'

'Why?' Anne said. 'You've got a good alibi, nothing to hide, nothing at risk here. Why get involved?'

'Ah, jeez,' Cynthia said. She started walking again, and Anne kept pace. 'George Ashby was a jerk, and a prick, and a liar, and a bigot, and probably a chicken thief, and sold his own mother down the river. But even so, you know, offing people isn't right. I'm sure whoever did it had a good reason, a damned good reason. But he shouldn't have killed the guy.' She paused. 'Maybe broken his kneecaps, I could see that. But murder — no way.' They walked out of the trees, and Cynthia's hair was the greenest thing in the landscape.

They bought sandwiches, apples, and drinks from the deli and, at Cynthia's suggestion, took them across the street, across the adjoining cow pasture, and down to the banks of a small stream. A broad flat rock jutted into the water, and they sat on it to eat their lunch.

'Little Pete Dixon,' Cynthia said. 'George got him through a work-release program out of Ukiah about three years ago.'

'Work release?' Anne said. 'You mean he was in jail?'

'And how,' Cynthia said. 'Grand theft auto and robbery. He stole a Cadillac, held up a convenience store with a fake gun, then trashed the Caddy during a chase with the cops.'

Pete had just turned eighteen, Cynthia said, and had no prior convictions, although he'd been picked up a few times for minor stuff. His father was a plastic surgeon further north, his mother an insurance salesperson, and both, Cynthia said, had driven Cadillacs, a fact which convinced George that Pete's crimes had been conscious acts of sabotage against a corrupt hierarchical political system. Or so George announced when he hired Pete as a part-time shipping clerk.

'This is all according to Carein,' Cynthia said, picking up an apple. 'Of course, she doesn't tell it the same way I do.'

When Pete's sentence was served, George hired him full time, found housing for him, and in return, received

Pete's rather vociferous allegiance and the protective benefits of Pete's physique and reputation.

'Course he doesn't look particularly rough,' Cynthia said. 'But don't let it fool you. Once Pete gets an idea in his head, it takes a nuclear explosion to get it out again. And he doesn't think about things, he just acts on them.'

Anne shivered. 'He said he didn't know why I'd killed George, but he'd find out.'

'Yeah, blame Thompson. And be careful around Pete Dixon, Anne. He's not too bright, but he stays bought. For Pete, that's a pretty dangerous combination.'

Anne folded the empty sandwich wrapping and stuffed it into her brown paper bag. 'What about Max?' she said.

'Max Allen.' Cynthia stretched along the rock. 'Let's see. He came to work here about four months ago. I think Carein knew him from somewhere; she's always picking up strays, you know, abandoned kittens, dogs, people. He needed a job and Jimi needed some help, so Carein brought him in, introduced him to George. He even had some technical training, a couple of correspondence courses in electronics, that sort of thing. But he worked out okay, according to Jimi.' She paused. 'Carein really went all out for him. She let him sleep on her couch until he found a place, fed him dinner, brought in lunch for him, washed his clothes. Brian thinks they have a thing going, but Brian's got a dirty mind.'

'You're sure they don't?'

Cynthia shrugged. 'Could be, but it's not likely. Carein's in her late forties, you know, and Max is about twenty, twenty-one, thereabouts. And there just weren't any of those vibes. I mean, they're close. Carein needs someone to mother, and I guess Max needs mothering, so it's like they were made for each other. But Max is really sweet. Withdrawn and kind of rabbity, I guess. Like he's always worried someone's going to blindside him. But just about as harmless as they come. Hell, he won't even kill pests, so for a while we had spiders all over the engineering room and mouse turds in the machines, until Mike came in one weekend and brought an exterminator.' She gathered up her litter and stuffed it into Anne's bag. 'So on Monday, there's dead spiders and mice all over the place, and Max just sat on the floor holding this dead mouse, and crying.'

She stood and brushed a few leaves from her jacket. 'I sure hope he comes in soon, before Carein becomes a total wreck.'

Anne, too, stood. 'Audrey seems pretty upset whenever his name comes up,' she said, following Cynthia across the meadow.

Cynthia made a face and pushed green hair from her forehead. 'Audrey,' she said, 'is weird.'

12

Audrey was in by the time Anne and Cynthia returned from lunch. Anne saw her as she signed back in; Audrey gave her a forlorn nod, sniffled, and continued down the corridor. Anne checked the message wall, found nothing pasted to it under her name, and walked back to her closet. She shrugged out of her down jacket, sat, and with a sigh reminiscent of Audrey, picked up the manual and tried to get to work.

Two hours later, she had determined that anyone trying to make sense of the manual's section on installation would need an economy-size bottle of aspirin and a geologic amount of patience. Were users really expected to open their own system boxes to plug in various circuit boards? She remembered a line from Pirsig's *Zen and the Art of Motorcycle Maintenance* — 'Assembly of Japanese bicycle requires great peace of mind'

— and wondered if George would have accepted it as a permissible morning computer quotation. At the very least, she thought, the manual needed a big warning that the system should not be plugged in during setup, lest an unsuspecting customer electrocute himself trying to get the sensors hooked up.

She pushed away from her desk. What she needed, she thought, was to set up the Growing Light system herself, from scratch. And for that she needed Jimi Hendrix Johannsen. She stood, stretched, and headed down the corridor.

Jimi was perched on a stool and hunched over his bench, his fingers busy with a tiny welding pencil and even tinier wires.

'Just a minute,' he said before Anne spoke, and bent closer to his work. She moved to one side and craned her neck. A clamp held a half-empty circuit board, punctured with small holes; Jimi threaded a small component through holes in the board, swivelled the board around, and soldered the component's wires to the other side.

164

'Just one more,' he muttered. He peered at a circuit diagram pinned to the wall, then leaned forward again. His huge fingers worked with sensitivity and precision, and in less than a minute another component was welded into place. Then Jimi pushed back, laid down his soldering pencil, and stretched.

'Oh, hi, Anne,' he said. 'What can I do for you?'

'I'm not sure,' Anne said, coming closer. 'I've been reading the installation manual, and I can't make heads or tails of it. I thought maybe if I could set one up myself, I could get a handle on it.'

Jimi's blue eyes blinked behind his thick lenses. 'You mean you're actually working?' he said with amazement.

Anne shrugged. 'As far as I know, I've still got a job here. Besides, what about you?'

To her surprise, Jimi chuckled. 'Here, let me show you something,' he said, and led her to the far end of the workbench.

A computer's system box lay open on the bench, connected by wires to a grimy monitor, a mouse, and a device that looked like a small cattle prod. Anne peeked inside the box, fascinated as always by the circuit boards, power supplies and other mysterious gadgets that, somehow, translated one kind of bewildering stuff into a second kind of bewildering stuff into something that appeared on a computer monitor and, with luck, made sense.

'Got any idea what this is?' Jimi picked up the cattle prod and grinned when Anne shook her head.

'This,' he said 'is the new Growing Light Aura Appreciator.'

He looked at her expectantly. *Oh no, Anne thought, not Jimi too.*

'Oh,' she said.

'Yes indeed, the latest innovation from the folk who bring you psychic gardening at its best,' he said seriously. 'You simply invoke the Auras option, pass the Aura Appreciator entirely around your body, and bingo! Growing Light assimilates your aura and uses it to focus the flow of your gardening energy.'

She looked at him obliquely. 'It does?'

'Of course,' he assured her, but something twinkled behind his lenses. 'Well, it

166

will as soon as we have the bugs worked out. Now here, take a look at this.' He pointed toward another peripheral device, this one resembling a hand-held calculator with a very large window. Jimi connected its cable to a port on the back of the system box and brandished it. A quick green light pulsed from the window.

Anne stared at it, and Jimi obligingly flashed it again.

'A bar code reader?' Anne guessed.

'Hey, you're not bad,' Jimi said. 'But no cigar. This, you see, is the Growing Light Past Lives Information Input Device. We don't have a fancy name for it yet.'

'Hold it a minute,' Anne said. 'You're not going to tell me that you pass that over your body and it reads your past lives.'

'That,' Jimi said, 'would not be scientific.' His grin broadened. 'No, you go to a special past lives regression specialist who is part of the Growing Lives Psychic Network. The specialist reads your past lives in the usual way — '

'The usual — '

'Hush, I'm explaining something,' Jimi said. 'In the usual way, and enters the

167

reading with the special Growing Light Past Lives Encoder. And the encoder then spits out a bar code which you, our customer, take back to your system. Then you use this device to read the bar code into your special tailored copy of Growing Light, and ka-boom!'

'Uh, ka-boom?' Anne said.

'Yeah, ka-boom. Your past lives are now part of your system, along with your astrological chart, your aura, and a whole bunch of other nifty stuff.' Jimi beamed.

'Great,' Anne said. 'It's not in the manual, is it?' Jimi shook his head, still beaming, and Anne frowned. 'Okay, Mr. Johannsen. Does it work?'

'Of course not,' Jimi said with glee. 'But it will, as soon as we have the bugs worked out. George had a guy in Berkeley working on it, you know, programming the code that'll get burned into the PROM that'll run the hardware that'll make the bar code that'll get read by the Past Lives Information Input Device that'll send the information to the program that'll help you become the best psychic gardener you can possibly be. Understand?'

'No,' Anne said bluntly. 'Not a single word.'

'Not to worry,' Jimi said. 'The programmer's angry at George anyway and won't do any more work until George pays him, which George won't. Or wouldn't. I know, 'cause he keeps trying to call. You want to see more buggy stuff?'

'I don't think I could handle it,' Anne said. 'Wouldn't it just be easier to use a software database for this?'

'Naturally. But not nearly as much fun.' He headed back toward his soldering pencil and Anne trailed along. 'So the answer is, no I'm not working. This isn't work. This is play. Work is supposed to get you someplace. This doesn't, and hasn't, and as far as I can tell, it never will.'

He lowered himself to the stool. Even sitting, he towered over Anne. 'And as far as putting a system together yourself goes, I can't help you. Max was supposed to pick up a spare from George this weekend, but if he did, he didn't bring it here. And even if we did have it, I don't think you'd be able to put it together. No,' he said as Anne started to object. 'I don't mean you couldn't, I just mean that if you expect to do it with nothing but the manual to help, it's hopeless. And that, Ms. Munro, is why we have site technicians, at a seventy-five bucks an hour, plus travel.' Jimi shook his head, his expression now serious. 'George Ashby may have been a lot of things, but he wasn't dumb.'

Anne sat on a vacant stool. 'So I've got to rewrite an installation manual that isn't supposed to help anyone install anything,' she said.

Jimi nodded. 'Yeah, but it can't look that way. If I were you, I wouldn't sweat it. Just, you know, change the words around, or use different ones, or something. You tech writer types can do that.'

'Sure,' Anne said. 'Change the words around, or use different ones.' She was silent for a moment, then said, 'Jimi, how do you stand it? All this, I mean — aura detectors and bar code past lives readers that don't work — is this what you wanted to do?'

Jimi shook his head. 'There's a recession on, Anne. And, look, you know my middle name. I grew up in a commune in

Humboldt County, home schooling and organic farming and multi-parent families. No grade school at all. The only college I could get into was a jaycee, then Lake Harris State.' He paused. 'My dads didn't like my leaving, but my mothers were pretty good about it. Anyway, I graduated from a backwater school at a bad time for finding work. This is what I took, and I think George hired me more for the commune than the degree.' He gestured with the soldering pencil. 'I'm looking, of course. Everyone here is looking, all the time.'

'Even Mike Thompson?' Anne said.

Jimi frowned thoughtfully. 'You know, I'm not really sure,' he said. 'I'm just not really sure.'

★   ★   ★

When she got back to her closet, she logged onto the network, found her way to her own sub-directory, and opened a new file which she called 'EDITNOTE.DOC', in preference to a couple of more colorful names she had in mind.

She had just finished typing herself a reminder to check with Cynthia about installation procedures when she heard voices in the hall, and looked up.

'There she is, Lieutenant,' said Mike Thompson, and he gestured widely at Anne's desk. Anne stared and Lieutenant Van Damme jockeyed his way around Thompson and nodded.

'Thanks for the, ah, guide, Mr. Thompson,' he said. Thompson didn't move. Van Damme looked at him for a moment, and Thompson shrugged angrily and moved away. Anne stood up.

'Lieutenant,' she said, hoping she didn't look too frightened.

'Nothing to worry about, Ms. Munro,' he said, and smiled. 'I just thought I'd return this. It was clean.' He held out her canvas tote.

'Oh.' Anne sat abruptly. 'Boy, I was afraid that — '

'And I'll need your signature,' he said. He spread a form over her desk. 'Here's what we took out of it. I think it's all back there, but I'd, ah, appreciate it if you could check.'

'Sure,' Anne said. 'But there wasn't anything in there, I don't think.' She looked at the form and turned red.

'Two diaper pins, pretty rusty,' Van Damme said, craning his neck a little to read. 'A number two Ticonderoga pencil, short, no eraser left. Two tampons. Three facial tissues, apparently used. A stick of gum, pretty brittle. I hope we didn't break it.'

Anne sighed and upended the tote over her desk. 'You forgot three pennies and the lint,' she said.

'No, there's the pennies. I don't think we catalog lint, though.' He smiled again. 'Everything okay?'

Anne signed the form. He folded it and put it in his pocket, then nodded at the photo of Danny.

'Cute kid,' he said. 'You got a minute to talk?'

Her stomach went tight again. 'Sure. Of course.'

'Maybe somewhere else,' Van Damme suggested. 'There doesn't seem to be room for another chair in here.'

Anne nodded and reached for her

jacket and purse. 'Do you mind walking?' she said, and Van Damme smiled again.

'I was hoping you'd suggest it,' he said, and stepped out of the room. 'Oh, hello again, Mr. Thompson.'

Thompson scowled at both of them and moved out of the way, and Van Damme followed Anne out of the building.

They walked in silence for a while, past the stand of pines and back into the sunlight.

'Sorry about your husband,' Van Damme said after a while. 'Tough way to lose someone.'

'You looked it up.'

'Yeah. Part of the job. At least, according to the Highway Patrol, it was pretty fast.'

Anne shoved her hands deeper into her pockets. 'People say that's supposed to be a consolation, but it's not, really. I'm glad Jeff didn't suffer, but he's gone just the same.'

'Almost two years now. Doesn't seem very long, does it?' A farm truck rumbled by, and he waited until the noise quieted. 'We didn't get any useful prints off the knife,' he said. 'Not that I was expecting any, but it would have helped.'

Anne thought for a moment. 'If I were Miss Marple, I'd ask if the hilt was wiped,' she said.

Van Damme shook his head. 'No. Are you Miss Marple?'

'Don't I have to be?' she said. 'Thompson's on my case, Jackson's on my case — what I need is someone on my side.'

Van Damme didn't respond. They passed the deli, and the road curved gently uphill, edged by bare apple trees.

'You were right about Ashby's hand, though,' he said at last. 'Forensics picked up fibers from his shirt sleeve, about where they'd be if his hand had pointed toward the computer.'

'That's great,' Anne said, excited. 'Did you check his hard disk yet? Is there something, you know, incriminating on it?'

The lieutenant shrugged. 'We don't have a report on it yet. You think Ashby tried to point out his killer?'

'No. But I think somebody else might think that.'

Van Damme looked at her with approval. 'Not bad, Miss Marple. According to the coroner, Ashby died almost instantly. Either somebody made a very lucky stab, or somebody knows a lot about anatomy. The knife pierced his heart.'

Anne thought again. 'If I *were* Miss Marple, I'd ask about the angle of the cut, wouldn't I? I mean, you can figure out how tall the killer is from that, right?'

'Yeah.'

He didn't elaborate. Anne bent down to pick a dark, wizened windfall apple from the edge of the road. 'If he died immediately,' she said, thinking it out, 'and his feet were toward the door, then he was probably walking back to his desk. Unless he was moved after he was stabbed?'

Van Damme shook his head. 'Nope. Except for the hand, he wasn't moved.'

Anne frowned at the apple. 'And he didn't turn around, so he must have known whoever did it. And maybe the killer was leaving, and Ashby just expected them to go.'

'Maybe.'

Anne stopped, and tossed the apple

into the winter orchard. 'Have I incriminated myself yet?' she asked with sudden bitterness, and to her shock, Van Damme laughed.

'Only if reading murder mysteries is a crime,' he said. 'I'll make it easier for you. The knife went in clean, which is amazing enough, but it means the killer didn't have to use a great deal of strength. Some, but it was a pretty sharp knife. So we're not necessarily looking for a large or powerful person.'

'Want to feel my muscles?' Anne said. 'I carry a five-year-old around a lot. He weighs forty-five pounds.'

Van Damme just smiled again. Anne hesitated, then said, 'There's a group of people who meet for breakfast every Tuesday down at Evvie's Café. They all used to work for Growing Light. I went in and talked to them this morning.'

Van Damme looked at her. 'And?'

'And I don't know. They hate him, I think. They were either fired or forced out. Maybe someone ought to talk to them.'

He pulled out a pad and pencil, and

Anne recited names.

'Does Miss Marple suspect any of them?' Van Damme said, putting the notepad back in his pocket.

'I don't know,' Anne said. The breeze tugged at her hair. 'What about that note?'

'What about it?' Van Damme said. 'It's not your handwriting, of course. But we didn't get any prints off it. Any reason you'd have Ashby's address on you?'

Anne shook her head. 'No, none at all. I'd never seen that damned thing before Jackson pulled it out of my bag.' She shivered quickly. 'Somebody put it there, Lieutenant. It wasn't there when I took my books out, before I left for lunch, and I didn't touch it after I got back. I didn't even get to my desk again. Why would someone want to set me up?'

Van Damme shrugged. 'Come on,' he said. 'We should be heading back.'

They walked for a while, then Anne said, 'You're not saying 'ah' a lot.'

'Ah,' he said. 'Caught me. It's just a mannerism. Makes some people feel more at ease.'

'I see. And is this just a mannerism, too? Being friendly, I mean?' He shrugged. 'Okay,' she said. 'Let's try this one. Why are you telling me all this?'

The lieutenant looked at her. 'It could be an interrogation technique,' he said. 'If this were a mystery novel, maybe I'd have romantic inclinations — no, wait.' He put his hands up, palms out. 'I don't, but we're speculating here. Or maybe I'd be convinced that you were innocent, and just trying to help you out.'

'Great,' Anne said. 'At the end of a mystery, everything's solved and you close the book, and all the characters disappear unless you read the book again. But in real life, somebody's still dead, and at the end of the mystery, some very real person's going to be in jail. I don't mind if it's someone who deserves to be in jail,' she said. 'I just don't want it to be me.'

Van Damme paused beside a gray Ford sedan and put his hand on the door. 'In either world,' he said gently, 'it's usually the killer's motives that count, not the detective's.'

He climbed into the car and Anne said,

'Wait, Lieutenant. Thompson wants me to drive down to Oakland tomorrow, to pick up some shipment. I don't suppose you could, maybe, tell him I'm not allowed to go?'

Thompson thought for a moment, then shook his head. 'No, it's okay. You've got a kid, a house, and a tenant who cooks. You'll be back.'

' . . . who cooks,' Anne echoed. 'How do you know all that?'

'It's my job.' He closed the door and rolled down the window. 'Another thing, Ms. Munro. That killer we've been speculating about? He, or she, was just about your height.'

13

Anne had just opened the main hardware manual and read the first sentence — '*Welcome* to the 'absolute best' in Integrated Ecological Psychic Gardening which will *enhance* and *expand* the life amplifying Experience that is so much a part of the expanded Universe of the Spirit of the Gardening psyche that has EVER been developed!' — when Lena rapped on the open door and, not waiting for an invitation, walked in and sat on the corner of the desk.

'I want to talk to you about this,' she said, waving Anne's job description.

'Okay.' Anne pushed her chair back and looked at Lena. George's widow, she thought. It sounded odd.

'This looks as if you're supposed to rewrite everything in the building,' Lena said. 'Is that what George wanted you to do?'

Anne nodded. 'As far as I could tell.

My instructions weren't exactly clear. I was supposed to — wait, let me get this right.' She closed her eyes for a moment, concentrating. 'Develop an overall company style that, let's see, immediately says, 'This is Growing Light'.' She looked up at Lena, who looked back. 'I'm sorry, he wasn't much clearer than that, except that the style was supposed to grow from everything about Growing Light. People and philosophy and the whole shooting works.'

'That sounds like George,' Lena said after a moment. 'And have you done it?'

'I started work yesterday,' Anne said. 'I've barely looked at the manuals.'

'But you *have* started.' Lena tapped the hardware manual. 'Any conclusions?'

Anne put her shoulders back. 'I read through the installation manual,' she said. 'It's horribly written, awkward, and impossible to follow. I just opened the hardware manual. You want to hear the first sentence? It's gibberish, and I don't expect the rest to be any better. No, I don't have any idea about an overall company style. Right now, I think the major job is to translate all this stuff into English and see if it makes sense. If not, someone will have to do a complete rewrite, from the bottom up.'

'Someone?' Lena said. 'What about you?'

'What about me?' Anne replied. 'Yesterday I was ready to quit. Now Mike Thompson and the sheriff think I killed your husband. I didn't, but it doesn't make this place seem like a good bet for long-term employment, does it?'

Lena looked at her for a moment. 'No, I suppose not.' She glanced down at Anne's job description. 'Growing Light is going to take a lot of work,' she said. 'I'd like you to stick it out, if you can. Forget the company style drivel and just make the manuals make sense. Talk to Jimi. If there's any vaporware in the manuals — you know, stuff that doesn't exist yet — just toss out that part. I want some materials that talk about what we've actually got.' She stood away from the desk. 'I'll have Cynthia bring you the software manuals.'

'Lena?'

She turned at the door, her frizzy hair

bright in the light from the hallway. Anne hesitated, abruptly unsure, then said, 'I'm sorry, this may be out of line, but — doesn't anyone care that he's dead?'

'George?' Lena said. She frowned and came back into the tiny room. 'George Ashby is dead,' she said, shook her head, and sat on the desk. Anne watched her in silence.

'Twenty-five years ago,' Lena said. 'I think those words would have killed me. Isn't that strange? He was this thin, intense, wild kid from the east coast, and I was a nut from northern California. I don't think I thought he walked on water, but you know, I sure thought he was something great.'

Another small silence came, and Anne said, 'Maybe he was.'

'Yeah, or maybe I was crazier than I thought.'

They had met in San Francisco, Lena said, not so much part of the hippie drug culture as of the radical student underground. 'Baby Bolsheviks, my dad called us,' she said, smiling. 'I guess we were. None of us ever went hungry except by choice, none of us ever went cold unless we wanted to — and none of us did a thing except talk big talk. Sure, we protested, but we weren't into blowing things up. If we did that, we might not have a choice about being cold and hungry.'

She had brought George home to Lake Harris County, and to her delight, her parents hated him on sight. So she married him, in a nude pre-dawn hot-tub ceremony on the banks of the Harris River, and Lena had gone back to school to get her degree while George found a job.

'He worked for one of the oil companies,' Lena said. 'Very uptight, structured place.'

Anne nodded. 'He mentioned it to me.'

'Yeah. He lasted four days, then he mooned the manager and walked out.'

George had drifted from job to job, while Lena worked part time in San Francisco and graduated with a degree in engineering. Then Lena found jobs, well-paying ones, while George tried his hand at one thing after another. In the late seventies, Lena started working with computers.

'And that's where it all started,' she said. 'Growing Light, the whole thing. I just kept tinkering, mostly for fun, for something to do. George . . . ' She sighed. 'George had a lot of friends.' She shrugged. 'At first, I guess I bought the whole package. You know, all the left-over Baby Bolshevik rhetoric translated into whatever was current. Drugs, retreats, ESP, TM — You name it, George did it, and I went traipsing along behind. Hell, I was as much a disciple as any of them. God knows my family had enough practice with that. Then, five years ago, my folks died, and things started falling apart. I'd started the company by then. It was pretty simple, crop planning software and a few moisture sensors. That's all I ever wanted it to be. And it did pretty well, better than I'd expected. Pretty soon I was writing papers and going to conferences and making money, and I suppose George couldn't accept it. I thought if I let him work in the company, he'd take it better.' She laughed. 'God, talk about putting your brains on hold!'

She'd found him in her office one morning, in the process of firing her chief programmer. She averted that, then George started sleeping his way through the female employees. Lena was used to that, although George had promised fidelity once AIDS became an issue, but her employees started quitting, morale disappeared, and one day she realized that her new employees were all, one way or another, on George's side, and convinced that she, Lena, was outdated and dragging the company down. She confronted him, and George moved out.

'He filed for divorce,' Lena said. 'My folks left me some money, so George claimed that he had no income, and the judge gave him control of Growing Light.' Lena laughed again. 'I wanted to kill the bastard. It was like, piece by piece, he took everything I had, everything I was, and screwed it over, changed it around, took it away or made it his instead of mine, instead of ours.'

She stood and smiled at Anne, a full, open, honest grin. 'You know, though, I am sorry that he's dead. Not George now, not this George. But God, you should have known him in the Sixties. Carein did, you know. I think that's why he hired her, she used to be part of the circle.' She shook her head. 'That woman,' she said over her shoulder as she left the room, 'that woman's a wreck.'

Anne sat still for a moment, thinking about it, then bent back to the manual.

Ten minutes later Mike Thompson marched in, waving his own copy of Anne's job description, and demanded to see the work she'd done on the company style.

'The manuals don't need revision,' he announced. 'They're just fine the way they are. But we need that style, and if you can't give it to us, I'm sure we'll find someone who can.'

He marched out without waiting for a response, and Anne put her head down on the desk.

Anne, girl, you're going to have to fake it, she thought. *Work on the manuals, make up some notes on a company style, try to keep everyone happy, and try to catch a murderer*. She groaned and opened the hardware manual again, and Carein stuck her head through the door. She did look like a wreck, but an excited one. Brian grinned over her shoulder.

'He's here,' she said with enthusiasm. 'Everybody's supposed to be in the lunchroom. Hurry up, come on, we can't keep him waiting.'

Anne rose wearily. 'Who's here? Do I have to bring my chair?'

'No, just come. He's here, Reverend Hankins.' Carein disappeared, and Anne hesitated. Could she be fired for refusing to have her aura cleaned?

'Anne, come on,' Brian said, grinning. 'You appreciate the absurd, don't you?' He held out his hand. 'Besides, if you don't show up, Mike'll really be convinced that you offed the boss.'

'Damn,' Anne said, and followed him down the hall.

14

The Growing Life staff milled around the lunchroom, muttering. Pete Dixon earnestly explained to Mike Thompson that George would have *wanted* Mike to have his aura cleaned. Audrey complained that Lena was making her go through the books for the past two years and was threatening to call in an auditor. Jimi, slouched in a corner, winked at Anne and played with his soldering pencil: trying to balance it on one end, then on the other, then twirling it through his fingers like a cheerleader's baton. Anne admired the way he avoided snarling his fingers in the pencil's cord. Brian had brought a sheaf of papers with him and was bent over them. Cynthia came into the room and stood beside Anne.

'I've got copies of the disks,' she said under her breath. 'Do you have a computer at home?'

Anne nodded. 'Yes, an IBM clone.'

'Great. Give me your address later and I'll meet you there after work.'

Anne nodded again as Carein, in the doorway, clapped her hands.

'Everyone, quiet, please.' She looked around. 'Reverend Hankins has come a long way for us, so let's try to make his work easier, okay? Reverend, this is the staff.'

Reverend Hankins wore a clerical collar under a Hawaiian shirt, a cherry nose that looked to have been broken a number of times, and a friendly expression, which disappeared when he came into the room. He stepped back suddenly.

'Good Lord,' he said. 'Tension, anger, fear . . . ' He grabbed Carein's hand. 'Can you see the blue? It's just thick, I've never seen it so thick.' Carein peered at the air and nodded. 'And look, there, at the dark red. A definite torrent of life-denying energy.' He peered around the room at about hip-level. 'I've never seen so many wide open first chakras. This may be difficult, very difficult.'

He walked all the way in, shaking his head. 'It's a good thing you called,' he said earnestly. 'You guys got a load of work to do here. I don't know if I can clean this up in just one session, but I'll try.'

'Thank you,' Carein said. 'What can we do to help you? Clear the room, meditate . . . '

'No, that's not necessary,' Hankins said. 'I'll need two straight-back chairs. With this much negative energy, I'll have to work one at a time, but you don't have to go away. Oh, and I need a drink. Beer, if you've got it.'

'Beer, Reverend?' Brian said. 'Isn't that evil, or something?'

Hankins shook his head. 'What is, is, my friend. Psychics are no different from anyone else, and I like a beer before a big job.'

'We,' Mike Thompson said, 'maintain a drug-free workplace. Uh, you want some mineral water?'

Hankins sighed. 'That'll do.'

Pete Dixon produced two chairs and Hankins sat in one of them, accepted a mineral water from Carein, and drank. Then he wiped his lips and put the bottle beside him.

'How about a muffin,' Pete said, gesturing at the breakfast meeting leftovers that still lay on the table.

'Naw. Maybe a doughnut later, though,' Hankins said. 'Okay, gimme a minute.'

They watched as Hankins planted his feet flat on the floor, dropped his hands palms up in his lap, and closed his eyes. He sat that way for a minute. Anne looked at Cynthia and raised an eyebrow; Cynthia shrugged.

'That's better,' Hankins said. 'Okay, let's see. Might as well tackle the heavy cases while I've got a lot of energy.' He glanced around the room again and winced.

'You,' he said, pointing at Audrey.

Audrey jerked toward the door, but Carein caught her.

'It's okay, he's going to help you feel better,' Carein said. 'It doesn't hurt, there's nothing to be afraid of.'

'Yeah,' Hankins said, and explained to the group that he never read minds without permission. 'I'm just going to adjust your chakras and try to clean out your auras a little, bring in some healing. You guys are repressed, got a lot of tension, it's so thick in here I can barely see the walls. Besides,' he went on, 'nothing happens unless you want it to. I can sit here and heal 'til hell freezes over, and if you don't want it, it won't happen. I'm just a way to let you help yourself, that's all. What is, is.'

Audrey still looked apprehensive, but she let Carein guide her to the second chair and help her to sit.

'All righty,' Hankins said. 'Just sit like me. No, don't cross your arms or legs. Feet flat on the floor, hands in your lap, palms up. Great. Okay, just close your eyes and try to relax.'

'Uh, do you want me to like meditate or something?' Audrey whispered.

'No, don't do that. Just sit there and relax, let me do the work.' With that, Hankins closed his own eyes.

After a minute he opened his eyes, stood, and placed his hands palms down about a foot over Audrey's head. He pressed the air around her head, neck, and shoulders, then down along the rest of her body.

'Clenched tight,' he said, moving his

hands back above her head. 'This'll take a little time, honey; you just keep relaxed.'

Anne sidled up to Carein. 'What's he doing?'

'Adjusting her chakras,' Carein whispered back. 'Extremely important. Closed chakras are very destructive.'

'Not destructive,' Hankins said. 'Just very denying, don't let cosmic and Earthly energy work within.' He suddenly moved his hands away and shook them hard.

'Got the seventh,' he said. 'Let's work on the sixth.' His hands moved down to Audrey's eye level.

'What's a chakra?' Anne whispered.

'It's like a kind of power node in your body,' Carein said. 'You know, where energy gets shared out inside you. If they're not, like, the way they're supposed to be, they can really screw things up.'

Anne watched as Hankins worked his way through all seven main chakras, finishing with the secondary ones in Audrey's palms and the arches of her feet. Then, according to Carein, he started work on the aura. He passed his hands through the air around Audrey's body, pressing, pulling, occasionally grabbing handfuls of nothing and shaking them away into the air. The first time he did that, Pete Dixon jumped out of the line of fire.

'It won't hurt you,' Carein said. 'Other people's energy doesn't really want to be in your aura, so it doesn't go in.'

She explained that Hankins was altering the shape of Audrey's aura, moving energy from high to low places and getting rid of the excess. Finally Hankins cupped his hands above Audrey's head like a funnel and stood still, then did the same at her feet. Then he sat for a moment.

'Okay,' he said. 'We're done. Put your hands together, then put your head between your knees.' He did the same, and after another minute, he said, 'Great. Stand and stretch. How do you feel?'

Standing, Audrey swayed for a moment. 'Weird,' she said, and Hankins nodded.

'Yeah, that's normal. Listen, I got your seventh and fourth chakras opened, and worked on closing up your first a bit. There's more orange in your aura now

— got rid of most of that dark blue and some of the dark red, but there's still a ways to go.' He hesitated. 'You should think about your fifth chakra.' He put his hand on his throat. 'There's something you're blocking. Your fifth was detached, you know. I got it linked up again, but it's still pretty tight.'

Audrey nodded, eyes wide, and retreated backwards. Hankins gulped the rest of his mineral water and asked for another.

'Now you,' he said, pointing at Mike Thompson.

Anne slid around the room to stand next to Lena.

'Listen,' she said. 'Can I just wait at my desk? I mean, I'm not really doing anything here.'

'Not so,' Hankins said unexpectedly. 'We're pumping a lot of energy through this room. Just by being here you're bound to pick up some of it, some of the healing. And that'll make my job a lot easier.'

So Anne stayed while the Reverend Hankins went through the same routine with Mike Thompson — 'Lots of gray here, son, lots of dark blue and dark red.

Let go of the fear, boy. Open it up. And for God's sake don't go disconnecting that sixth chakra again, it was hard enough linking it up.'

Carein was next. 'Wild,' Hankins said when he'd finished with her. 'There's silver around your hand chakras. You ever been telekinetic? You know, moved something without touching it?'

'I, I don't know,' Carein said, looking flattered.

'I wouldn't be surprised,' Hankins said. 'I only see that in telekinetic, very rare. You got problems with your sixth, too, something you don't want to see. And try to keep the third opened, you're gonna need it. Okay,' he said, swiveling to look at Anne. 'You're next.'

It was, Anne discovered, very soothing to sit for twenty minutes, directed to relax, eyes closed: like doctor's orders to take a vacation, she thought, and tried not to smile. She could feel Hankins nearby, hear the shuffling hush of her coworkers, and smell the thickening air of the room and the slight acridity of the reverend's sweat, but for the life of her, she couldn't perceive any changes within, except for an increasing desire to nap.

'Okay, clasp your hands, then head between your knees,' Hankins said at last. 'Now stretch. Walk around, make yourself real. You got a pretty closed fifth, girl. Lost someone close to you, eh? It takes time to heal, but you had some orange in you already, and I like that yellow around your head. You'll do okay.'

Mike Thompson muttered something under his breath, and Hankins, looking visibly tired, asked Lena to sit. 'Open up the fourth,' he told her. 'There's healing going on, but you've gotta love yourself and love the world, sweetheart. No way around it . . . '

By the time he finished with Lena and started on Pete, he looked exhausted but insisted on continuing. Brian, Jimi, and Cynthia took only five minutes each.

Finally the Reverend Hankins, bathed in sweat, fell back into a chair. 'That's a decent beginning,' he said, panting. 'There, see, more orange and less dark blue — the positive is overcoming the negative. Can you see it?'

Carein nodded enthusiastically, and Anne closed her eyes. The Reverend Hankins might be full of bull, she thought, but it was bull he apparently believed, heart and soul.

'Now then,' Hankins said, straightening with a visible effort. 'I've reconnected chakras and got some adjusted, but not all of them, and the auras still need work. I'm not gonna leave this job half done. Wouldn't be right. I'm coming back tomorrow, okay?'

Lena and Mike nodded.

'Good. Between now and then, you all be real careful. Your auras are fragile right now, real fragile. Tomorrow we'll really flush 'em out, balance out the cosmic and earth energy, give you guys some steadiness to work with. So tonight, purify your bodies, no fights or arguments. And above all, *no* psychic shocks.' He peered at them. 'Can you do this?'

'Do what?' a new voice said suspiciously.

Sheriff Jackson filled the lunchroom door, looked at the Reverend Hankins, and snorted.

'Never mind,' he said. 'This Max Allen guy that turned up missing? We found him.'

'Where?' Mike demanded. Carein grabbed the back of a chair, eyes wide.

'Where? I'll tell you where. Stuck under a bridge near the reservoir is where.' Jackson looked belligerent. 'Stuck right there in Lake Harris County's drinking water, that's where we found him. With a couple slices in his wrists. Max Allen is dead.'

In the shocked silence that followed, Reverend Hankins looked around the room and put his head in his arms.

'Just look at those auras,' he said unhappily.

15

'He must be mistaken,' Carein said again, just as serenely as the first time. 'Max *can't* be dead. It's not possible.' She turned to Reverend Hankins and smiled. 'It's just some silly mistake.'

Jackson had left immediately after his announcement, taking a doughnut with him and leaving Van Damme behind. Now Van Damme took Carein's hands in his and leaned forward.

'Ms. Forest,' he said, 'I'm afraid there's no mistake. We found his driver's license on the body, and — '

Carein smiled at him. 'Oh, Max was always loaning things to people. Or misplacing them; he used to misplace things all the time. So that doesn't prove anything, Lieutenant.' The corners of her mouth twitched. 'It doesn't, does it?'

Hankins wrapped an arm around her shoulders. 'I'm going to get her home,' he said. 'Okay, Lieutenant? This — ' He nodded quickly at Carein. ' — this stuff is gonna break any minute now.'

'Maybe the hospital . . . ' Lena suggested.

'Oh, no, that's not at all necessary,' Carein said, that terrible smile still on her face. But Hankins nodded.

'A last resort,' he said, and turned Carein to face the door. 'Come on, honey, I'll give you a lift. Can you remember your address?'

'Of course I can,' Carein said as he led her out. 'It's on a real power node. We don't have that many here, but I found one. That's why Max is okay, you know . . . '

A minute later, the front door closed and they saw Reverend Hankins appear in the parking lot. He helped Carein into his battered blue Dodge Monaco and a minute later, accompanied by exhaust fumes, they drove out of the lot.

'I don't suppose,' Anne said into the quiet, 'that there could be a mistake . . . '

'No, it's positive,' Van Damme said. 'She and, ah, Max Allen — they were close?'

'Carein's always adopting some loser,' Thompson said, and everyone looked at him. 'So what?' he continued, grinning. 'Case solved, right? Obviously Max murdered George, then killed himself.' Thompson looked pleased. 'All neatly wrapped up.'

'No,' Audrey said loudly. 'No, that's not it. That's not it at all. George drove him to it, you know.'

Van Damme raised an eyebrow. 'You want to tell me about it?'

But Audrey shook her head until her blond hair flew. 'No, I've gotta talk to Carein. I mean, like, I've really got to talk to her, you know? Right now.'

'Tomorrow,' Lena said. 'Carein's in no shape to talk to anyone. I want her left alone. Whatever was going on between her and Max, tomorrow's soon enough to find out about it. You're sure it was suicide?' she said to Van Damme, and the lieutenant nodded. Lena blew out her breath.

'We don't have a time of death for Allen yet,' Van Damme said. 'Probably any time between Monday morning and that afternoon. The, ah, coroner's office will call when they have it pinned down.'

'So it could have been Max,' Thompson insisted.

'No,' Audrey shouted. 'George was, I mean, right in Max's face, like he always did to scare people, and Max couldn't, and, and — '

She waved her arms wildly. Lena captured them, and her, and pulled the younger woman in close. Audrey buried her face in Lena's neck and held on.

'Another idiot hysteric,' Thompson announced.

'You know, Thompson,' Brian Stein said, 'you're a real turd.'

'Oh, yeah?' Thompson said. 'You know, Stein? You're fired.'

'He's what?' Lena demanded, abandoning Audrey to spin around and stick her nose in Mike's face. 'He's *what*, Mr. Thompson?'

The effect on Mike was startling. Thompson took a rapid step backwards into a chair and sat abruptly. Lena pursued her advantage.

'Just where do you get off, *Mr.*

Thompson? No one, do you hear me, no one fires my employees except me, is that clear?'

Thompson gaped, and Anne remembered Audrey saying that George was — what were her words? — 'right in Max's face.' Lena, it seemed, had picked up the mannerism, and its effect on Thompson was amazing.

'Ah, excuse me,' Van Damme said. Lena swung around to look at him, and Thompson quickly slid sideways out of the chair and went around the table. Brian laughed.

'What?' Lena demanded, then took a breath. 'Sorry, Lieutenant. Mr. Thompson has a bad effect on me.'

'A bad effect on you?' Thompson hooted from his safe position across the table. 'What about your little performance last Friday night, huh? Jumping up at the awards dinner and yelling that George stole Growing Light from you?'

'He damned well did,' Lena retorted. 'All that crap about innovative programming and all that — I wrote the programs to begin with, and George damned well knew it and so do you. If anyone deserved that award, it was me!'

'Well you didn't get it, did you?' Thompson said.

Lena went for him, but Thompson slid behind Van Damme.

'Anyway, I've got a contract,' he said over the lieutenant's shoulder. 'George and I worked on it for weeks, we'd just gotten it all signed, the lawyer's filing it for us. Growing Light is mine, and so is everyone who works here.'

'I'll believe it when I see it,' Lena retorted.

'Fine,' Thompson said. 'I'm seeing my lawyer tomorrow morning, ten o'clock.'

'And I'm seeing mine,' Lena said furiously.

'Oh, shut up!' Audrey yelled. 'I don't care who owns this dumb company, but I know that Max didn't kill George. And he didn't take that fancy knife, either, 'cause I saw him the whole time he was there, on Sunday night, and he didn't go near the kitchen or anything.'

'Wait a minute,' Lena said. 'Wait, hold it. What fancy knife?'

'Yeah, what're you talkin' about?' Pete demanded.

Anne glanced at Van Damme, but he just looked bland. He probably hadn't told anyone, she realized, so only she and Jimi knew what the knife looked like.

'The knife that killed George,' Jimi said calmly. 'He brought it in sometimes, to cut cakes for parties and stuff. The hilt was shaped like a person. Silver, I think.'

'A person,' Lena repeated. 'Silver? The last presentation knife? That son of a bitch had my presentation knife, and he kept it in the *kitchen*?' She turned to Van Damme. 'They were in my family for generations, a present to my great-grandfather, and that son of a bitch lost one of them years ago and my family damn near disinherited me. Then when we separated, the bastard swore he'd lost the other one; he even signed a deposition about it. But he had it anyway? And he kept it in the kitchen and used it to slice *cake?*'

'Doesn't matter where he kept it,' Pete Dixon said. 'But Audrey's right, no way Max coulda done George. He didn't have the balls.'

'But Audrey does,' Thompson said maliciously.

'Stop!' Van Damme's commanding voice cut through the resulting noise. 'Ms. Lincoln, maybe you'd better come down to the station with me.'

Audrey started crying again, but Jimi stood, towering over the lieutenant, and spread his hands.

'Why?' he said. 'I told her which knife it was, 'cause I saw it when Anne and I went back to guard George's office and waited for the cops.' He blinked down at the lieutenant. 'You didn't say not to say anything,' he said. 'She's got an alibi, all those messages — '

'She faked the times,' Thompson said.

'And I'll bet she can prove every one of them,' Jimi continued. 'What's the matter, Mike? First you jumped on Anne, then Max, then Audrey — you're real eager to pin this on someone, aren't you?'

Thompson looked at Van Damme, who just raised his eyebrows. Thompson straightened his back and put his shoulders back. His paunch stuck out even more.

'The rest of you may not care that George Ashby was murdered,' Thompson said. 'But I sure as hell do, and I want the person who did it strung up. And I'm sure as hell wondering, Lieutenant Van Damme, just what's taking the sheriff's office so goddamned long to find out who did it. Do you have any answers for me?'

Van Damme just looked at him, then turned to Audrey.

'We'd like to get your statement formally,' he said. 'More about Max Allen then George Ashby. Do you understand?'

'Not until I talk to Carein,' Audrey said stubbornly.

Van Damme hesitated, then nodded. 'Okay, I'll come by tomorrow afternoon. Ah, three o'clock. And I expect you to, ah, be here.'

'After I talk to Carein,' Audrey insisted.

Van Damme just looked at her, and finally she nodded. 'Okay, like, three,' she said.

'Good. Oh, and Ms. Ashby, could I have a word with you? I'd like to hear more about the knives.'

Lena hesitated for a moment, then

nodded and followed him out. At the door, she turned back and glared at Mike Thompson.

'Ten o'clock tomorrow,' she said. 'With lawyers.' She glanced at the rest of the staff. 'It's almost four o'clock. Everybody go home.'

★   ★   ★

However, and without any great discussion, instead of heading home, Anne, Brian, Cynthia, and Jimi drove to the Casa Vaca, known to the Growing Light staff as the Greasy Taco. Anne arrived late. When she walked in, the others waved at her from a booth in the far corner, and she started back toward them.

'*Con permiso, señorita,*' the counter man called to her. 'We don't serve the tables this time of day. You want something, you gotta pay up here for it first.'

Anne found a <u>refresco</u> in the cooler, paid for it, and took it to the table with her.

'Sorry I'm late,' she said as Jimi stood to let her in. Van Damme had caught her

211

as she was leaving, to tell her that Toby Sanchez, of the Tuesday Morning Breakfast Club at Evvie's, had disappeared that afternoon and seemed to have left Lake Harris County. The sheriff's department had alerted other law enforcement agencies, and Van Damme said he hoped to have news of Sanchez's whereabouts by the next afternoon. Anne wasn't quite sure how she felt about this, and still hadn't made up her mind as she slid down the leatherette bench. Jimi sat beside her and stretched his legs into the aisle; they took up a lot of space.

'No problem,' Cynthia said. 'Brian was just telling us that Thompson is a dangerous maniac, but that's not news.'

'It'll be news if he gets the company and fires your ass,' Brian said.

'I can't believe George signed any contract with him,' Jimi said. 'It would have been stupid, and George wasn't stupid.'

'He didn't,' Brian said. 'I've got proof.'

They looked at him, and Anne said, 'For God's sake, why don't you take it to Lena? Or Van Damme?'

But Brian just shook his head. 'When the time's right,' he said. 'But just wait, it's a real bombshell. It'll blow that bastard right out of the water.'

'Promises, promises,' Cynthia muttered, and raised her bottle of Corona beer.

Anne sipped at the orange <u>refresco</u>, then turned to Jimi.

'You said George kept that knife at his house, the one Lena called a presentation knife — '

'Yeah.' Jimi shook his head. 'I guess it was real old or something. George'd bring it in to slice stuff, and give us this big song and dance about not getting hung up on material stuff. I didn't know it was Lena's.'

Anne frowned. 'How did it get from George's place to the office? It seems like Max was at George's on Sunday, and I guess Audrey was too.'

'Yeah, George was boffing Audrey,' Brian said.

'Boffing?'

'Yeah, you know.' Brian made a graphic gesture with his hands. 'I thought it had cooled down, but I guess not.'

'George had to have it,' Cynthia said. 'He told me once that if he didn't have sex every other day, his semen would back up into his bloodstream and poison him.'

Anne hooted, but the others just looked at her.

'You don't believe that,' she said in amazement.

Jimi shrugged. 'Maybe not, but George did. Anyway, so I guess Audrey could have brought it in, or Max, but I don't believe it.'

Anne privately agreed with him, and thought about the missing Toby Sanchez again.

'Who knew where George lived?' she said.

Everyone, they assured her. George held lots of meetings at his home, and occasional staff parties. Besides, Cynthia said, the place was easy to break into, especially if you knew George.

'He had an alarm system,' she said. 'With a code, you know, that you punch in to turn it off? Every time he fired someone, he'd have me or Jimi come up to reprogram his code.'

'Yeah,' Jimi said. 'Four digits: zero one, zero two. His birthday, you know. So first he'd have the month first and the day second, then he'd put the day first and the month second. Never varied. You could figure out the code just by counting backwards from the last firing.'

Anne blinked. 'And everybody knew this?'

'Sure,' Brian said. 'I think it was one of George's head games. He'd explain it to you in confidence, then wait to see if anyone broke into his house.' Brian shrugged. 'Nobody ever did, that we know of. Unless someone did it to steal that knife.'

'Catherine of Aragon, falling on hard times again,' Anne murmured.

'Beg pardon?' Jimi said.

'Catherine of Aragon,' Anne repeated. 'The figure on the knife hilt.'

'No way,' Jimi said, and the others nodded. 'That knife had a guy on it. George never said who it was, but it sure wasn't a woman.'

'But it had to be,' Anne said, confused.

'I looked at it, after George was killed. Here, it looked like this.'

She sketched rapidly on a napkin and handed the drawing around.

'See, a woman's figure, round head-dress, and the cartouche on her midriff, the H and C intertwined and the Tudor rose. It had to be Catherine.'

'Maybe it was,' Jimi said. 'I didn't look at it real close, you know, Monday. But George's knife had a guy on it; he used to make this big song and dance about how right on it was to have a guy on a knife. Something about penetration.'

Anne sat back. 'But that means that — that George wasn't killed with his own knife. So — where did the Catherine knife come from?'

Jimi shrugged.

'I don't really care,' Brian said. 'I mean, whoever did George is gonna be caught eventually. What I'm interested in is not letting Thompson do us.'

'You don't have Thompson and Sheriff Jackson breathing down your neck,' Anne retorted. 'I do.' She took another drink. 'I know an antique dealer in Berkeley.

Maybe I'll talk to her tomorrow, she might be able to help.'

'How?' Cynthia said.

'I don't know,' Anne replied. 'But the knife that I saw was a museum-quality piece, so maybe we can dig up some history on it. It can't hurt.'

'That's right,' Brian said. 'You've got to go to Oakland tomorrow anyway.' He drained his beer and stood. 'Look, I think you don't have to worry about Thompson. I mean, maybe Jackson was pretty rough with you, but everyone knows you didn't do it. I mean, why would you? But if you want to look into stuff, go ahead, and good luck. Me, I'm gonna go dig up some evidence.'

They filtered out of the restaurant and stood for a moment in the parking lot, then Jimi touched Anne's arm.

'Here,' he said, handing her a slip of paper. 'If you want to check things out, give this guy a call.'

Anne looked at the paper. Peter Simpson, it read, followed by a Berkeley address and phone number.

'The past lives programmer,' Jimi

explained. 'He claims George ripped him off, and he's pretty angry. Might be worth checking into.'

Anne nodded and put the paper into her jacket pocket as Jimi folded himself into a rusty Volkswagen bug and chugged off. Cynthia confirmed that she'd be over that evening after dinner and patted the hood of an ancient bathtub Hudson painted an improbable candy-apple turquoise.

'Jeremiah Hudson, the love of my life,' Cynthia said with affection. 'Lives off gas, oil, spare parts and my paycheck. You don't know a good mechanic, do you?'

Anne nodded, thinking of Carl Nielsen and his constant tinkering on his ancient Ford truck. 'Yeah. You'll meet him tonight.'

'Hear that, Jeremiah my love?' Cynthia crooned as she slid behind the wheel and hauled the door closed. She had covered the seats in bright red velveteen, and the dashboard gleamed. Jeremiah Hudson coughed, shuddered, then came alive with a deep basso growl and moved onto the street.

Anne slid into her own sensible import wagon and sat for a moment, holding on to the steering wheel. It was only Tuesday evening, she thought wearily. Only a day and a half since George had died.

Then she took a deep breath, relaxed her shoulders, and drove home.

16

Carl hadn't cooked that evening, but had brought home leftovers from Evvie's. When Anne walked in the door, a sweet, tangy smell filled the house. Danny wrinkled his nose, but after a single taste, ate his portion with enthusiasm, agreed to a bath after dinner, demanded that she read *Green Eggs and Ham* for the seven hundredth time, and slid into a peaceful sleep. Anne stood over him for a moment before kissing his forehead and quietly closing the bedroom door.

'Here, I saved this for you,' Carl said, handing her the front page of that morning's *Intelligencer*, the same issue she had seen at Evvie's. George's murder occupied the upper right-hand corner, complete with a photograph of George and Mike taken, according to the caption, at the Redwood Empire Human Potential Association's awards dinner last Friday night. Anne was tempted to toss the thing away, but on second thought she folded it and slid it into her tote bag.

Carl listened while she told him about the events of the day, starting with what she had learned at Evvie's that morning, and ending with the revelation about the second knife. As she finished, a car pulled into the drive. Carl, looking surprised, glanced out the window.

'It's Cynthia Baker,' Anne said, heading for the front door. 'She's got the backups for George's hard disk.'

'Oh, yeah, right,' he muttered. 'What's she driving, an old Hudson? Neat car.' He trailed after Anne into the living room.

But the minute Cynthia entered, Carl backed up and stared at her hair. She noticed it and laughed.

'Not to worry,' she said. 'I only eat lizards in private. Anne, where's your system?'

Carl stood between them and the desk, and he moved back to let them pass.

'I'll get some coffee,' he muttered.

Cynthia stared appreciatively after him. 'Nice buns,' she said. 'He live here?'

'In back,' Anne replied. 'He's my

tenant; he rents the cottage behind the house. He fixes cars, too.'

'Nummy,' Cynthia remarked as she slid her hand along the system box and flipped the switch. The computer growled and displayed its start-up screens. Cynthia took a handful of diskettes from her bag and stacked them beside the keyboard.

'360s,' she said. 'I figured you might have an older system, so I copied everything from the one-point-two-meg disks. What is this, a 286?'

Anne rested her hand on the monitor, remembering. 'It was Jeffs business system,' she said as Carl came in, bearing a tray with cups, coffeepot, and fixings. 'So let's see, it's a 286 with one meg on-board RAM and a 40-meg hard disk.'

'Yeah,' Carl said. 'With dual overhead cams and a double framistan on the floozy-gidget running at two hundred rpm in overdrive.' He plunked the tray down on the coffee table and glowered at the computer.

This time, Cynthia's laugh was whole-hearted. 'Don't sweat it,' she told him. 'Just means that this is an okay machine, a little outdated but not obsolete. At least, not this month. Let's see what we've got.'

She typed in a few commands, and the screen blinked and presented one of George's memo files.

'What's that mean?' Carl said, bending over their shoulders to stare at the screen. 'Good progress with self-actualization? Huh?'

Cynthia shrugged. 'Means that George wanted to say something positive without saying anything at all. Look at the next line. 'Tell Max to get in on time'. Typical George-babble, all of it, start with gibberish then get to the subject. That last line, that's the heart of it. Here, let's look at this one.'

Words scrolled up the screen.

''Mike — forget it',' Anne read. 'Insisting is non-accomplishing and obstructive.' Insisting on what?'

Cynthia shrugged and tapped the keyboard. Heads together, the three reviewed a memo to Jimi Johannsen about the 'ability of the system to empower self-assertion' via the aura reader; a note to Brian demanding that he order new copies of a manual;

and a series of letters to George's lawyer suggesting, among other things, that Lena Ashby be examined by a psychiatrist before any final settlement was reached. There was also a vituperative letter to Peter Simpson, the past lives programmer in Berkeley, which caused Cynthia to snort and Carl to turn red and beat a hasty, if temporary, retreat to the kitchen. Anne printed out copies of all these documents, and put them in her tote.

The last file was titled MYLIFE.DOC and dated the Saturday before George's death, but the file resisted their efforts to view it. After typing in a few rapid commands, Cynthia said the file was probably encrypted, and produced what she called a 'hex dump'. The results looked like garbage. Anne blinked, watching Cynthia's fingers fly over the keyboard while the monitor screen shifted and danced.

'What's encryption?' Carl said.

Encryption, Cynthia said, was a scheme whereby the computer scrambled the contents of a file. The scrambling couldn't be undone unless one had the key, and if the scheme involved a long key, Cynthia said, then trying to break the code would be difficult, if not downright impossible.

'Unless . . . ' Cynthia tapped at the keyboard, frowning. 'Look, we've got to start with some basic assumptions. First, George was a cheap bastard. I mean, he could have bought us a decent word processing program, and instead he loaded in a shareware program. It works, but only barely. So I don't think he'd go buy an expensive encryption program, it just wasn't like him. Hell, it could even be something he wrote himself.' She laughed. 'In which case, we're in real trouble. But it's probably a pretty simple-minded substitution scheme — you know, where 'a' is always 'l' and 'b' is always 'x'. If you know the key, it's simple to break. If the key doesn't have too many characters, I should be able to break the code.'

'How?' Carl said.

'Write a program to try out all the combinations, and see what we get.' Cynthia pushed back from the keyboard and stretched. 'Tell you what. I've got a 486 at home. I'll copy MYLIFE onto my hard disk and try to decrypt it. We can look through the results tomorrow night; it should be done by then.' She tapped a series of commands, and the drive lights on the system box blinked and glowed. 'Of course, if he used a long key, we're back to square one.'

Carl shook his head. 'You understand all that stuff, huh?'

'Yeah, but I can't figure out why my car diesels after I turn off the ignition. I'll bet you can, though.'

'Sure, it's probably your timing,' he said. 'Your Hudson acting up?'

'That's Jeremiah Hudson to you, friend. Yeah, we've both got timing problems.' She cocked her head. 'Interested? I'll let you take a look someday, if you'd like.'

'Uh, sure,' Carl said, then muttered something about washing up, and retreated to the kitchen.

'He's not taken, is he?' she said wistfully, and Anne laughed and shook her head.

Fifteen minutes later, Cynthia refused another cup of coffee and gathered the disks together. 'I'll put together a program tonight and try it out tomorrow. It'll take some babysitting, but I'll find something to do while it's running.'

'But you've got to go to work,' Anne said, holding out Cynthia's jacket.

Cynthia grinned. 'No sweat. I feel a real bad attack of PMS coming on. That always scares the crap out of Thompson. You break your leg, get pneumonia, total your car, he expects you at work. But just mention getting your period and he turns green and runs.'

Carl left a minute after Cynthia did. Anne yawned as she put away the coffee cups, then called Alicia of Alicia's Antiques in Berkeley, and filled her in on the events of the past two days.

'A silver-hilted presentation knife in the figure of Catherine of Aragon,' Alicia's precise voice repeated. 'I'll run a search through the database. With luck, I should have something for you by tomorrow.'

'What database?' Anne said, repressing another yawn. 'You don't have a computer.'

'And you, Anne Munro, are out of date,' Alicia said. 'I happen to have a fine system, tied in by modem to the National

Antiquarians Database and various universities. I'll see you tomorrow, Anne. Now go to sleep.'

Alicia hung up. Anne dug out Peter Simpson's phone number, then shook her head and re-cradled the phone. If Simpson was that mad at Ashby, he might not agree to see her at all. Better just to drop by, she decided.

Besides, one more conversation that day was more than she could take. She turned out the lights and went to bed.

17

Wednesday morning dawned bright and cold, the sun a small yellow disk in a pale blue sky. Despite this, the morning weather report promised a fast-moving storm by late afternoon, and Anne made sure Danny took his rain jacket with him. She drove Danny to school and walked him to the kindergarten play yard, where Mrs. Prizwalski presided over Early Morning Childcare. Anne stood with her for a moment, chatting about the brightness of the day. When talk turned to the murder, she made her excuses and captured Danny. He kissed her goodbye at lightning speed and ran back to the jungle gym. Auralia's face, she noted, was no longer covered with buttons and glue, and she seemed to be playing happily with Penny and Jackie, and no hard feelings apparent.

Anne sat in her car for a moment, watching oak leaves catch the light and scatter shadows across the school parking lot.

Beyond the oak, two large ravens bickered over a scrap near the playground picnic tables. Finally, with a small impatient gesture, she put the car in gear and pulled out onto the Melville-Santa Bolsas Road.

Before leaving home, she had called the Growing Light offices to remind everyone that she was driving to Oakland. It was the first time she heard the company's phone message, and she listened to the background of New Age music and the machine's measured, soothing voice assuring her that communicating with her was something the entire company was eager to share as soon as possible. She managed not to laugh on tape.

Santa Bolsas Road wound between pastures and farmlands and through Santa Bolsas itself. The town boasted some buildings dating as far back as the 1850s, but most of the downtown had been built at the turn of the century and in the two decades following. During the California boom times of the 1970s and 80s, Santa Bolsas, like the rest of Lake Harris County, had been too far away, and too poor, to participate in the orgy of demolition and square-box reconstruction. As a result, the town's tree-lined streets ran between gingerbread Victorians and solid iron-front buildings; picket or wrought-iron fences edged lawns or elaborate flower gardens, and as far as Anne knew, not a single parking meter graced the entire county.

The road crossed Santa Bolsas Creek, entered the narrow pass in the eastern hills, crossed the Harris River over a 1930s WPA bridge, and scooted her through the southern end of Sonoma County before depositing her at Highway 101, where everything stopped. The morning traffic was bumper to bumper, and Anne waited until a truck driver gestured and made room for her. Waving, she slid her small station wagon into the traffic. On the radio, a traffic reporter briskly announced a major blockage on tiny Lakeville Highway, and she decided to stay on 101 through San Rafael rather than risk the smaller two-lane road through to Vallejo.

Now, creeping along with the commute traffic through Novato, Anne hoped that Cynthia's program would work. With luck, that night she'd have something solid to show Van Damme, something that pointed a finger at someone other than herself. In the meantime, there were sensors to pick up along the Oakland waterfront, and what she hoped would be a long and informative meeting with Alicia.

Driving over the Richmond-San Rafael Bridge and through Richmond reminded her again of why she and Jeff had been so happy to leave the East Bay. By the time she negotiated the usual hideous backup near the Bay Bridge and through downtown Oakland to the waterfront, she realized that somewhere she had misplaced the rhythm of city driving. She had no problem with the freeways, they were too clogged to be frantic, but the city streets distressed her — people down here thought stop signs were suggestions. She pulled into the parking lot of a waterfront diner and held on to the wheel for a moment, catching her breath, before locking the car and going in search of a cup of coffee and directions to the warehouse.

The woman behind the counter looked Anne over and shook her head.

'Honey, you be lost,' she said, reaching

for a coffee cup and pouring steaming black liquid into it. 'You miss the Berkeley exit, girl?'

Anne laughed and relaxed. She asked for directions to the warehouse and listened while the waitress and two truckers disagreed with each other. Eventually an Asian woman in an AC Transit uniform interrupted, issued concise directions, and returned to her breakfast. Anne finished her coffee and left the diner.

To her relief, the warehouse was run by much the same kind of people. With rowdy friendliness, they found the shipment of sensors, dealt efficiently with the paperwork, and sent her on her way. She called Alicia from a pay phone near Jack London Square and got back into her car, relaxed and in possession of her city driving skills again.

Alicia's Antiques occupied a small space at the corner of Adeline and Ashby in Berkeley. Anne circled the block three times before finding a parking space, then walked past the rows of antique stores, pausing to peer in the windows. Bedsteads and highboys and rugs; dolls and lace and vintage dresses; engraved silver urns and tableware behind black iron bars. On the sidewalk, a ragged man glowered and demanded money from passers-by, and Anne ducked into Alicia's shop before he spotted her. The bell on the door jangled.

Spode, Alicia's watch-cat, stalked around the counter and came to demand a pet.

★   ★   ★

Anne knelt to stroke him, and the bell behind her jangled. She looked over her shoulder as the ragged man tramped in. He howled something unintelligible and thrust his hand, palm up, at Anne. Spode hissed and backed away.

Before Anne could blink, Alicia herself stormed from the back room, planted hands on her narrow hips, and glared.

'Don't even think of it,' she announced. The man stopped. 'I am sick and tired of chasing you out of here. If I see your ass in my shop one more time, I'm going to kick it up and down Ashby Avenue, do you understand?'

He blinked and took a step back. 'Yeah, okay, lady — '

'*Now!*'

He jumped backwards, and the door snapped shut.

'Well, that's much better,' Alicia said, and patted her fluffy white hair into place. 'Anne, my dear, do straighten up and assume a bit of dignity. We are not, after all, rugrats, are we?' Behind silver spectacles, Alicia's eyes twinkled, and she offered Anne one dainty be-ringed hand. Anne took it and stood, smiling down at her tiny friend.

'You never cease to amaze me,' she said.

Alicia laughed as she turned away. 'Oh, you mean The Howler? Every morning for the past two weeks. I declare, I've simply lost my temper. I have a snack set up on the Regency. Do come along now, I'm famished.' She took her seat at a Regency table set with linen, silver, fine china, and a pastry box. 'I'm quite sure the poor man has a sad story, but that's no excuse for rudeness. No sugar, no milk, correct? I don't comprehend how you can drink coffee that way.'

They spent the next half hour catching

up on each other's lives. Alicia asked questions about Growing Light and George Ashby's death, demanding details Anne had not given her the night before.

'Very interesting,' she declared finally. 'Well, let's clear this away and take a look, shall we?'

The bell jingled again, and Anne cleaned the table and took the silver and china into the back room while Alicia dealt with a lady who was interested in the Wedgwood but wasn't quite sure it would go with her new house. Eventually she bought two Delft bowls and a small Royal Copenhagen figurine, complained about the price, and left.

'Business has been booming ever since the Great Fire,' Alicia said, joining Anne in the back room. 'Here, don't wash those, I'll take care of it later. Nothing like a catastrophe in the richest part of town to move the pricey goods.'

Alicia's books, alphabetized and neatly aligned, filled a ten-foot shelf. A thin film of dust covered their tops. Below them, on a Louis XIV table, stood an impressive-looking computer system with a color monitor.

It blinked companionably as Alicia sat down and tapped the keyboard. The screen moved through various menus and 'please wait' notices.

'Best investment I ever made,' Alicia declared. 'Aha, here we are. So, we choose era, like this.' She tapped in a menu choice. 'Now then, if your knife has the Tudor Rose and it really is Catherine, then it had to have been made between 1509 and 1533. Unless it commemorated her marriage to Edward; that was in 1501.'

'I don't think so,' Anne said. 'I'm pretty sure the letters were H and C, intertwined below the Rose.'

'Well, knowing Henry, he wouldn't have wasted money too often. So we assume it was commemorative of the coronation, correct? 1509. Very well, then . . . '

She tapped more instructions into the keyboard, and Anne looked around the shop. Alicia had done well in the past year; the shelves were crowded with sparkling china and crystal, and vintage jewelry gleamed within the display counter.

'Now, then, your knife probably started life as a commemorative figurine. At least, that's often the case. So, let's see about our sub-categories here. Commemorative, figurines, silver, and special emphasis on gift lists. That should do it. Aha, there we are,' Alicia said and tapped a few more keys. Her printer started chattering.

'Created in London in 1509, probably late winter or early spring since the marriage took place on June 11.' She pointed at a line on the screen. 'Listed among the wedding and coronation gifts presented to the Spanish envoy on June 24, during the coronation banquet. Two of them,' Alicia said, pausing to make sure Anne understood the significance of that. 'Catherine, and Henry himself.'

'Yes,' Anne said. 'Jimi mentioned that George's knife had a male figure on it.'

'The figurines probably traveled to Spain later that year, perhaps as early as August, and ended up in the treasury of Ferdinand and Isabella, Catherine's parents,' Alicia said. 'Who, thirty-three years later, funded Columbus' first voyage. But that, of course, isn't material until a bit later. At some point during the next two hundred years, the figurines were mounted as knife hilts — a common fate for such objects. The next mention listed them among the presentation gifts given by Charles II to José de Gálvez. This poor gentleman had the task of sailing to the New World and setting to rights the deplorable finances of Mexico. At which point they disappear from history.'

The printer finished clattering. Alicia picked up a sterling letter opener and separated the pages, evened them, and handed them to Anne.

'I must say,' Alicia said, 'that whoever did the mounting must have done a fine job. Imagine, after all these centuries. Catherine still being sharp enough to murder that, ahem, gentleman.'

'It didn't take a lot of strength,' Anne replied, looking at the papers. 'Van Damme said it was a lucky hit.'

Alicia frowned and tapped the printout.

'Spain,' she said contemplatively. 'Toledo steel? That would make sense, and explain how the knife kept such an excellent edge. I'll check that in a bit, whether the foundries were . . . later, definitely later. Now, then, what next?'

Anne folded the papers and slid them into her tote. 'You know,' she said slowly, 'tracing its origin is only part of it. After that, I have to figure out how it made its way into George Ashby.' She frowned. 'I have the name of someone here in Berkeley who might know something. I thought I'd go by and see him before I head back north.'

Alicia's eyebrows rose. 'Know something in what way?'

'Well, he used to work for George, programming. And Jimi said that George got mad at him and refused to pay him, and it just seems like a good idea to check it out.'

Alicia sighed. 'I suppose it does, considering that this Jackson person seems ready to toss your trim backside in the slammer. I assume that you'll be careful.'

'Of course.' Anne reached for her jacket.

'And young Danny? How's he taking all of this?'

Anne frowned. 'I haven't told him. Here I try to teach him that the police are his friends and help people and protect us from bad guys, so how am I supposed to reconcile all that with the fact that this particular man thinks that Mommy is one of the bad guys?'

Alicia nodded. 'Well, nobody ever told you that raising a child would be simple, did they? I'll try the California history databases. They're not entirely satisfactory, but perhaps I can trace your sword or knife hilt, or whatever.' She walked with Anne toward the front door. 'Of course, there's quite a bit of precedent for taking a figure or the like and making a ceremonial hilt from it. Poor dear, as if she didn't have enough troubles, ending up on that piece of cutlery.' Alicia opened the door and stuck her head out. 'The coast, my dear, is clear, at least for the moment. Take advantage of it.'

Anne gave Alicia a quick hug and walked rapidly toward her car.

18

Anne started her car and eased out into the traffic on Ashby. Over the radio, an announcer cheerfully burbled, 'Round the Bay newstime is exactly ten-fifteen.'

Anne made a right turn onto old Grove Street, now Martin Luther King, Jr. Way, and glanced at the slip of paper Jimi had given her. Peter Simpson lived in west Berkeley, below Shattuck but above Sacramento; not the best part of town, but not the worst. For a moment she thought about calling first, then remembered George's vituperative letter to Simpson. If someone had sent her a letter like that, she thought, she'd be furious. She wondered just how angry Peter Simpson was.

The address turned out to be a small cottage tucked behind a larger brown-shingle house. She followed a brick path between the brown shingle and a hedge of roses, into and across a tiny patio and to the equally tiny cottage in the rear. Smoke curled from a brick chimney. She mounted the steps and rang the bell.

'Go away,' a voice yelled from inside.

'Mr. Simpson?' Anne called.

'I don't want any, I don't have any opinions, and I can't afford it. Go!'

'Mr. Simpson, I work at Growing Light,' Anne shouted through the door. 'I need to talk to you.'

The door flew open and a wildly bearded face came out. 'You got money for me?' the beard demanded.

'No, I — '

Simpson started to slam the door, but Anne blocked it with her foot.

'Mr. Simpson, I'm trying to learn about George Ashby,' she said firmly. 'I think we ought to talk.'

Simpson kept pushing at his door. 'You tell Ashby,' he said, 'that if he wants to talk to me, he'd damn well better pay me what he owes me, that black-hearted lying son of a bitch.'

'I'd be glad to,' Anne retorted. 'Except that somebody murdered that black-hearted lying son of a bitch, and that's what I want to talk to you about.'

For a moment Simpson kept pushing, then the door swung wide open.

'Murdered him?' the programmer repeated. 'You mean the bastard's *dead?*'

Anne took a deep breath. 'Undeniably and reliably dead, Mr. Simpson. May I come in?'

'Oh, hell,' Simpson said. 'And I'll just bet he took my money with him. Yeah, come on in.'

Anne ignored the less-than-gracious invitation and stepped inside. A bewildering pile of computer equipment occupied the top of a table near the window, and spilled over onto the windowsill and the floor beneath. Printouts, magazines, photocopied sheets, and other detritus teetered along the couch and across the floor, stopping well short of a tall hearth on which stood a metal fireplace. Flames glowed behind a screen, and defunct computer components littered the hearth, which extended into the tiny kitchen. Simpson marched into the kitchen and emerged with two chipped mugs and a pot.

'Earl Gray,' he said, dropping the pot

on a corner of the computer table. 'It's all I got.'

He dumped magazines from an easy chair for her, then perched on the wheeled typing chair in front of the computer.

'I gotta call my lawyer,' he said. He tapped his keyboard, and a blank blue screen came up. 'I'm filing suit against Ashby, I mean, I filed before all this came down. Who did him? When did he die?' He typed the date, then looked over his shoulder. 'What's your name?'

Anne told him and sketched in the events of Monday morning, while Simpson listened and made notes on his computer.

'You work for him?' Simpson said when she finished.

'It was my first day,' Anne said.

'And you drove all the way down here just to let me know?' Simpson snorted. 'I don't believe it.'

'I need to find out who killed him. Because Mike Thompson and the sheriff seem to think I did it, and I didn't.'

'Hah!' Simpson leaped from his seat

and paced about the tiny room, adroitly avoiding paper piles while peering at Anne. He had small brown eyes under thick, curly brows which gave him the appearance of an animated brown bush. A rather malicious brown bush, Anne amended, as Simpson stopped pacing and spun toward her.

'You think I did it,' he crowed. 'You're here because you think I killed George Ashby! That's a hoot.' He convulsed in laughter.

Anne tried not to wince and wondered just how sane he was.

'So you want to know where I was and all that, my — what do you call it — my alibi! Hah! Well, let's just keep it in the air a little longer, shall we?' Simpson said with glee. 'Damn it, I need to talk to my lawyer. I did it? Hah! What I wouldn't give — that bastard's been stealing my program codes for years, you hear me? I mean, sure, he used to pay me, but you know what I found? Do you?'

'I have no idea,' Anne said.

'Hah!' Simpson dove into a pile of paper and emerged with a printout. 'You know what this is? Do you? It's my notes, that's what it is. Last month, I got a call from the — wait, I've got it right here — the Redwood Empire Human Potential Association, got that? They wanted to give that bastard an award, and you know why? For his innovative programming, that's why! And you know who wrote that stuff? Not the basic stuff, that's all routine, but the aura routine and the astrological importer and all that? Do you?'

Anne took a breath. 'You did?'

'Hah! I told them, I told them chapter and verse, and you know what those assholes told me? Do you know? That George Ashby put his name on all of it, every single last line of code! That bastard couldn't program worth a damn, oh no. But he could program enough to get into *my* code and overwrite my name in it and stick in his own goddamned name, and file a goddamned copyright on it, and that's what that bastard did.' Simpson sat down, then jumped right back up again. 'Well, I want you to know, I convinced them! Sent them the code, date-stamped and everything. I guess that just about fried it for him, didn't it?'

'I'm afraid not,' Anne said, carefully setting down her teacup and gauging the distance to the front door. 'They gave him the award anyway. Last Friday night, at some big awards dinner.'

Simpson stared at her. 'You're fooling, right?' he demanded. 'More of George's bullshit mind games, right?'

'I'm afraid not, Mr. Simpson. Last Friday night.'

Peter Simpson's jaw dropped, then he mumbled something, and to Anne's astonishment, he fell back in his chair and started to cry.

'He did it again,' Simpson sobbed. 'You know, that bastard's always coming out on top. Like when he sent me out of that goddamned foxhole and I took out the enemy and *he* got the medal . . . '

'I beg your pardon?'

'1909,' Simpson said, and sniffled. 'And in 1853 when he aced me out of the land in Tennessee, and — hell, all the way back to Greece when that little bastard got the Phoenician import charter when it should have gone to me!'

Anne started to rise, but Simpson paid no attention.

'And, my God! When was that, sometime during Alexander, when we got into that scrape in Egypt — or maybe that was Darius — I'd forgotten about that . . . '

He turned to the computer and started banging at the keyboard.

'Those temple carvings,' he muttered. 'I'd forgotten about those, and he stole them and sold them to that Macedonian general, and . . . '

Anne quietly let herself out, and didn't stop moving until she reached her car, got inside, and locked all the doors. Then, still under tight control, she drove until she was back across the Richmond-San Rafael bridge before pulling off the freeway in central San Rafael and sitting for a while in a gas station parking lot, just holding on to the steering wheel. After a few minutes her shoulders relaxed, and she thought about Peter Simpson again.

Egyptian temple carvings and Phoenician import charters and Macedonian generals; she started to giggle. The image of George Ashby chasing Peter Simpson through time, like some vengeful agent of wrath — an intense blue-eyed maniac in pursuit of a harried brown bush . . . Still laughing, she made her way to the women's room. It was locked. The gas station attendant gave her a strange look when she asked for the key, but handed it over.

★   ★   ★

By the time she negotiated the horrible left-hand turn off 101 toward Santa Bolsas, she knew her laughter to be a thin edge of hysteria. The thought sobered her. The clouds lowered, promising rain, and traffic was thin over the two-lane WPA bridge; the road ran through the middle of Santa Bolsas, past the iron front buildings on Main Street and the ugly new Lake Harris County National Bank building at the intersection of Main and School Streets. The clock in the tower above the Lake Harris Historical Museum and Research Center read 1:00. Her stomach growled. She thought about stopping at Evvie's for lunch, then decided against it. Carl would be working, and hungry to know everything she'd learned that morning. And, she thought honestly, she really didn't even know that herself.

Beyond Santa Bolsas' tiny downtown, the sidewalks disappeared into a tangle of weeds and ditches, and the occasional homemade billboard. At the western edge of Santa Bolsas, she pulled into the skinny parking lot in front of Wolen's Bait Grocery & Deli ('Open Sundays,' the sign proclaimed). Rain spangled the windshield as soon as she stopped the engine, and she hurried inside.

A large stuffed hawk screamed silently from the rafters, lording it over a prized collection of swordfish, bass, and a huge marlin Mitch Wolen had caught in Alaska. The wall behind the counter boasted eight-by-ten photographs of Mitch's father, Abraham Wolinski, with an enormous salmon caught off the coast.

'Why aren't they stuffed too?' Danny had asked old Abraham the first time Anne brought him into the store.

'Stuffed?' Abraham echoed. 'Stuffed,

the child says. To stuff salmon, you goyische kopf, is a sin. Salmon you only photograph. Then!' The old man dipped into the deli counter. 'Then the salmon you smoke, then the salmon you eat!' He leaned over the counter to stuff a sliver of salmon into Danny's mouth, and the child had been a fan of lox and cream cheese ever since.

Now, Abraham's son Mitch Wolen took her order for a tuna on rye and a cup of coffee.

'Hear tell Jackson's on your tail,' he said in a whisper, leaning across the counter. Anne raised her eyebrows.

'Millie Beckson,' he went on, still whispering. 'She told Betty Cartwright at Betty's Boutique and Unmentionables, and Betty told Abraham, and Dad's ready to get up a petition and picket City Hall.' Mitch grinned. 'He's getting ready to picket Melville, too; got a sign ready and everything. It says, 'Save People, Not Fish.' '

Anne laughed. Last summer, the Melville Piscine Emancipation Front had picketed Wolen's and blocked the Santa

Bolsas-Melville Road for four hours during the height of the weekend tourist traffic, chanting 'Fishing is murder' and preventing avid fishermen from reaching the coast. Abraham's one concession to the picketing had been to mount a sign above the deli case. 'Our Tuna,' it said, 'is Dolphin Estranged.'

'Not to worry,' Anne said. 'Tell Abraham that Jackson hasn't got me yet.'

She took her sandwich and coffee and sat at one of the two tables Mitch kept at the back of the shop, before a homemade mural of wide-mouth bass cavorting amid hawks, and a lopsided American eagle that Abraham had insisted on painting himself. The sandwich, as always, was delicious, and the coffee hot and extremely strong.

Anne dug into her tote and pulled out the list she had made Monday night. She went over it, adding information gleaned over the past day and a half, and sat back to look at it.

Mike Thompson still headed the list, but Audrey's hysteria yesterday might point to a motive. Certainly Max Allen, dead or not, had moved up the list of suspects. And now there was Peter Simpson to consider, and the mystery of the Catherine and Henry knives — if Henry was, indeed, mounted on the knife that had not killed George Ashby. And what about Carein? Anne shook her head, puzzled, and folded the list back into her tote before paying Mitch and driving back to Melville.

On the way, she passed Danny's school. The yards were empty, even the ravens taking shelter against the increasing rain. Just past the school, rolling fields and the occasional truck farm passed by, interspersed with wholesale nurseries and dairy farms. The hills shouldered in near Inez and the road wound upwards toward Melville and, beyond it, the pass to Bodega Bay. The wipers thwacked and squeaked, and Anne found herself seduced by the idea of driving past Melville and through the pass to Highway 1 on the coast, and north out of California, out of Oregon and Washington, through Canada, and into the cold calm distances of Alaska. More north wasn't possible, but she could turn east and south, through the provinces and across half the continent, then down, not along the East Coast but through the Rust Belt and the fertile Midwest, down to Mexico . . . Danny at her side, learning to eat new foods, speak new languages, never bound to one place or one time, always moving, learning, seeing and hearing and tasting the exotic, the strange, the wonderfully new —

The car jolted over a cattleguard and Anne shook her head, putting aside thoughts of grand and improbable escapes. The day had darkened with heavy rain; the wipers barely kept up. Anne slowed and downshifted for the climb up the foothills toward Melville and Growing Light. The road snaked here. A dense stand of eucalyptus bordered one side, and on the other, the hills fell with increasing steepness toward the farmlands below. Sometimes livestock or deer wandered onto the road, oblivious of traffic — and always, it seemed, at night or in the rain. Anne kept watch for them, so intently that for a while she did not notice the headlights approaching behind her.

When she did notice them, she shook her head. Probably one of the local kids, still convinced of immortality and ready to break his neck or somebody else's by driving too fast in dangerous conditions. By now the vehicle behind her seemed far too close. Anne flicked on her emergency blinkers. That often slowed them up a bit.

Instead, the headlights seemed to accelerate, filling her windshield. Anne pumped the brake and prayed that the idiot would pass her. The windshield flared around her and light stabbed down from the rear-view mirror, blinding her. She pumped the brake harder, hit the horn, clutched the steering wheel with her right hand and reached for the window crank with her left. If she could only see, at least out the side . . . It seemed that time slowed, that she had plenty of time to grab the lever, feel the resistance in the brake pedal, marvel that she was doing all these correct things in a rational order. A sliver of visibility through the side window, but the eucalyptus trees flew by much too close. She corrected and returned one hand to the horn, pounding on it, and was jerked back as something fast and solid hit the back of the car. The small wagon slewed wildly. She wrenched on the steering wheel and felt the tires grip the road before the other vehicle hit her again, harder this time. She heard the hiss of rubber over gravel and then, sickeningly, over nothing at all.

19

'Good lord, Terry, she's alive!'

Anne raised her head. For a little while, after the impact, she had sat enveloped in motionless silence, then for a while after that she shook so hard that she had to hold onto the steering wheel and close her eyes. Noise everywhere: a constant drumming above her, what sounded like cattle bellowing, a distant siren, then the voice again.

'She's alive, I say! Get over here!'

More bellowing outside, and a hand reached through the window and touched Anne's shoulder.

'You okay?' the voice said.

'I think so,' Anne whispered.

The voice shouted, 'Can you hear me? You okay?'

The shout cut through her head like a knife, and she closed her eyes. 'Yes, I think so,' she said, more loudly this time.

The head retreated. 'Says she's okay!' it

reported at top volume. The siren became louder.

Really, she thought. *Such a fuss.* She tried to straighten up. It was much harder than it should have been, and she discovered that she, and her car, rested at a steep angle.

'Now don't you move, girl,' the voice said at a more reasonable volume. 'My man and me, we took that first aid thing down at the church, and they said you're not supposed to move 'til the ambulance gets here. So you just rest easy. You cold?'

'Yes,' Anne whispered.

A moment passed, then something warm and wet slid over her shoulders and arms. 'You need it more'n I do.' The voice paused. 'You fall asleep or something up there?'

'I did not,' Anne said, straightening anyway and opening her eyes. The sirens were closer now. A light bobbled toward her up the hillside, and in its occasional light she saw a woman's face under a rubber hat, peering at her.

'Someone hit my car,' Anne said. 'Up on the road. Had his high beams on.'

The woman thought for a moment as the sirens screamed and stopped.

'There's crazy people runnin' round with blood in their eyes. My boy says that, got it off a song somewhere. You're lucky, girl, me and my man were closin' up the barn when we see you come off the road. Called 911 right away, and come right up here. Now don't you move; here comes the fire truck.' She removed her head from the window. 'Down here,' she bellowed. 'Says she's okay, least she can talk. Now *don't* go turning your head, girl!'

In the rear view mirror, Anne saw the Emergency Medical Technicians approaching cautiously, scanning the land.

'No lines down,' one called, and another shouted that Anne's car didn't seem to be leaking gas. A thin blond woman in a blue uniform reached the car.

'Just hang on a minute,' she said. 'We gotta stabilize the vehicle. You okay? Did you pass out?'

'No, I don't think so.'

'That's good,' the woman said. 'Don't move your head, okay? I'll be in with you in a second.'

A moment later, the woman was in the car and had Anne's head in a strong and unrelenting grip.

'Hey, I'm okay, really,' Anne said. 'Just sore, that's all.'

'Look, I'm just trying to help you,' the EMT said. 'You could have a back injury, and I'm not taking any chances.'

Seconds later, her neck was enveloped in a huge brace, but the EMT didn't let her go. Other hands checked her pulse and breathing, and relayed a string of numbers out the window.

'I'm cold,' Anne said. 'My chest hurts.'

'We'll get you a blanket, just hang on.'

Rain drenched her as they maneuvered her from the car, keeping her neck and back straight, and strapped her to a backboard. Overhead, a leafless California walnut spidered against the sky. Anne closed her eyes against the rain as they carried her up to the ambulance. Once inside, the EMT started palpating her chest.

'Who's the president?' she said.

'Huh?'

'The president. What's his name?'

Anne told her, and continued to answer questions about the date and other trivia as the EMT finished her exam.

'Lucky you had your seatbelt on,' she said. 'Looks like you've got some bruises, but nothing's broken.' She launched into questions about allergies and health history, while her colleague called the hospital and Anne tried to get a word in edgewise about the car that hit her. A sheriff's deputy wrote it down, and looked at her.

'I know you,' the man said. 'You were up at that place in Melville, where that guy was murdered.'

'I work there,' Anne said. She remembered Mike Thompson talking about health insurance, and panic hit her.

'Where are you taking me?' she demanded.

'Santa Bolsas Memorial,' the EMT said. 'They'll take great care of you.'

'No, you can't! Look, I'm okay, just some bruises. Can't you just let me go?'

'Sorry, ma'am, it's regulations. You gotta be checked over. Besides, what if something's wrong that we can't check here? You've gotta be checked over by a doctor.'

'Look, you don't understand. I don't

have medical insurance — I can't pay for it,' Anne said desperately. 'There's a waiting period at my job, I just started there, I can't pay any hospital bills, they'll take my house — '

'No, they won't,' the EMT said. 'Your job right now is to get better, and my job is to help you do it. Nobody's gonna take your house, now you just calm down,' the EMT said. 'Calm down. I really don't want to have to restrain you.'

Anne closed her eyes and took the trip to Santa Bolsas Memorial in a fog of misery, punctuated by the soft whine of the siren and the smack of rain against the ambulance roof.

★　★　★

Half an hour later, she lay on a table in a corner of the emergency ward. Someone moved nearby, but she had to squash her chin into the neck brace to look. Lieutenant Van Damme sat beside the bed, doodling into his pad.

Anne looked around for a moment, noting the white curtains that divided her from the rest of the ward; the gleaming wall-mounted monitors that were not, thank God, connected to her; the bustle of the doctors and nurses and technicians on the other side of the curtains. She felt stiff from her neck to her hips.

'Welcome back,' Van Damme said. 'I'm happy to report that Doc Emerson says you're the luckiest woman in Lake Harris County. Nothing broken, nothing harmed. A few bruised ribs and a neck strain, that's the extent of it. That's the good news.'

Anne just looked at him sideways.

'The rest of the good news is, I think I can get you qualified for Victim's Assistance through the county. The EMT said you were worried about medical bills. VA will take care of that.'

'Victim's Assistance,' Anne echoed. 'How?'

'It all depends on where we go from here,' Van Damme said. 'We've towed your car. I think it's totaled, but you can argue with your insurance agent about that.'

Anne rolled over a bit to look at him. He smiled and waited.

'That,' Anne croaked. She wet her lips and tried again. 'That's the bad news.'

Van Damme shook his head and his smile went away. 'No, the bad news is that somebody lost some paint on the back of your car — square in the middle and along the left-hand bumper. Pretty recently, too. Mabel Hillegas said you said something to her about someone hitting your car.'

Anne wet her lips again and tried to take a deep breath. It hurt, and she lay still for a moment, then told him about the ride from Wolen's toward Melville, the rain and the twisting road, the high beams and everything she'd done, and the final silent fall through nothing.

'But why would someone want to hit my car?' she said. 'Why would someone want to hurt me?'

Van Damme laid his pencil in his notebook, then leaned back in the chair. 'Well, Miss Marple,' he said, 'I was hoping that was something you could tell me.'

For a moment that didn't make any sense, then it did. Anne rolled onto her back again and stared at the acoustic tiles on the ceiling. 'God, it must be the sedatives,' she muttered. 'Look, if I tell you what I've been doing, are you going to get mad at me?'

'If it led to someone trying to run you off the road and kill you,' Van Damme said, 'then yes, I probably am.' He leaned forward and, unexpectedly, took her hand. 'But I'm more likely to get mad at whoever didn't like what you've been up to. Either way, I think you'd better tell me.'

Anne turned her hand so that his fingers laced through hers and, holding onto him, told him about her conversation with Alicia and about meeting Peter Simpson. She thought of telling him about the backup copies of George's files, but on impulse decided not to. Van Damme took up his pencil and notebook and made her repeat certain details.

'It seems to me,' he said after a while, 'that someone knows you're poking your nose into this case, and that someone wants you to stop. You following me so far?'

Anne tried to nod, and couldn't. 'So?' she said.

'So I don't want you poking into this either,' he continued. 'Look, Jackson's almost seen the light here. He knows there's no evidence linking you to Ashby's death, and if he weren't such a fool he'd have seen it from the beginning. That note doesn't make any difference. Thompson — I figure him for the bully type. He latched onto you that first day because someone like that has to blame somebody, and you were handy.'

'What about Thompson?' Anne demanded. 'He's never told us what he was doing Monday morning. His office is right next to George's — he could have snuck through the bathroom, stabbed George, and snuck right back out. Hell, he's even got a bathroom to clean up in.'

'Yeah, I know. Trouble is, George spurted a bit, know what I mean? Thompson didn't have a chance to go home; everyone says he didn't change clothes. Aside from the office, we didn't find any other traces of blood.'

Anne frowned at the ceiling. 'Maybe he

wore something protective. Maybe a plastic garbage bag. I saw some in Pete's room; he could have used one of those.'

'Sure. But Lena Ashby could have done the same thing.'

'No,' Anne said. 'George was alive when Lena left; he came out to tell Audrey those lies about my husband. And Audrey would have seen her come back in, if she did.'

'Yeah. We checked her alibi. She went from Growing Light to her lawyer, the transit times check out, and both the lawyer and his secretary swear she was there at the right time.'

Anne peered at him. 'And Thompson?'

Van Damme shook his head. 'He was on the phone to his own lawyer. We've checked that, too.'

'Wait a minute.' Anne battled both headache and sedatives for a moment. 'What about this. Thompson calls his lawyer, talks, puts him on hold, goes in and stabs George, comes back out, finishes the conversation, gets rid of whatever he used to cover himself with . . . No, huh?'

'No,' Van Damme echoed. 'Or, that is, probably not. Thompson's hiding something, and could be that he killed Ashby, but somehow it just doesn't click for me.'

'Hah.' Anne looked at him sideways again. 'That famous detective's intuition?'

Van Damme didn't smile. 'Sometimes it works. This time, I don't know. But something tells me that this was a spur-of-the moment thing, and something tells me that we're looking for a woman here.'

At that, Anne pushed herself up, ignoring the soreness in her midsection.

'And just what,' she demanded, 'led to that brilliant conclusion? Is there something female about stabbing someone? Or was it that George got it in the back? And will you stand up so I can glare at you without straining my eyes?'

'Hey, calm down,' Van Damme said, rising. 'We're talking intuition here, okay? I'm not being a sexist, Ms. Munro.'

'Bull,' Anne muttered, and settled back. 'So?'

He stared at the white curtain. 'I don't know. The more I hear about Ashby, the more I think he liked messing with people's heads. That stuff he said about your husband, things the other people told me. By the way, I tracked down your Tuesday Morning Breakfast Club, and they told me the same sort of thing. And we did find Toby Sanchez. He's visiting his sister in Lakeport. He spent all day Monday at the unemployment office, so he's out of it.' Van Damme transferred his gaze to Anne, but he still looked like he was staring at something far away. 'I get the feeling that Ashby went out of his way to hurt people. Emotionally, I mean. Yeah, some of it was real-world, firing people and all that, but mostly I think he played mind games. And something tells me that a woman would have objected to that more than a man would.'

Anne bit her lip. 'Toby hasn't found work, then, and I don't think the others have either. This is just a guess, okay, but what if Ashby was giving bad references for them? I mean, we're in a recession, and employers can be real picky about who they hire. So all it would take, really, would be one or two, oh, insinuations, know what I mean? You know, so-and-so isn't really stable, or had family problems. Or did drugs. That might drive someone to kill him. I mean, God, people have families to support, bills to pay. A lot of folk, we're one paycheck away from the Santa Bolsas Family Shelter or eating out of garbage cans.' She looked away from him. 'Your family's on the line, your kids, and something like that comes down, it's not that hard to see how that could just snap someone, just push them over the edge.' She looked at him. 'That's why it's so important to get into those computer files of his. I mean, I think he thought he walked on water, you know, the sort of person who wishes he had someone following him around writing down how brilliant he is all the time.'

'A Boswell,' Van Damme said.

'Yes, exactly. And since he didn't, I'm willing to bet he did it himself. And if we can get into his computer files, we'll get a better handle on who he was messing with when he died.'

They looked at each other for a moment, then Van Damme sighed. 'I'm going to tell you to lay off,' he said. 'Nobody thinks you killed Ashby, but someone doesn't want you looking into things. Damn it, Anne, someone tried to run you off the road, and it's sheer dumb luck that you weren't hurt worse, or even killed.' He reached out, un-fisted one of her hands, and held it. 'I don't want you getting hurt,' he said.

Anne gaped. 'You don't want . . . ' she echoed. 'Uh, listen, Lieutenant, I'm not sure what you're getting at.'

'Do you have any idea,' he said earnestly, 'just how much trouble it would make for me if you got yourself killed? It's hard enough dealing with a pack of, well, ah, *different* people, just on Ashby's murder and Allen's suicide. I don't want it to get any more complicated than that.'

Anne stared at him a moment longer and then, irresistibly, started to laugh.

'Are you okay?' he said, and reached for the white curtains.

'Oh, yes,' Anne said, forcing herself to sobriety. Van Damme hesitated, and in that moment she twisted to swing her legs over the side of the bed. 'What time is it?'

He frowned and consulted his watch. 'Three forty-five. Why?'

'I've got to get out of here,' Anne said, and paused. 'Weren't you supposed to see Audrey at three o'clock?'

Van Damme shrugged. 'I put it off when I heard about your accident.'

'Indeed.' Anne looked at him curiously. 'Listen, would you tell them to get my clothes? And tell them I'm leaving?'

'But you can't,' Van Damme said, alarmed.

'Nonsense. You said Doctor Emerson took care of me? Better call him, then. I'm busting out of this joint.'

Van Damme didn't think that was such a good idea, and kept saying so to Anne, and then to Dr. Emerson and his nurse. Dr. Emerson checked Anne over, said she was free to go but to wear the neck brace for a week, and marched off to cope with another emergency. His nurse came back with Anne's clothes and a small bag full of muscle relaxant and painkiller samples, and shooed Van Damme out of the cubicle.

'You take these; the doctor wrote down the dosages for you,' she said, helping Anne into her shirt. 'Victim's Assistance is all well and good, but if we give you a prescription you'll have to pay for it first, and God only knows when you'll be reimbursed. But don't you worry about our bill, we'll send it to the county and if they don't cough up, then it will eventually get to you.' She inspected Anne's hair critically, then dragged a comb from her pocket and worked on Anne's head while she recited a string of instructions.

'There,' she said, stepping back to inspect her handiwork. Then she leaned forward and whispered, 'You give Jackson hell. Abraham, Mitch Wolen's dad, I bought some fish from him yesterday and he told me all about it. That's just about the final straw, you ask me. Me and Betty Cartwright and Millie Beckson, we got a recall petition started. So you just remember, you got friends on your side, girl.'

With that she nodded emphatically, draped Anne's jacket over her shoulders, and ushered her into the waiting room.

'You take good care of her,' she said to Lieutenant Van Damme, favoring him with a basilisk glare. 'You hear me?' The nurse marched back into the ward.

Anne looked at Van Damme and smiled. 'And there you are,' she said. 'Shall we go, Lieutenant? We can still get to Melville before quitting time.'

'There's no need,' he said. 'I already called and told them, and said you wouldn't be in today.'

'Well, won't they be surprised, then. Come on, let's go.'

Van Damme's mouth pinched down. 'I am going,' he said, 'to drive you home.'

'Nonsense.' Anne glanced at the waiting room clock. 'It's four o'clock; there's plenty of time to get to Growing Light and see what's going on. Then we can pick up Danny at daycare.' She walked to the door. He didn't follow, and she had to turn her entire body to look back at him.

'Well, come on,' she said. 'If I'm going to get Victims Assistance, then we'd better find a victimizer, hadn't we?'

'Damn,' Van Damme said, catching up with her. 'You're as bad as Sam Jackson, you know that?'

Anne smiled and let him lead the way to his car.

20

Rain sheeted over the windshield, and the tires hissed through puddles on the road. Anne made Van Damme stop so that she could peer at the broken fence and the ruts in the meadow where her car had gone over the side. The leafless California walnut bore a gash in its side, and Anne felt sorry for it. She shivered and wrapped her arms around herself.

'You still want to go to Melville?' Van Damme said as he put the car in gear.

'Oh, yeah,' Anne said. 'Somebody tried to kill me back there — who'd take care of my little boy if something happened to me?'

Van Damme didn't respond, and they made the rest of the drive in silence.

The Growing Light parking lot seemed almost deserted. Van Damme parked beside the Volvo. The rain had turned its dusty cover into a dense mud that dripped onto the pavement; Van Damme came around to help Anne out of the car, and they walked together into the building.

To Anne's surprise, Brian Stein poked his head around the partition separating Audrey and Carein's office from the reception room. He gawked, then scrambled out to her.

'My God, we weren't expecting you,' he told Anne. 'You look awful, you ought to be home in bed. Why isn't she home in bed?' he asked Van Damme.

The lieutenant shrugged. 'She's a stubborn lady.'

Brian shook his head. 'An accident on that road . . . It's a wonder you can walk at all. Look, they've stuck me with the phones, can you believe it? Pete's out, Audrey's out, Carein's out, Cynthia's out — you'd better pretend the accident damaged your ears or they'll put you to work.' He looked at her. 'It didn't, did it? Damage your ears?'

'No,' Anne said. 'Some bruised ribs, but that's all. Where's everybody else, Brian?'

'Hah,' Brian said. 'Hiding, that's where they are. Come take a look at this.'

He led them down the corridor and

stopped at the message wall.

'Feast your eyes,' he announced, sweeping his arm toward the wall. Anne stopped beside him.

'Good Lord,' she said.

Taped to the memo wall was an immense photocopy of a legal document titled 'Partnership Agreement'. Anne read it quickly, moving from the recitation of the parties (George Ashby, hereinafter Original Owner, and Michael Thompson, hereinafter Prospective Partner), through a list of whereas and heretofore clauses, and down to the bottom line, in which for good and valuable consideration, the receipt of which was hereby acknowledged, aforesaid Original Owner hereby granted to aforesaid Prospective Partner, free and clear of any encumbrances, a full and undivided fifty percent (50%) interest in the business known as Growing Light, including its assets, liabilities, et cetera and so forth. Original Owner and Prospective Partner reserved the right of first refusal to buy each other out, and in the event of the death of either party, the other party inherited the entire company.

There followed two signatures, a date, and a notarial seal.

'Lena,' Brian said, 'is spitting nails and shitting bricks.'

'I'll bet,' Anne said. 'When did this show up?'

'This morning,' Brian said, and went on to recount how Mike and Lena had spent the morning at their respective lawyers' offices. Mike had come back first, armed with a document which, he said, his lawyer had registered with the County Recorder's Office. Thompson then hogged the copier for half an hour while he made progressively larger copies of the document, pinning the largest one on the wall moments before Lena charged in the door.

'It was a full-fledged brawl,' Brian said with relish. 'Verbally, I mean. Lena had an opinion from her own lawyer about how Growing Light was legally hers, and they stood here and screamed at each other. Then Lena locked herself in her office, and Mike locked himself in his, and God knows what they've done about the bathroom.' He shuddered happily.

Anne peered at the notarial acknowledgment. It was dated the past Saturday and signed by a John Lifeblood, Notary Public in and for the State of California, County of Lake Harris. She closed her eyes briefly, memorizing the name, while Van Damme questioned Brian about the particular whereabouts of Carein, Cynthia, and Audrey.

'Cynthia called in sick,' Brian said. 'Carein didn't show up, so I called her house.' He pursed his lips. 'That Hankins character answered. Said she was asleep, but he thought she was doing better. Her aura, you know, something about colors and all that. I tried calling Audrey but she didn't answer. Maybe Mike knows where she is.'

'What about Pete Dixon?' Anne said.

'Oh, Pete's out running errands. Mike sent him somewhere first thing this morning. He came back about half an hour ago, saw Mike, then took off again.'

Anne looked at Van Damme.

'Body shops,' he said. 'Mr. Stein, I need a phone.'

Brian gestured toward Audrey's desk,

told the Lieutenant how to get an outside line, then came back to Anne, avidly curious.

'Tell,' he demanded. 'Everything.'

Anne just looked at him. 'When did you get in today?'

'Around eight,' Brian said, drawing back. 'I haven't left since; Mike wouldn't let me leave these damned phones. I had to have the deli deliver a sandwich, and that bastard wouldn't even reimburse me for it. So? Tell!'

She took a deep breath and stopped when it made her ribs ache. 'Someone ran me off the road,' she said. 'Came up behind me fast, with brights on, and hit my car twice.'

Brian shuffled backwards until his legs hit the dusty couch. He sat down hard.

'Someone tried to — to hurt you?' he said, still staring.

Anne nodded, just as a door slammed open and Mike Thompson shouted, 'Goddamn it, Stein, I told you that you're *answering* the phone today, not calling on it!' He stormed around a corner and stopped when he saw Anne.

'What're you doing here?' he demanded.

'Showing up,' she replied. 'Surprised to see me, Mr. Thompson?'

He frowned. 'Van Damme said you were in the hospital. You should be home in bed.' His frown deepened. 'What about those sensors?' he demanded. 'I know you picked them up, I called the warehouse. I warn you, Ms. Munro, those sensors are my property and I want them, in perfect condition. Where are they?'

'In her car, or what's left of it,' Van Damme said, coming around the partition. 'Which is at the department's yard. You'll get your sensors, Mr. Thompson.'

'Yeah, well, they'd better be in good shape. Any damage and she's paying for it.'

Anne opened her mouth, but Van Damme shook his head at her. 'All in good time. That's, ah, quite a document, Mr. Thompson.' He gestured at the memo wall.

A huge smile spread over Thompson's round face.

'Yes, it is,' he said with pride. 'George and I worked on that agreement for months; there's copies of it all over his disk. You'll see all of 'em, when you look in his computer.' He turned back to the lieutenant. 'Have you done that yet?' he said. 'Checked George's computer?

'Ah, I believe the department is taking care of that,' Van Damme said.

Thompson's smile broadened. 'Well, you'll find them all in there, every single version. George and I worked for months on that contract, we got it just where we wanted it.'

Anne kept her expression neutral, thinking about the back-up disks. If there were any partnership agreements on them, they must be in the encrypted files.

'I see,' Van Damme said. 'I assume your lawyer can confirm — '

'The hell he can,' Lena Ashby said, coming around the corner. She had abandoned the Growing Light uniform of blue jeans and sweatshirt, and wore a severely tailored three-piece suit, the sort of thing Jeff used to call a Full Corporado. Her high heels clicked against the worn linoleum of the hallway.

'My lawyer,' she said, 'talked to George's lawyer, and George's lawyer says he never heard a thing about it until this, this ridiculous document showed up Tuesday morning.' She jerked her head toward the Partnership Agreement. 'I believe this entire thing is fraudulent, and I want to file a complaint.'

Thompson hooted. 'Give it up, Lena! I won, fair and square, and like I said before, I want your ass out of my building by five o'clock. Or I'll call the sheriff.' He rose up on his toes and bounced. His belly bounced too. 'Trespassing, you know.'

Lena's smile, in return, dripped poison. 'Afraid not, Mr. Thompson,' she said sweetly. 'George may have had control of Growing Light, but I, Mr. Thompson, own the damned building.'

'No you don't,' Thompson said. 'George told me he bought this building himself.'

'George,' Lena said, 'couldn't breathe without lying.' Her smile grew. 'In fact, Mr. Thompson, I own just about every-thing in the building, too. Computers, furniture, rugs and all. It was in my name originally, and I never signed it over to that bastard. Matter of fact, he owed me nine months' rent when he died. I guess I can collect that from you, Mr. Thompson, can't I?'

Then Lena Ashby, three-piece suit and all, stuck her belly forward, bounced on her toes, and hooted at Mike Thompson before turning smartly and clicking her way back to her office. Her door smacked shut, and Brian Stein collapsed with laughter.

'You're fired!' Thompson shrieked. 'I'm calling my lawyer — you're fired, Stein, you're out of here!'

'You can't fire me,' Brian shouted at Thompson's retreating back. 'Who'll answer your stupid phones?'

Thompson's door slammed shut. Anne and the Lieutenant looked at each other for a moment, then Van Damme glanced at his watch.

'It's getting late. Mr. Stein. Can you, ah, tell me about the other people here today? Where they, ah, were all day?'

Brian's face sobered. 'God, I forgot about the accident. Anne, are you sure you're okay?'

When she nodded, he turned to Van Damme.

'I got in just before eight,' he said. 'Jimi was already here, and Cynthia called around eight-thirty and said she couldn't come in. She called back a little while ago to talk with Anne, after the lieutenant called. I told her about the accident.' He paused. 'I think Jimi left for half an hour around noon or one, and came back in about twenty minutes. Thompson got in around eleven-thirty, and Lena got here at noon. Neither of them left again, I don't think they trust each other alone here. Pete was in at eight-thirty, then gone until about three. He spent a while with Mike, then went out again. And that's it.' He spread his hands and froze. 'My God, Anne, do you think that Pete — '

'We don't think anything right now,' Van Damme said, but Anne knew that the sheriff's department was busy calling auto-body shops. If Pete Dixon had dents on his shiny red pick-up truck, he'd want them fixed immediately.

'I think I'd like to talk to Mr. Johannsen,' Van Damme said, and headed back toward the engineering cubby. Anne tried to shrug at Brian, thought better of it, and turned to follow the lieutenant.

'Anne, wait,' Brian said. He reached into his shirt pocket and pulled out a sheet of paper. 'Here,' he said, thrusting it at her. 'Remember I said I had something about Thompson? I found it, but after this morning I don't know what use it is. You take it, okay?'

'Okay,' Anne said, raising it up to look at it. It was handwritten in bold black felt-tip pen, addressed to Mike Thompson, and dated a week earlier.

'Don't wave it around,' Brian said. 'Just look at it later.' The phone rang, and he headed back around the partition. Anne slid the paper into her purse and walked to Jimi's area. As she entered, Jimi's phone clicked. Brian's voice said, 'Jimi, is Anne in there with you?'

'Yes I am,' Anne said.

'Call for you.' The phone clicked again, then started ringing. Jimi lifted the receiver and handed it to her.

It was Carl, frantic with worry. Cynthia had come by, having gone to the hospital and found Anne already discharged.

'Are you hurt?' Carl demanded. 'Why the hell aren't you at home? You want me to get Danny? God's love, Anne, if Aunt Millie finds out about this . . .'

Anne calmed him down, said she'd be grateful if he would pick up Danny from daycare, and promised to be home within an hour.

'Cynthia's on her way,' Carl said. 'She said she'd bring you home. You want me to come instead? I can get Danny and go right up there.'

Anne thanked him, declined the offer, reiterated that she was okay, and hung up the phone.

'You see?' Van Damme said. '*Everyone* thinks you ought to go home.'

'Yes, I see,' Anne replied.

Jimi, looming over her like a solicitous redwood tree, ushered her to a stool. Anne smiled, not wanting to go into the details of her accident yet again, and after a moment Van Damme continued with his questioning.

Jimi couldn't prove that he hadn't left the office, but swore that he hadn't. Anne, remembering that Jimi drove an ancient

Volkswagen bug, knew that he couldn't have forced her off the road — bug headlights were distinctive, even set on bright, and she would have noticed. But Jimi had something else on his mind. He shoved a clutter of electronic components aside and opened a three-ring binder on his desk. Van Damme leaned over to look at it and Anne, on the high stool, peered over his shoulder.

'Okay, this looks like nonsense if you don't know what it is,' he said, trailing a finger down a listing of computer code. 'It's the original program code for the astrological module, you know, the one that deals with birth date and rising sign and all that. But George didn't write it. It's got his name on it, sure, right up here, see? But it's not George's style.'

'It doesn't look like any style at all,' Van Damme said. 'How can you tell?'

'Here, check this out.' Jimi flipped the pages to another section. 'Here's the code for the office system, you know, the dumb quotations and menus and all that? George did write that. Now, look here.' He flipped back to the first sheet. 'Here's where all the variables are defined, this whole section here. Now, see, in George's code, there's no section like that. George makes 'em up as he goes along.'

'What's a variable?' Van Damme said.

'It just means a piece of data that's stored in the computer's memory, and you manipulate it. You don't want a number or word there permanently 'cause it can change. For example, say you want to write a program to divide any number by any other number and get a result. So the first number is your first variable, and the second number is your second variable. Then the program just says, in code, get a number and put it in the first variable slot, then get a second number and put it in the second slot, then divide the first number by the second number.' He blinked behind his thick lenses. 'You with me so far?'

'Yeah,' Van Damme said. 'So?'

'So that way, you can use that piece of code for any division problem. You know, it's like algebra, sort of, A divided by B equals C? So A is the first variable and B is the second, and you just slide in your numbers. Otherwise, you'd have to write a whole piece of code for every single problem you needed to work out.'

'Okay, so George makes them up as he goes along, you said.' Van Damme shifted, and Anne peered over his other shoulder. 'So what does that prove?'

'Nothing yet, but look at this here, on the first set. Look at the names of the variables.'

Anne squinted at the code, following Jimi's finger down a series of lines that included words like vasyear, vasmo, vasday, vassign, and vasrise.

'The 'v' is for variable,' Jimi explained. 'The 'as' is for astrology, because that's what this module is about. So, V As Year, is variable, astrology, year. V as mo is the month, day is the day, sign is for the sign and rise is the rising sign. See? It makes sense.'

'Okay,' Anne said. 'I can see that.'

'Good,' Jimi said. 'Now, look at George's code. Let's see, I'll find a variable — here we go. X.' He looked at them triumphantly. 'See?'

'No,' Van Damme said.

Jimi sighed. 'It's like this. You know that V As Mo is variable, astrology, month, so every time you see it in the code, you know what it is immediately. Like this, see, it says take the month and day and call it V As Date, then search the signs database for a place where the date fits, then take that sign and put it in the V As Sign variable. See?'

Anne nodded. 'Yes. It's pretty clear.'

'If you say so,' Van Damme muttered.

'But look here. George just calls his variables X, or A, or Z1, or G2 — you can't tell what they are by looking at them.'

'So George's name is on the code for the astrology module, but he didn't write it,' Anne said.

'Yeah, I think Peter Simpson wrote it; it reads like his code. And look at this.'

Jimi flipped to the back of the book, which comprised a jumbled series of notes, letters, and doodles. 'Look here.'

He pointed at a photocopy of a letter to Peter Simpson, the same letter Anne and Cynthia had found on the back-up disks. Ashby not only accused Simpson of obstructionist incompetence and lack of internal development, but ridiculed his programming skills, his sexuality, and his hairstyle. It concluded with the statement that George refused to pay Simpson anything at all, and pointed out that there was no written contract between them.

'God, Simpson was right,' Anne murmured. 'George really did rip him off.'

'Oh yeah,' Jimi said. 'And what makes it worse is that for a while, Simpson was George's pet. He'd have him up for a whole week at a time, give him all kinds of space here, loan him a car, put him up in his own house. You'd have thought that the guy walked on water, or at least that George thought he did. Then, with no warning, Simpson is all of a sudden the Great Satan around here. He's not allowed in the front door, nobody's supposed to talk to him — Audrey brought up his name at a staff meeting once, something about paying him, and George just froze her out.' Jimi shook his head, bewildered. 'In some ways, you couldn't blame him. Simpson wasn't easy to get along with. Not a bad programmer, all in all. But nuts, definitely nuts.'

'I know,' Anne said. 'I saw him this morning. He said George had it in for him all the way back to Alexander the Great.'

21

Van Damme took the program binder and stuck it under his arm, and was just helping Anne from the stool when Audrey Lincoln rounded the partition and saw them. She nodded and stood aside while Brian, Lena, and Mike Thompson crowded in. Audrey's nose was red and her eyes looked puffy; she held a crumpled sheet of paper in her hand.

'Good, you're here,' she said. For once, she didn't look nervous.

Brian, with avid curiosity, squeezed himself into a space between the end of the work bench and a file cabinet, and Lena perched on the bench itself, as far from Mike Thompson as she could manage. Thompson, looking extremely put out, planted himself in the doorway and his fists on his hips.

'This had better be important,' he said. 'I've got a lot of work to do.'

Audrey, looking at Van Damme, ignored

him. 'I've got something to say, like to everybody. I've even got, you know, notes and everything.'

She unfolded the paper she held. Van Damme put his hand up.

'Ah, one moment, Ms. Lincoln,' he said. 'Are you sure you want to do this?'

Audrey just glanced at him, unfolded the paper, raised it, and paused at the sound of tires squealing outside.

'That's Cynthia,' Brian said.

'Good.' Audrey nodded again, then glanced at the lieutenant. 'I went to Carein's today, and I told her all of this first, and she said it was, you know, important that I tell everybody. Just in case, you know. So I'm doing this for Carein and for Max. Okay?'

Van Damme shrugged and Cynthia came in. She looked around and pushed her way to Anne.

'Are you okay? What are you doing here, anyway?' she demanded.

'I had to come,' Anne replied. 'You look awful.'

'I was up all night.' Cynthia looked around. 'What's going on?'

'Audrey seems to have called a meeting,' Thompson said with disgust. 'Can we get on with this?'

Cynthia started to say something, then looked at Audrey's face and pressed her lips together. She moved over to stand behind Anne.

'Okay, good,' Audrey said, and shook her piece of paper. 'My name is Audrey Lincoln,' she read. She paused for a moment, then went on, 'I'm writing this just in case something happens to me before the sheriff finds out who killed George Ashby. There's some stuff I need to share.'

'Audrey, wait,' Cynthia said. 'Maybe you should have a lawyer first.'

'I don't need one,' Audrey said. 'It's, like, I haven't done anything wrong, you see? I've just gotta say this. To everybody.'

Audrey glanced at her notes, then said to Van Damme, 'Last Friday afternoon, George Ashby invited me to his house for dinner on Sunday. George did that a lot, because we used to be really friendly.'

'I'll bet,' Lena said, but Van Damme frowned at her and she closed her mouth.

'When I got to George's place, he hadn't even cooked dinner. I wasn't really surprised, because George was like that. I mean, he was always inviting someone over for something, then making someone else do all the work. So I told him I wasn't going to cook and maybe we'd better go out to eat. Then George said he didn't want to eat anyway and we went into the bedroom.'

'I knew it, I knew it, I knew it,' Brian whispered, but subsided when Van Damme frowned.

'Afterwards, George said he would call out for pizza and I went to take a shower, and when I got out I heard the doorbell and figured it was the pizza man and that was real fast, and there wasn't any robe in there so I just, like, wrapped a towel around myself and went out. But it wasn't the pizza man, it was Max, Max Allen, and he had his back against the wall and George was leaning at him, you know, that way George does so you really feel trapped and everything.'

'Hah!' Mike Thompson said.

Audrey glared at him. 'You don't know

anything,' she said coldly, and went back to her notes.

'So I came out and Max saw me and he made this kind of noise, like he was moaning, and he tried to get out the door but George wouldn't let him. And I'm all, what's going on here and George is all, I told Max to come over, and Max is all, I'm supposed to pick up a computer and George says that can wait because he really wants to get behind Max's problems. Then Max tries to leave again and George locks the door and makes Max sit on the couch and makes me sit on the couch too, and then he says he knows what's wrong with Max and that I'm supposed to fix it and he's going to help too. George, I mean. He was going to help me fix Max. And then — '

'Hold it a moment, Ms. Lincoln,' Van Damme said. 'Do you, ah, know what George was going to fix?'

'Sure,' Audrey said. 'Max was, like, he couldn't get it up, you know. I mean, everybody knew it.'

'Everybody?' Van Damme said.

'Yeah,' Brian said, but this time he

didn't sound flippant. 'Yeah, George made sure of that.'

'So then,' Audrey continued after taking a deep breath, 'so then George tells Max to kiss me, and Max doesn't want to do it and I don't much either. I mean, Max is an okay kind of guy, you know, I mean really sweet, but it's like I'm not really into, you know, in front of other people. But George just laughs and says we like our jobs don't we, and he doesn't think we'd ever find work in this economy, especially Max. So Max like moans again and George starts telling Max that he's gotta confront his problems and get behind getting healthy again, and he's still right in Max's face, that way he always did to scare people. George is like listing all this stuff he says is wrong with Max and Max is like crying, just sitting there on the couch real stiff, you know, real upright, and he's just, like, there's tears and snot and everything and George just keeps telling him all this crazy mean stuff and some of it's not even, like, true or anything.'

Audrey was crying too, back straight

and hands trembling. Jimi leaned over and put a hand on her shoulder, but Audrey shook it away.

'So then George goes, is Max ready to get behind reality and Max is still crying and he doesn't say anything, but George just smiles and, like, starts to take his clothes off. I mean, George takes his own clothes off, this robe he's wearing, and says Max and I should get naked too, and then Max, like, looks at George and throws up, I mean he really barfs. Then he like runs for the door, and George just starts to laugh, you know, and Max gets the door unlocked and George is still laughing and he yells after him, he's like telling Max he's useless and fired and then I'm running out of there, you know, trying to catch up with Max and tell him it's okay, it's gonna be okay, but Max gets into his truck and he can't start it and then he can and then he's like, you know, gone, he's driving off but he's all over the place, 'cause he's still crying probably.

'So I go back inside and George is still, like, laughing, and I just get dressed and get out, and George doesn't say anything,

I mean like not a word, not even when I'm walking out, except when I'm like starting my car he comes over and he's all, I'll see you Monday, and then he goes back in and I hear him laughing some more. So I went home.'

Audrey folded the paper held it out to Van Damme.

'It's just, like, what happened. I mean, notes, but I signed it and everything,' she said.

Van Damme took the paper and looked at it, then looked straight at Audrey. 'Ms. Lincoln, did you kill George Ashby?'

Lena suddenly moved away from the work bench and took Audrey in her arms. Audrey stiffened for a moment, then relaxed against Lena's shoulder and shook her head.

'No. But George Ashby killed Max Allen, Lieutenant. Maybe not with his hands, you know, but he made him die.'

'I see.' Van Damme kept looking at her. 'Do you think Max Allen killed Ashby?'

Audrey shook her head again, and shrugged. 'I don't think so. But I wrote that, you know, like if maybe he did, then somebody should like, tell why.'

'Audrey,' Lena said, 'why you? Why wouldn't Max tell this himself?'

'Because Max never talked about anything personal,' Jimi said unexpectedly. 'I've worked with him for months, and not a word about where he was from, or went to school, or where he lived — damn,' he said with sudden vehemence.

'All we knew about Max,' Cynthia said, 'was that he was a sweet guy.'

'Yeah, and the lies George told about him,' Brian said.

Van Damme sat on the edge of the table and clasped his hands between his legs. 'Were they lies? From what Ms. Lincoln said, Mr. Allen didn't seem like a very stable character.'

'What does that matter?' Cynthia demanded. 'If Max had problems, he didn't want them talked about, or he'd have done it himself. George Ashby lied about everybody; it was some crazy game with him, playing with people's heads. Like he did to Anne last Monday, about her husband. Like he's done to everyone here, at one time or another.'

Van Damme looked down at Audrey's papers, then up again. 'We still don't have a time of death on Max Allen,' he said. 'I appreciate everything you've told me, but until we know when Mr. Allen died . . . ' He spread his hands.

'Audrey,' Lena said. Audrey stepped away from her. 'Why did you do it? Sleep with George, I mean. Why?'

'I can't type,' Audrey said with simple dignity. 'I can't run a computer or anything like that. I mean, I graduated from high school two years ago and all I've done is like waitressing. So he like gives me this job, bookkeeper, and I've got this desk, and a paycheck — and I can add and subtract stuff, I can run an adding machine. If I lose this job . . . ' Her voice trailed away.

Lena's face, Anne thought, was fascinating. Disbelief, pity, anger, confusion. Finally George's widow said, 'Bookkeeper. And you just added and subtracted stuff?'

'Sure,' Audrey said. 'I mean, George and Mike gave me all the numbers. And that's what bookkeepers do, isn't it? Just add and subtract?'

'Oh, child,' Lena said, and put her arm around Audrey's shoulders again.

Anne glanced around the crowded room. Cynthia glared at the floor, Jimi beat one fist into an open palm, and Brian Stein, leaning back in his chair, shook his head. 'Poor Max,' he said.

'Oh, bull,' Mike Thompson said. 'Well, that's it, isn't it? George pissed Max off, and Max did it. I always knew he was unstable, and this proves it.' Looking extremely satisfied, Thompson swaggered out.

Van Damme shook his head. 'Ms. Lincoln, I'm afraid you'll have to come down to the station with me. This paper is fine, but we'll have to ask you some questions.'

'Yeah, I know that,' Audrey said. 'It's okay, I'll go. Carein said I should.' She buttoned up her raincoat.

'Wait a minute,' Cynthia said. 'Audrey, how did Carein take all this? I mean, she was really close to Max.'

Audrey blinked. 'Gee, I really don't know, you know? She just sat there and that aura cleaner guy held her hand, and she like just listened and didn't say a word. And when I was done, she's all, you've gotta go tell them, tell all of them. But she was real quiet, know what I mean? Like it wasn't a big surprise or anything — like maybe she already knew.'

22

Ed and Millie Beckson were waiting when Cynthia eased Jeremiah Hudson into the driveway, and Ed rushed down to help Anne from the car.

'Gladys called Millie from the hospital,' he said, handling Anne as though she were made of crystal. 'Nice car,' he told Cynthia. She nodded. Both she and Anne had been quiet on the ride home, wrapped in their own thoughts. An image kept repeating itself behind Anne's eyelids, of Audrey weeping, and the shadowy figure of Max Allen fleeing in tears into the night. Eventually she forced the image away, knowing that she would be with Danny in a few minutes; seeing his mother in a neck brace would be bad enough without having to watch his mother cry.

Inside, Millie supervised as Ed ushered Anne to a nest of orthopedic pillows and foam inserts piled on the couch. Ed peeled off Anne's coat and shoes, settled pillows and foam around her, covered her with a blanket, and, as a finishing touch, propped a bed table over her lap.

'You just behave yourself,' Millie said when Anne protested. 'Going off the road, and then gallivanting all over the county when you should be at home and in bed. I swear, Annie Munro, sometimes I think you lack the brains God gave the billy goats.'

Anne looked at Cynthia, who just spread her hands. 'She's right, you know,' Cynthia said, and Millie favored her with a nod.

'Carl told me about you,' she said. 'You're not that bad.'

Cynthia turned away, but not before Anne saw her smile.

Ed made a few more adjustments to the nest. Then and only then did Millie holler down the hall. Carl came out with Danny clinging to his back like a monkey.

Danny looked over Carl's shoulder at her, his eyes wide.

'Mommy,' he said in a little voice. 'Are you going to die?'

Anne cursed and pushed aside blankets, bed tray and everything else.

'Of course not, pickle,' she said. 'Come give me a hug, okay?'

Danny wriggled off Carl's back and ran to her, and she clutched him, rubbing her face against his silky hair. 'I'm fine, honey,' she murmured. 'Just a little bunked up — like when you fall down and hurt yourself, you know? I'm kind of sore, sweetheart, but I'm going to be fine, I promise you.'

He pulled back a little and looked at her anxiously.

'That's a big Band-Aid,' he said, touching her neck brace. 'Did you get a real big owie, Mommy?'

'No, honey, it's not cut or anything. The doctor just wants me to wear this for a while, to make my neck feel better.'

'Oh. Ed told Millie that our car got broked, like Daddy's did,' he said. 'But when Daddy's car got broked, it made Daddy dead.'

'But I'm not dead, Danny. I'm okay. And we'll just have to get a better car, won't we? You can help me pick it out, would you like that?'

'Uh huh,' Danny said, starting to smile. 'Can we get a red one? That changes into stuff, like Inspector Gadget's?'

Anne laughed. 'Maybe we can, pickle.'

He grinned, mashed a kiss into her cheek, and let her go. 'Me and Carl, we're cooking dinner,' he said. 'Okay?'

'That's fine, sweetheart. You go ahead.'

She watched while Carl and Danny disappeared into the kitchen, then turned to Millie Beckson.

'How dare you,' she whispered. 'You remember how Jeff died — what did you think he'd think, me in a car wreck and all these goddamned pillows and everything? Good God, Millie!'

'I told him you were okay,' she said, unperturbed. 'Better that he worry and get over it, than you go around pretending you're just fine when he knows damned well you're not. You gonna stay down, or does Ed have to spend the night here?'

Anne tried to shake her head, and couldn't. As far as she knew, neither Ed nor Millie knew the truth about the accident, and she wanted to keep it that way for a while longer.

'I'll be good,' she said, and Ed tucked her in again.

'You see that you are,' Millie said, then unexpectedly leaned down and brushed her lips across Anne's forehead. 'Sorry you took it wrong. Maybe I was a bit bossy there, but heavens, somebody has to be.' She straightened and reached for her coat.

'Me and Ed, we've gotta go,' she said. 'We've got a meeting down to the church, see if we can't get a recall on the spring ballot.'

Anne settled back among the cushions. 'You know, Millie, I appreciate your help, but you don't have to recall Sam Jackson just because of me.'

'I'm not,' Millie said. 'That boy made a promise to the county, and he hasn't kept it. Them weirdos in Melville hate him because he's got it in for them, and the rest of us hate him because he's a lazy bum. Folk get ripped off and roughed up and just last month, some punks from outside the county came in and lifted four hundred fifty-six dollars off Burt's steakhouse, and Jackson still hasn't caught 'em. And the tourists, good Lord, they just act like they own the place, littering and getting drunk and all sorts of stuff, and what does Jackson do? He arrests Arnie Ingle's boy for ridin' his bike without a helmet! Next thing you know, people will be cutting each other up down to the roadhouse again! And all Jackson does is jaw it up and get his picture in the paper. Huh!'

'Right on,' Cynthia said. Millie nodded at her with approval and marched out.

'Now, you stay down and get some rest, you hear?' Ed said. 'When we come back from the church, I don't want to see any lights on in here.'

Anne rolled her eyes, and Ed closed the door behind him.

'You're a lucky woman, Anne Munro,' Cynthia said. 'Wish I had someone like that to keep an eye on me.'

'No, you don't,' Anne said. 'She'd have you in sweater sets and a page-boy haircut inside a week. Did you get into the files?'

Cynthia pulled up a chair. 'Oh yeah,'

she said. 'I was up all night writing that damned program, then fixing it, but it worked. I haven't read the printouts yet. I found the right key just before I learned about your accident, and it finished printing just before I left. Want to take a look?'

'No. Wait until Danny's asleep,' she said. 'We can tell Carl about Max then, too. But I don't want to upset Danny anymore.'

'I can see that,' Cynthia said. The two women looked at each other for a moment, each itching to get into it, then Cynthia jumped up.

'I'll go help in the kitchen,' she said. 'Oh, by the way, you know what the encryption key turned out to be? MYBOSWEL.'

Anne started laughing and Cynthia trotted off toward the kitchen.

Dinner appeared a few minutes later. Tonight's menu was crisp fried chicken and mashed potatoes with gravy, steamed winter vegetables, and homemade dinner rolls hot from the oven. They sat around the table and for a while the only sounds were those of eating.

Eventually Cynthia pushed herself away from the table and raised her water glass to Carl. 'Any others at home like you?' she said.

To Anne's amazement, Carl turned bright red. Then, to her further amazement, he said, 'Afraid I'm the only one. Think I'll do?'

To cap it off, Cynthia, in turn, blushed. Anne choked and turned to wipe gravy off Danny's chin.

'Peach pie for dessert,' Danny said. 'Carl made it. He didn't make it here, he made it at Evvie's but he brought it home. And ice cream too — didn't you, Carl, huh? Can I get it now?'

Dessert was served, and through it Anne kept a surreptitious eye on her friends. They did their best, but kept eyeing each other and smiling.

Damn it, they're adults and it's their business, she told herself, and pushed the subject away while she supervised Danny's bath and bedtime story and eventual slide into sleep. Tonight he insisted on taking every stuffed animal he owned to bed

314

with him, and Anne tucked them all in together. If a bed full of lumps comforted him, she was not going to object.

By the time she returned to the couch, her entire midriff ached. She took a muscle relaxant, then looked through the printout of George Ashby's decrypted files while Carl and Cynthia finished the dishes.

'My God,' she said when the others joined her. 'It's hard to read through the psychobabble, but there's enough in here to give a motive to everyone in Melville. Listen to this.'

No one at Growing Light had escaped George's speculations or plots, from Jimi Hendrix Johannsen ('someday, I have to get that guy to admit that he's a freak') to Brian Stein ('you can't trust a Jew, no matter how good he is'). But the most telling entries were made the Saturday before his death.

'According to George,' Anne reported, 'the affair with Audrey was over. He wrote that she was keeping him back, but he invited her over for one final, uh, event on Sunday. And he says that he told Max to come too. Here, listen: 'It's time to break through that guy's barriers and make him face his sickness once and for all. And my sweet Audrey is just the one to do it.' '

'Sickness?' Carl said.

Cynthia closed her eyes. 'George said that Max was impotent,' she said, and told him about Audrey's speech that afternoon at Growing Light.

Carl frowned. 'So maybe Max did kill George. Maybe George pushed him *too* hard.'

'It's possible,' Cynthia said. 'I don't like it, but it's possible.'

Carl shook himself, looking grim, and went into the kitchen. He came back with a bottle of brandy, with which he spiked his own coffee and Cynthia's.

'None for you,' he said to Anne. 'Won't mix with the sedatives.'

'I know,' Anne said. She lifted the papers again as Cynthia reached for her coffee cup. 'You know, maybe Max had a great motive for killing George, and maybe he even had the opportunity to do it — we don't know when he died. But I keep thinking about what everyone says about him, about how he was fragile, and lost, and it just doesn't make sense to me.'

'Me, either,' Cynthia said. 'I say we keep looking. What else is in that file?'

'Other stuff, about Peter Simpson and Lena. But you know what's not in here?' She tapped the pages. 'There's nothing in here about a contract between George and Mike, not a word about a partnership. Mike said he and George had been working on the contract for months, that there were copies all over George's hard disk.'

'What partnership?' Carl said.

Anne told him about the partnership agreement, then remembered the paper Brian had given her. She dug it out of her purse and spread it over the bed tray. It was dated the previous Thursday.

' 'Mike: You're not on the right psychic plane for this sort of major lifestyle change,'' Anne read. ' 'Hang in there, work on it, tune yourself and you'll reach a higher plane of self-actualization. Then your havingness will flower into something that would make a partnership make sense between us, but right now there's dissonance between our levels of being. So just concentrate on your self-conceptualizing. I'll know when you're at the right place. Until then, shut the hell up.''

'Jeez,' Cynthia said. 'That's George's handwriting, all right. Laying the George-babble on pretty thick, wasn't he?'

'This thing was dated last Thursday,' Carl said. 'And that agreement was dated Saturday?'

Anne nodded. 'Carl, would you get me the phonebook?'

He brought it, yawning. One book was enough to cover all of Lake Harris County, with parts of Sonoma and Marin tossed in for good measure. Anne turned to the Ls and ran her finger down the page.

'There he is,' she said at last. 'John Lifeblood, Melville. He's got to be the one who notarized the partnership. And it looks like he lives just down the road from Growing Light.' She reached for the phone.

A few minutes later, she had an

appointment to see John Lifeblood at ten-thirty the next day, to get a school document notarized. Satisfied, she hung up the phone.

'What document?' Carl said around another yawn.

Anne smiled. 'The school sent a field trip authorization home with Danny yesterday. It doesn't need to be notarized, but it can't hurt, can it?'

'I suppose not,' Cynthia said. 'But what good will it do?'

'I don't know,' Anne replied. 'But I'm going to find out.'

Half an hour later, Carl staggered off toward the cottage and Cynthia, assured that Anne wasn't worried and didn't want overnight company, pulled on her jacket. She promised to come by in the morning to give Anne a lift to work.

Anne finally took a painkiller, then worked her way out of her clothes and into a nightshirt. She checked on Danny, turned down the heat, and climbed into bed. Just as she was drifting off, the phone rang.

'Wake up, Anne. These country hours

you keep are ridiculous,' Alicia's voice said.

'Alicia, please . . . '

'I have some fascinating information about your Catherine knife,' Alicia said, ignoring her. 'Did that get your attention?'

Anne turned on the light and pulled herself up. 'Yes, yes it did. What have you found?'

'Two tidbits. One historically interesting, and the other positively delicious.'

It had taken some work, Alicia said, but she finally got authorization to browse through the university's California database. A passing reference in an early history of northern California mentioned a pair of silver-handled knives, one with the figure of Henry VIII and the other with the figure of Catherine of Aragon, in the possession of Frances Hopkins Harris. According to the account, the knives had been given to Harris by General Mariano Vallejo, when Harris purchased his land from the general.

'There's no doubt about it,' Alicia said. 'I could track it further, but it appears

320

that somehow those knives made their way from José de Gálvez — you remember Señor Galvez and his difficult mission on behalf of Charles II, of course — to the Vallejo family. Not at all far-fetched, considering. But the second tidbit is absolutely toothsome.'

'Okay, Alicia,' Anne said. 'Consider yourself begged.'

Alicia gave a happy sigh and launched into the story. She had explained her quest on a computer bulletin board used by northern California antique dealers and antiquarians. This afternoon, a retired dealer responded with a piece of interesting information.

'He had a shop in the Haight in the sixties and early seventies,' Alicia reported. 'And he remembered the Catherine knife quite clearly. He said a young woman brought it in. A young *hippie* woman, Anne, tattered and long-haired and rather pregnant. She wanted to pawn the knife. Well, my informant is an antique dealer, not a pawn broker. He made her a very generous offer for the knife, not knowing precisely what it was but very sure that it was both old and rare. The young woman refused to part with it. My informant tried to trace the knife, but of course we had neither computers nor databases back then and had to do things the hard way. Eventually he gave up the chase. Of course, if he'd actually possessed the knife, it would have been a different matter. Anne, are you still there? You haven't fallen asleep, have you?'

'No, I'm still here,' Anne said, wide awake now. 'Alicia, did he say when all this happened? What year, maybe?'

'Better than that. He took notes while he was trying to track down the presentation knife, and like most of us he's compulsive about keeping things. The young woman visited him in the fall of 1971. October, to be precise. He didn't have the specific date.'

Anne took a deep breath, ignoring the ache in her ribs. 'Alicia, you are a wonder,' she said.

'Naturally. Now go back to your reprehensible rural sleeping pattern, and call me tomorrow. I believe you owe me lunch.'

The phone clicked as Alicia disconnected.

Anne re-cradled the handset, then leaned back against the pillow, thinking. San Francisco in the early seventies. George and Lena, the student underground — could Lena have been pregnant?

Her bedroom door creaked open and Danny appeared, clutching his battered beloved stuffed cat. Anne had been expecting him.

'Hello, pickle,' she said as she pulled the covers down.

Danny knuckled his eyes, padded across the rug, and climbed into her bed. Looking serious, he pulled a pillow flat and pushed it against hers, centered Sylvester on it, dropped his head squarely on the cat's stomach, grabbed pillow and cat again, and scooted them both until he lay snuggled against Anne's side. It was how he had slept for months following Jeff's death, the two of them clinging together through the long hours of the night.

Now Danny said sleepily, 'Love you, mommy. G'night.' His eyes closed.

Anne turned off the light, moved carefully onto her side, wrapped an arm over her son, and followed him into sleep.

23

'Well, you didn't get your name in the paper,' Cynthia said the next morning when she picked Anne up. Anne maneuvered herself into the front seat and fumbled with the seatbelt, astonished at how sore she felt. She put a folded rain jacket on the seat. Cynthia handed Anne a copy of the *Intelligencer* while she helped Danny into the back seat and tried to buckle him in. Danny thought Jeremiah Hudson was the neatest car he'd ever seen and kept wriggling away from Cynthia to peer over the front seat at the dashboard, or slide down to the floorboards to see what he could find there. Cynthia tickled him into submission.

Anne glanced at this morning's update on the murder. Jackson announced that he had two suspects, and was following all the leads, and promised to have the murderer in custody by the weekend. A sidebar detailed the recall petition and listed some of the citizens' complaints against the sheriff; an op-ed piece chided the recall backers, pointing out that George Ashby's death had been the only murder since Jackson had taken office, and the sheriff was pursuing the matter diligently. Anne wondered if Van Damme had pulled strings to keep her accident out of the paper. Usually the *Intelligencer* printed details of every fender-bender in the county.

Yesterday's rain had disappeared, leaving the sky bright and cloudless, the air clean and sharp. Anne put the newspaper aside and rolled down the window, relishing the brush of freshness against her cheeks.

They dropped Danny off at school. Cynthia spent the next few miles creating grandiose scenarios having to do with Thompson trying to evict Lena from his company, while she tried to evict him from her building. The stream of chatter didn't abate, and Anne suspected that Cynthia created it to prevent Anne from asking about Carl. Anne resigned herself to the role of appreciative listener until they were into the farmlands beyond Inez and she asked Cynthia to pull over at a mailbox. The name on the box read 'Hillegas'; Cynthia drove down the long graveled driveway toward a small white house. A woman paused halfway between the house and the barn, then came toward them as Cynthia stopped the car and Anne slid awkwardly out.

'Mrs. Hillegas?' she called.

The woman nodded.

'I'm Anne Munro — you and your husband helped me yesterday, after the accident. I brought back your jacket.'

'Lord almighty,' the woman said. 'I didn't recognize you.' She took the jacket and eyed Anne. 'Got a bit of whiplash, it looks. How're you doing?'

'Okay. I guess I was pretty lucky. I just wanted to thank you, and let you know that I'm all right.'

Mrs. Hillegas looked embarrassed. 'Just being a good neighbor,' she said. 'Anybody would've done it. Glad you're okay, though. Listen, you want a cup of coffee?'

'Oh, no, no thanks,' Anne said. 'I've got to be going. But could I ask one question?

Yesterday, before the accident, did you see or hear anyone going by pretty fast, headed toward Melville?'

Anne didn't really expect an answer, but to her surprise Mrs. Hillegas nodded.

'My man did. Said he heard someone tearing up the road, just before he came inside to get me. Then I came out and looked up the road, and that's when I saw you go over the side.' Mrs. Hillegas's eyes widened. 'Think that was the car that hit you?'

'Maybe. Did your husband see the car? The one that was speeding?'

''Fraid not.'

Anne thanked her again, got back into the car, and waved as Cynthia drove back toward the main road.

It was close to nine o'clock when Cynthia slid Jeremiah Hudson into the parking lot and slowed, glancing around. 'Let's see,' she said. 'Lena's here, and Mike. That ought to be fun. Pete's truck isn't here. Jimi, Brian, and — Reverend Hankins's car, isn't it? The blue bomber? Wonder why he's back.'

She slotted Jeremiah between Jimi's

bug and Hankins's Dodge, and the two women walked into the building.

Carein sat at her desk, her hands folded in her lap. Reverend Hankins occupied Audrey's desk, a newspaper spread before him and a greasy white bag next to that. He looked up as they entered and rattled the paper. Carein smiled a little. She looked worn, and old.

'I'm much better,' she said. 'Harry's staying with me; he's keeping me centered until all this is finished.'

Hankins nodded, looking sad. 'Bad karma going down here,' he opined. 'Wanna jelly doughnut?'

Anne and Cynthia declined as he dug into the greasy white bag and pulled out a doughnut.

'Bad karma,' Hankins said again, biting into the doughnut. Filling flowed over his chin. Carein smiled and handed him a napkin.

Back in the reception area, Cynthia wrinkled her brow. 'She's in bad shape,' she whispered. 'Jeez, jelly doughnuts in her space. I don't like it, Anne.'

The memo wall had grown even more

impressive overnight. Now, next to and partially covering Mike's Partnership Agreement, was an even bigger enlargement of a property deed for the land and building that housed Growing Light. Lena had even provided gigantic copies of her last property tax bill, to show, Anne guessed, that she still owned the place.

Outside Anne's closet, Cynthia said, 'Are you sure you don't want to work with me and Brian?'

'Hey, I'm bruised but not disabled,' Anne said, and smiled. 'I'll call if I need anything.'

Cynthia shrugged and left, and Anne slid between the wall and the end of her desk. An hour and a half before her appointment with John Lifeblood. Sighing, she opened the Growing Light User's Manual and stared at its unintelligible first sentence. Then she tried the next sentence. It was no better than the first.

Twenty interminable minutes later, Cynthia came in and closed the door.

'I just talked to Van Damme,' she said. 'Have you seen Mike this morning?'

'No.'

Cynthia perched on the edge of the desk. 'He came marching in just after I sat down, and said that Jackson found all the partnership drafts on George's computer.'

'But that's impossible,' Anne said. 'He couldn't have.'

Cynthia looked grim. 'Well, he did. I called Van Damme as soon as Mike cleared out. He says the department's computer tech found them in a subdirectory called 'Partner', with dates on them starting six months ago.' Cynthia frowned. 'God damn it, Anne, I know I didn't miss anything when I backed up that hard disk. I've got a backup routine that starts with the root and just follows everything from there on, right on down the directory tree. There's no way — ' She slammed her hand against the desktop.

'Did you tell Van Damme about the backups?' Anne said.

'Oh yeah, I told him,' Cynthia said with disgust. 'He's gonna come get them this afternoon, but you know what that bastard did? He yelled at me for contaminating his goddamned evidence, that's what he did. Said there was no way we could prove that I didn't erase those files when I made the copies we've got. What's he expect us to do, sit around on our hands until Jackson — '

'God,' Anne said. 'If that's true, then we can't use the backups to prove that Thompson tampered with the computer.'

'Van Damme's point exactly. I asked him to bring a printout of the directory listings, all of them. Maybe there's some way I can figure it out from that. He got all snooty on me, you know, ah this and ah that, but he said he'd do it.' She blew her breath out hard, then looked sideways at Anne. 'I guess I should have thought of that, shouldn't I? Contaminating the evidence, and all that.'

'How could we?' Anne said. 'Look, it's not the end of the world. I'm still going to check out the notary; maybe we can salvage something here. Anyway, I'm the one who asked you to do it, so if there's anyone to blame, it's probably me.'

They looked at each other a moment, then Cynthia smiled ruefully. 'Ah, hell, at least I got a good mechanic out of this deal.'

Anne raised her eyebrows. 'Yes?'

'Yeah, I talked to Carl yesterday, when I went by your house before I came here to get you. He's gonna check out Jeremiah for me.'

'Really,' Anne said. 'Is that all he's checking out?'

Cynthia just looked at her, opened the door, and left.

★　★　★

The house would have been identical to its neighbors on the curving, relatively modern street, save for the signs and decals its inhabitant chose to display. Anne paused on the sidewalk to catch her breath after the short walk, and read them.

'Real Estate Services,' proclaimed a hand-painted swing sign imbedded in the ivy-covered lawn. The words were spelled out in the rounded multicolored psyche-delic lettering of the hippie era. Under it, another sign reading 'Notary Public' flapped in the light breeze; this one looked stiffly official. The 'Bookkeeping

Services' sign, suspended from the porch roof, was also plain and unadorned; under it, another said 'Fine EverLife Products Available Here!' This last one, a dark lavender on yellow, bore the logo of a nationally known multi-level marketing concern. Chained crystals dangled from the bottom of the sign, catching the clear winter light. Anne suppressed a smile: wasn't EverLife being investigated by some midwestern attorney general? She couldn't remember; multi-level schemes multiplied and collapsed at a remarkable rate.

She pulled her hands out of her pockets and climbed the front stairs, glad that she'd taken one of the muscle relaxants before walking over. Pots of aloe vera and other plants decorated the edges of the steps and the small porch; the front door sported a window in the shape of a crescent moon. The sound of drumming filtered from inside. Anne hesitated, then rang the bell.

A moment later, the notary public, real estate broker, bookkeeper, and member of a suspected pyramid scheme opened the door and smiled at her. The pungent odor of marijuana spilled out, along with more drumming. Bare feet, tie-died shirt, ragged jeans; Anne was surprised that he didn't wear love beads, too.

'Mr. Lifeblood? I called yesterday to have something notarized.'

'Oh, yeah, I do that,' John Lifeblood said, still smiling but not moving.

'Uh, good,' Anne said after a moment. 'Could I come in?'

'Oh! Yeah, of course, come on in, be at peace.' He pulled the door open further, and gestured her into what must once have been the dining room. Now it held a desk made of a door resting on two small chests of drawers, a couple of armchairs, and piles of boxes with the EverLife logo on them. They blocked a door which, Anne suspected, led to the kitchen.

'Hey,' he said suddenly, 'you got one of those things on your neck, you know?'

'Yes, I know. I was in an accident, but it's no big thing.' She pulled the field trip consent form from her tote and put it on the desk. 'This is for my son's school,' she said. 'I haven't signed it yet.'

'Oh, yeah, groovy,' Lifeblood said, adopting a professional look at odds with his headband and ponytail. 'Hold on, lemme get my kit, okay?'

He delved in a drawer and brought out a rubber stamp and a pad, shoved one into the other, and grabbed the consent form.

'Shouldn't I sign it first?' Anne said.

'Oh, sure, if you want to,' he said, and pushed the form back toward her. She found a pen on the desk, then hesitated again.

'I think you're supposed to check my ID,' she said. 'Aren't you? And have me sign your book?'

'Like, if you really want to,' Lifeblood said, starting to frown. 'I mean, it's all these uptight regulations, just tying people up all the time. You know, Big Brother and all that.'

'I just want to make sure it's legal,' Anne said mildly. 'Okay?'

He shrugged. 'Sure, if that's the way you want it. You wanna show me some paper or something?'

Anne produced her driver's license.

Lifeblood glanced at it, and raised his rubber stamp again.

'Do I sign your book now, or later?' Anne said.

He sighed and reached into the drawer once more. It took a while to come up with the notary records book, but eventually he opened it for her.

'There,' he said. 'Go on and sign it.'

Anne bent over the book and read down the list. The last entry was dated two months prior, and wasn't even complete. George Ashby's name didn't appear anywhere on it. Anne thought quickly. Lifeblood didn't seem the type to read newspapers, she decided.

'Wow,' she said. 'That's funny.'

'What?'

'Well, I called you because George Ashby, the guy I work for, said you notarized something for him last weekend, but I don't see his name here.' She looked at him innocently. 'Maybe he went to someone else.'

'Ashby?' Lifeblood frowned, then the frown cleared. 'Oh yeah, I remember him. Came by with some sort of legal paper. Yeah, I took care of him.'

'Last Saturday?'

Lifeblood waved eloquently. 'You know, days of the week, it's all just uptight Western craziness anyway. I mean, like, what's today, anyway? Tuesday or something? You just look outside, it's not raining, sun's out, all that great energy that comes down after the rain. *That's* what today is, not some uptight regimented *name* or something.'

'I think it's Thursday,' Anne said, and signed the book. Lifeblood banged the rubber stamp against the consent form and signed his name below that.

'Great,' Anne said, sliding the consent form back into the tote. She brought out the copy of last Tuesday's paper. Before leaving the office, she had folded the front page so that the headline was hidden.

'Oh, look at this,' she said, pointing to the picture of Ashby and Thompson at the awards dinner. 'There's the guy I work for.'

Lifeblood peered at the picture. 'Yeah, I remember him,' Lifeblood said. 'In a big hurry, you know. Came by at night. I told him, you gotta slow down, man, this kinda scramble just screws up your life, you know?' He tapped one of the faces. 'Slow it down, buddy,' he said to the picture. 'It's gonna get you good, you keep moving that fast.'

Anne looked at his finger. 'That's the guy who had you notarize the Partnership Agreement?'

'No doubt about it,' Lifeblood said. 'He got better after we smoked a bit, but I told him, better relax, belly like that on you, you're gonna strain your heart and your karma.' He shook his head. 'Tried to sell him some EverLife, but he wasn't into it.' He tapped the photograph again and said to it, 'Too bad.' Anne reached down and lifted his finger off Mike Thompson's face.

'Mr. Lifeblood,' she said, 'I think I need to use your phone.'

★   ★   ★

Van Damme, of course, wasn't in, and Anne didn't dare insist that they find him, not with John Lifeblood counting his inventory and, she suspected, listening to

338

every word. She succeeded in leaving a message asking Van Damme to meet her at Growing Light immediately, then held the phone to her ear a while longer, pretending to listen while she thought. Her middle ached again. Could she make a citizen's arrest? If Lifeblood chose to run, getting away from her would be laughably easy. But she didn't dare tell him she wanted him to talk to the cops.

Finally she re-cradled the phone and turned to the notary, stepping back from the desk so that she stood between him and the door.

'Mr. Lifeblood,' she said, 'I'm going to make you a deal.'

'Groovy,' he said. 'You wanna buy some EverLife?'

Anne closed her eyes and sent a brief prayer of thanks heavenward.

'Yes,' she said. 'I really do. And I know that a lot of folk at the office would be interested, too. Besides, I left my checkbook there. If you want to come with me, I can write you a check for the notarization, and maybe for some of the products, too.' She smiled. 'Maybe you'd like to bring a box along?'

'Oh, yeah, that would be really fine,' Lifeblood said. He winnowed through the boxes. 'Yeah, here, introductory packs. You're gonna like these, they got vitamins and skin creams and all kinds of really great junk, you know, I swear they make you younger; you can lose weight, get that skin tone back. You're gonna just love this stuff.'

'I'm sure I am,' Anne said.

'Like, this is karma, pure and simple,' he said. 'Hey, wait, I gotta get my shoes.' He dumped the box and disappeared into the next room. Anne held her breath until he came back, carrying a pair of sandals.

'Like, the EverLife people, they told me, you just gotta want it enough, you know, you just gotta think positive and all this good stuff'll just come your way, and like, man, they were right,' he babbled as he strapped on the sandals. 'Like, I've never really done a presentation before, you know? This'll be my first time, but I've practiced, just like they said. I got it all down.' He lifted the box onto his shoulder and sighed happily. 'Wow, I feel, like, nervous, you know?'

'I'm sure you'll do just fine,' Anne assured him, and followed him out of the house.

24

Lifeblood kept up a steady stream of talk as they walked the quarter mile back to Growing Light. Going past the parking lot, Anne noticed Pete's red pickup blocking Lena's car. Resisting the urge to check the truck's front bumper, she pushed open the front door and led Lifeblood into her office. Pete's space was unoccupied, and she assumed he was closeted with Thompson.

'Listen, I'll get some folks together. You wait right here for a minute, okay?'

She closed the door on him, rushed to Cynthia's office, and explained.

'Brian, you call the sheriff's office and get someone over here immediately,' she said; but Brian, looking out the window, shook his head.

'No need,' he replied. 'If that's not an undercover cop's car, I'll go back to New York and mug tourists. You want me to get Thompson?'

'God, no,' Anne said. 'He wouldn't go with you anywhere. Cynthia, could you — '

'Sure thing,' she said. 'Brian, you get everyone else. Lunch room, right?'

They scattered. Anne went back to her office, slid inside, and closed the door again.

'Wow, they sure don't give you a lot of space, do they?' John Lifeblood said genially. 'I mean, like, this is claustrophobic.' In the tiny room, the smell of marijuana was even more dense, and Anne wondered if he'd smoked a roach in the past few minutes.

'Yeah. Listen, get your box, everyone wants to see you and this place is too small,' she said. Before going out, she checked the hallway in both directions, then led him into the lunch room. He dumped the box on the table and started emptying it, and Anne looked out the window. Van Damme was taking his own sweet time coming into the building, and she cursed under her breath, then noticed a couple of squad cars parked across the street. She bit her lip and helped

Lifeblood unpack his products.

Jimi ambled in first. 'Brian buzzed and said you got something to show us,' he said, puzzled. 'What is this stuff?'

'The greatest twenty-five bucks you'll ever spend,' Lifeblood assured him. 'Listen, man, just hang on until everyone's here, okay? I got a presentation and everything.'

Anne introduced them. 'Mr. Lifeblood notarized the Partnership Agreement,' she said.

'Oh. Yeah,' Jimi said, and folded himself into a chair. He gave Anne a look of immense curiosity. John Lifeblood looked critically at the bottles and boxes he had dumped on the table, then began rearranging them into what Anne supposed was a more pleasing configuration.

Carein, Hankins, and Van Damme entered in a clump. Carein clung to Hankins's arm, and Van Damme came around the table to Anne. Today he carried a briefcase.

'What now?' he demanded.

'Oh, Mr. Van Damme,' she said, 'this is John Lifeblood. He notarized George's partnership agreement. Didn't you, Mr. Lifeblood?'

'Huh? Oh, yeah, sure thing,' he said, still fussing with his boxes.

'So?' the lieutenant demanded.

'He's got some fascinating stuff to sell, and a whole presentation, don't you?' She didn't wait for Lifeblood's response. 'I'm sure it's going to be interesting. Listen, why don't you go stand by the door? You'll, um, have a better view there, won't you?'

Van Damme looked at her as though she had lost her mind, but retreated to the doorway and leaned against the wall near the coffee machine. It hissed at him.

Lena entered, opened her mouth, then saw Van Damme and looked puzzled. He leaned forward to whisper to her, and she turned and helped him hold up the wall. Last of all came Pete, followed by Thompson and Cynthia Baker.

'Now what the hell is this all about?' Thompson demanded, pushing his way into the room; and John Lifeblood looked up at him and smiled radiantly.

'Hey, wow, this is really great,' he said. 'I mean, when I signed on with EverLife, they told me this kinda thing would come down; you know, personal contact and all that. Way to go, George. Way to go.'

'George?' Pete Dixon said.

'Yeah. That's his name, right, man? Remember you came in to have that thing notarized? I didn't know you worked just down the road, man . . . ' As the shocked silence continued, John Lifeblood looked around, confused, and blinked. 'Hey, I'm sorry, guy. You want I should call you Mr. Ashby?'

'The man's insane,' Thompson said.

'The hell I am,' Lifeblood said. 'You come to my house, split a doobie with me, I notarize your stuff, and then you hand me this bull? I don't gotta stand for this.' He started packing up again.

'I'm afraid you do, Mr. Lifeblood,' Van Damme said, moving to block the door. 'Are you sure you can identify this man?'

'Come on, man, do I look like a fool? I share some of my hard-earned dope with someone, you're damned straight I'm gonna remember him. That's George Ashby. I notarized his stupid contract for him.'

Lena started to laugh. 'I knew it,' she

sputtered. 'I told you it was a forgery, Lieutenant, didn't I?'

'Lieutenant?' Lifeblood echoed. 'Ah shit, man.'

'Deep shit,' Brian said with satisfaction, and looked at Thompson. 'Well, *Mr.* Ashby? You gonna tell us about it? And maybe about killing George, too?'

Carein gasped and took a step but Hankins held her back. Pete Dixon leaned forward, glaring.

'You kill George, man?' he said. 'I'll rip your bloody lungs out.'

Thompson feinted toward the door, but Van Damme and Lena blocked it, and Jimi moved over to stand before the window. Pete started around the table toward Thompson.

'I didn't do it,' Thompson shouted, looking at them wildly. 'I didn't kill George; he was already dead when I got in there. But he was going to make me his partner; we'd been talking about it, we got all those contract drafts on his computer. You just ask the Lieutenant, he'll tell you.'

'Yeah.' Van Damme took a sheaf of

papers from his briefcase and handed them to Cynthia. 'The directory listings you wanted,' he said. 'I had to print them myself, but damned if I know what they mean.'

Cynthia flicked through the pages, then grinned. 'Piece of cake, Lieutenant,' she said happily. 'Look at this.' She spread a page against the wall. 'Right here. It says 'Partner', then 'DIR' in angle brackets — that means 'directory', Lieutenant. And following that is the date and time the directory was made. And that date and time, Lieutenant, is eleven fifty on the day George died.'

'After George's death,' Jimi said. He looked at Thompson. 'You little toad,' he said. 'When did you get that thing notarized, anyway?'

'On Saturday,' Thompson insisted, but Lifeblood shook his head.

'No way, man. I mean, names and dates are all uptight crap, but man, you and I got stoned and watched *Monday Night Football*, remember? Raiders and the Broncos, and during the third quarter a ref said offside against Oakland and we cracked up, man. At least I did; you didn't know what the hell was so funny.' He squinted at Thompson. 'Man, that shoulda told me something right there.'

'All right,' Thompson shrieked. 'All right, I forged the signature. It's not that damned hard, anyone can do it. But he was dead when I went in there, so I just got my disk and loaded in the agreements. But I didn't kill him, I swear to God I didn't, he was already dead!'

'Right,' Anne said. 'Then you planted that note in my bag, the one with Ashby's address on it. You faked that faint, too, when we went in and found George's body.'

'I had to,' Thompson said miserably. 'His goddamned hand was pointing at the computer. I had to move it. God, and he was dead and everything. But that's all I did, I swear it.'

'Man,' Pete Dixon said, shaking his head. 'You really jerked me around, and I don't like that, Mike, I don't like that at all. Maybe you didn't kill him, but you ripped him off. You'll fry, Mr. Thompson. You'll fry good.'

'Oh I will, will I?' Thompson retorted. 'And what about you, Pete? What about you and that errand yesterday?'

Pete just sneered. 'You're a goddamned liar,' he said. 'Everybody knows that. Can't believe a goddamned word you say.'

'I wouldn't be too hasty about that,' Van Damme said. 'A mechanic in Petaluma remembers you and your truck, Mr. Dixon. You brought it in around four thirty, said you'd hit your girlfriend's car, wanted him to fix the bumper.' Van Damme stood away from the wall. 'Scrapes looked a lot like what you'd get if you hit another car. Twice, say. On a real rainy, twisty road in Lake Harris County.'

Anne held her breath, waiting, while Pete Dixon glared at the Lieutenant, then turned toward Thompson.

'You set me up, you bastard,' he said. 'You said nobody'd find out. You said by the time the bitch got back to work, everything would blow over. Hell,' he said, shouting now, 'you even gave me the money to get my goddamn truck fixed!'

'Don't let him hurt me!' Thompson shrieked, diving behind Reverend Hankins.

'Keep him away from me!'

'Man, you made your own karma, you gotta sit in it,' Hankins said with distaste, moving himself and Carein away. 'Lieutenant, you gonna get this man outta here? Yeah? Well, take the other one too, his aura's really screwing things up for everybody.'

Van Damme gestured behind his back, and the door filled with uniforms. Thompson refused to let them take him until Pete Dixon was cuffed and Mirandized for attempted vehicular homicide. Then he listened sullenly as Van Damme read him his rights, and let two deputies take him from the room. But he dug in his heels and stopped at the door, glaring over his shoulder.

'You just remember,' he said. 'Whoever killed George Ashby is still out there. Any one of you could be next — and I sure hope you are.'

The deputies led him out. Lifeblood tried to follow but Van Damme caught his arm. 'Not so fast, Mr. Lifeblood.'

'Hey, I didn't do nothing,' Lifeblood protested.

Van Damme smiled. 'Let's see, the Secretary of State's office issued your notary's license. I'm sure they'd like to talk to you about how you used it.'

'Ah, crap,' Lifeblood said as he, too, was cuffed. 'The EverLife people didn't say nothing about this.'

Anne heard a deputy reading rights as Lifeblood was led out. The voices faded, and in the ensuing silence Anne glanced at Carein. Carein looked at her and slumped against Hankins. The reverend put his arm around her, and Anne took a deep breath and reached for Carein's hand.

'Carein?'

Carein looked at her.

'It's about my place on the memo wall,' Anne said. 'When you told Audrey to set it up, it was down near the floor, wasn't it?'

Carein nodded. 'Silly place for it, wasn't it? Then I guess Audrey moved it, and I didn't figure it out. So I put your memo, about Harry I mean, I put it in the old place.' She smiled and patted Anne's cheek. 'So you knew I came back that morning, didn't you? Did you know about Catherine, too?'

Anne nodded.

'I knew you were smart,' Carein said. 'From that very first day, you know, I just knew you were smart. But it's okay, you don't have to, like, do the whole detective bit. It's all over with now anyway.'

'I know,' Anne said with compassion. 'Carein, do you want to tell us why?'

25

'He was mine, you know,' Carein said simply. Hankins handed her a cup of water and she took a sip from it.

The lieutenant cleared his throat. 'Ms. Forest, I'd advise you not to speak without an attorney present.'

'Oh, but I have one,' Carein said, and smiled at him. 'Harry's a lawyer, or he was one, before he decided to help people in a more meaningful way. He's got a license and everything. And Harry says I need to share this, you see. Because otherwise I can't grow.'

'You just tell it your own way,' Hankins told her. He let her go, and she transferred her smile to him, then pulled a chair from the table and sat.

'I was seventeen that year. You know, 1970, living in San Francisco, hanging out on Haight Street, just digging the scene. That's where I met him. George I mean. On Haight Street, outside the

Drug Store. He was handing out flyers, and we just got talking, the way it happened, you remember,' she said to Lena. 'You remember what it was like.'

Lena nodded, staring at Carein.

'So pretty soon I was helping out. George and Lena had this big apartment off Ashbury near the park and we'd all get together and, you know, party all night and all that stuff. It was so, so different from Connecticut, you know, different from everything I ever knew. I mean, free love and acid and talking about how we were going to change the world. It was like wonderland. You remember, Lena, right?'

'Yes,' Lena said. 'Oh yeah, Carein, I remember.'

'George was just like this, this god or something.' Carein closed her eyes. 'He'd just, like, spin like a star, and ideas and poetry and music, they'd all just spark out of him, and we'd sit there and listen and it was like we were listening to the future, you know, like we were listening to life. We'd get together, maybe three people, maybe fifteen, and we'd talk all night, and listen to music, and dance, and get stoned. And get up the next morning and help the Diggers feed people in the Park. It was really fine, for about half a year or so, and then I got pregnant.'

Lena sat down on the table. 'God,' she said. 'We just thought you'd disappeared, or that your folks had stolen you back. God, Carein, I never knew.'

'Oh, I didn't want anybody to know,' Carein said, opening her eyes to stare earnestly at Lena. 'I mean, when I figured it out, I just kinda dropped out, you know? It wasn't anything *you* ever did. And kids, you know, they weren't really part of the equation. That's what George told everybody, remember that? That until the revolution, it was stupid to have kids.' She spread her hands, looking at everybody. 'It was wonderful, it really was, but it wasn't really enlightened. I mean, us, the women, we made the food and served the food and listened and all that, but it's not like we were really supposed to be, you know, equal or anything.'

'Yeah,' Lena said, still looking at

Carein. 'And we went along with it, didn't we? We swallowed the whole line, for a while at least.'

'Yeah, well, by then I was gone,' Carein told her. 'I kinda told George where I'd be, but he never came around looking for me.' She paused and sipped at the water. 'So anyway, I got some money together and went back home, and I had the baby. I mean, there weren't any legal abortions, not back then; and I knew a girl from home, she'd died from one, you know, where you meet some guy in a hotel room and he does something to you and disappears? I mean, me and another friend, we found her; she just died there in that hotel room, all alone.'

Hankins put his hands on her shoulders. 'It's past, Carein. It's all gone past. It's over.'

Carein swallowed and nodded. 'So I didn't want to die that way,' she explained. 'So I had the baby, and he was great. I didn't know he'd be like that, you know? He pulled my whole life together, this whole new little soul. I had the baby and it hurt, then they put him on my belly and, like, the sun came out.' She reached out and grabbed Lena's hand. 'It's just like the sun came out, after all the fog.'

'I nev — ' Lena said, and tried again. 'I never had kids.'

'Yeah,' Carein whispered. 'I know. It's okay.'

Carein had moved herself and the baby to a commune in New England, and supported herself and the child with homemade jewelry that she sold at various fairs and flea markets. The commune folded after a couple of years and she moved on, from one alternative lifestyle to another, from New England into the south and down to the southwest. But it had been a good life, she said, smiling. When her son was sixteen he wanted to leave, to try it on his own. She tried to talk him out of it but he insisted, so he went off to live with some friends. Carein moved with another group of people to Canada, but it was cold up there, and her son was down in southern California and that seemed a very long way away. After three years, this commune, like others, dissolved, and Carein, alone again, felt the need to return to California. An old friend from the sixties told her how to find George, and George, in turn, gave her a job at Growing Light.

'It just seemed like, you know, part of the cycle,' she said to Lena. 'It's just that, well, back then was the best part of my life. And now my boy was gone, for three years he was out of my life, and he was living in some place — it wasn't like where I'd raised him; it sounded, I don't know, dark and, and bad somehow. And I didn't have the vision anymore, I couldn't just reach out and help him, I couldn't talk to him anymore. So I just wanted to go back, go back to the beginning again, and maybe I'd find what I'd lost, find the vision and the energy and the love again. You know?'

Jimi fished a neatly folded handkerchief out of his pocket and handed it to her, and Carein wiped her cheeks. Anne folded her arms against her stomach, feeling the bandages poking through, but she couldn't take her eyes from Carein's earnest, ravaged face.

'But you know, George was different,

Lena. He'd changed. I tried not to see it, I made all kinds of excuses for him; but when he tried to make fire it was just kind of flat, like it was just sounds now, just only sounds. Like he'd forgotten how important words are, and they were just noises to make with your mouth, to make other people do what he wanted. Just only sounds. And I tried to help him work it out, you know, we'd talk and I gave him books and crystals, and made teas and all sorts of stuff, and he'd laugh and take them, but he'd never, you know, follow through. It was like it was all some game to him, where he knew the rules and nobody else did but you had to play by them anyway.'

She looked at Lena anxiously. 'George lied, Lena. He lied about everything.'

'I know,' Lena said. 'I know.'

Carein was quiet for a minute then, and Van Damme said, 'Is that all, Ms. Forest?'

She shook her head. 'No. No, it's not. My boy, he had some problems with his friends, so he came out here. And I knew about George then, but I thought I could bring him back. It's like, he brought me alive all those years ago, and now maybe the reason I was here was to give it back, to help him the way he'd helped me. So I thought it would be okay, I thought maybe I could help him, that he'd be better being with me, and that somehow I could help George come back too. So I let him come up to be here. I let him, I asked him.' She shook her head, ignoring the tears. 'I asked him to come home. And George gave him a job, and, you know, for a while it was working out okay. I mean, I didn't tell anybody that Max was my boy, 'cause he wanted to make it for himself, and I could understand that; that was all right.'

She stopped for a moment and closed her eyes again, and nobody spoke.

'Breathe deep,' Hankins whispered. 'All the way. Clear it all out, honey; you're almost there.'

Carein filled her lungs and slowly released the breath, while Hankins kneaded her shoulders.

'I'm sorry,' she said after a while. 'This is kinda the hard part. You know, all last week George was really on Max's case, he really hurt him bad; and Max wanted to take off, he wanted to leave me again and he was so frail, you know, it's like anything could knock him over, knock him out. I couldn't lose him, not again. So I told him. About George.' She paused again. 'He seemed to take it okay, you know, he really seemed to go with it; and then he didn't come home Sunday night, not at all. And I called everyone he knew, and I drove all over the place. That's why I was in late on Monday; I was just, like, driving all night trying to find him. And I never did.'

'Carein,' Anne said, 'what happened Monday morning?'

Carein took another cleansing breath. 'Monday, after you and George came in, and after Lena left, I tried to talk to him, because I knew Max had been up there on Sunday night. George didn't want to talk about it; he said I was not, you know, forwarding the process by getting uptight about Max. He just wouldn't listen to me. So I went home, to get the knife.' She looked at Anne. 'He gave it to me, you know. Back then. The knife with Catherine on it.'

Anne nodded. 'You tried to pawn it in San Francisco, didn't you?'

Carein smiled. 'Yeah, but the guy wanted to buy it, and I just couldn't, you know, it was all I had of George, of that year. I used it to cut Max's cord when he was born. And I thought maybe if George saw it, and I told him about Max, then he'd understand, you know; he'd love Max the way I did.'

She breathed deeply again and took another sip of water. 'So I went home and got it out, and I brought it back. I guess Audrey was in the bathroom or something, so I just went into George's office. And he said all that garbage again, you know, about self-acceptance and havingness and all that, all those noises he didn't believe. And I got mad and said he didn't believe any of it, that he just used it to jerk people around.' She looked up, wide-eyed. 'And you know what he did? He laughed and said I was right. And then he told me about seeing Max that night, and what he tried to do, and how Max cried and ran away. And that's when I showed him the knife, and told him that

363

Max was his son. 'Cause you know, all that free love; but it was only George, just only George for me. Always just only George.'

Lena gasped and held herself, staring at Carein. Jimi came around the table and knelt to hold Lena tight.

'You know what he said?' Carein's voice broke. 'You know what he told me?'

Hankins tightened his grip on her shoulders.

'He said he didn't care,' Carein said. 'He said he didn't *care*. He said that Max was my sickness, not his. And he laughed at me, and he turned around and walked away, and I just, I just, I couldn't do anything else, you see? It's like there was nothing else left to do.' She turned in the chair and clung to Hankins, sobbing. He held her and looked over her shoulder at Van Damme.

'She didn't know she'd killed him,' he said. 'She told me she just hit him and ran, because now she knew that Max was hurting. But she didn't mean to kill him, Lieutenant. He just — he just died.'

Carein shook her head against Hankins's

belly and said something that nobody could hear. Then she straightened up and said it again.

'I didn't know until I came back, and I came back because I hoped Max had come in, or someone had heard from him. But then George was dead, and Max might be still out there, might still be needing me.' She turned to Van Damme. 'I didn't know he was dead,' she said raggedly. 'I didn't know my little boy was dead.'

Anne closed her eyes and put her face against the wall. In the distance a siren wailed. For a moment the lunch room was silent, then Lieutenant Van Damme did a strange and unexpected thing. He got on his knees before Carein Forest and took her hands.

'Ms. Forest,' he said, 'you know I have to take you in.'

'Oh, yes,' she said. 'Don't feel bad about it. It's your job, Lieutenant. You can handcuff me if you like.'

'I don't think that will be necessary,' Van Damme said as Lena stood away from Jimi's arms and came around the table. The siren came closer.

'Lieutenant, listen,' Lena said, coming around the table to stand beside Carein. 'Any legal fees she needs, I'm gonna pay them. And you make sure they treat her right, got that straight?'

'Got what straight?' Sheriff Jackson demanded, shoving his way into the lunchroom. 'I heard on the radio you're transporting prisoners from here, Van Damme. You forgotten who's sheriff in this county? Just what the hell are you trying to prove behind my back?'

Van Damme looked startled, but Cynthia crowed and delved into her pocket.

'Sheriff Jackson,' she said, favoring him with a grin. 'Just the man I wanted to see. I've got a petition here you might want to sign.'

Anne looked at Jackson's apoplectic face, and regardless of the ache in her midriff, started to laugh.

*   *   *

'I'm closing the whole thing down,' Lena said much later. 'But you can stay on, if you like.' The wall clock read four-thirty

366

and winter darkness was starting to fall.

Anne glanced at Jimi, Cynthia, and Brian and said, 'Lena, that doesn't make a whole lot of sense.'

Lena smiled. 'Yes it does. Growing Light, all that aura stuff and past lives decoders and astrology modules, they were never part of what I had in mind. I'm closing it down. I'm going to re-engineer the thing from the ground up, make it into something that's useful in the real world. And I want to do the same with the company, too. Get out of this building — hell, get out of Melville entirely. Hire some competent people, maybe even my original staff, if I can find them and they want to come back. And you four, if you want to stay on.'

'Not me,' Brian said after a moment. 'Nothing personal, Lena, but I've had enough of country living. I'm headed for Seattle.'

She shrugged. 'I looked at your marketing plans. They're good, Stein. If you change your mind, let me know.' She looked around the lunch table. 'What about the rest of you?'

Jimi leaned back, letting his chair rock on its rear legs. 'No more aura detectors?' he said. Lena shook her head. 'All of it gone?'

'All of it,' Lena said. 'We keep the moisture and temperature sensors, but they'll need work. They were supposed to be near the heart of the system, but I think they just got pushed aside to make way for all the nonsense George stuck in. No, they're out.'

Jimi tapped his soldering pencil against his lip. 'I'll think about it,' he said.

'How about the company?' Cynthia said. 'You know, structure and responsibility and all that stuff George used to spout.'

'It's very simple,' Lena said, lacing her fingers together. 'I'm the boss. If Anne stays, she's head of tech writing and she can hire subcontractors or whatever she needs, but she runs that department. We'll still need site technicians, customer service people, and I'm hoping you'll agree to head that. I don't want a big company here, and I do want lots of talk, lots of ideas.' She spread her hands. 'Listen, at first we're going to be making this up as we go along, finding out how to make the company work better, how to make people work together. I'd feel a lot better if I didn't have to do it alone.' She looked across the table at Anne. 'How about you?' Lena said. 'You've had it pretty tough here. I'd like you to stay on, but if you don't feel you can, I'll understand.'

Anne sighed and touched the neck brace with her fingertips. 'I don't know, Lena. I need the job, but . . . ' She sighed again. 'How do I know you're not going to, to change somehow? That you're not going to become a lunatic like Mike, or George?'

Lena put her head in her hands and started laughing. Startled, the others looked at each other uneasily.

'Oh lord,' Lena said at last, catching her breath. 'Anne, I can't guarantee you a single damned thing. But I will say your chances with me are just about the same as anywhere else. And at least,' she said, still grinning, 'with me, you'll know what to look out for.'

Anne looked at her for a moment, then stuck her hand across the table. 'Okay,' she said. 'Sign me on.'

'Yeah, me too,' Cynthia said, and Jimi nodded.

Brian shook his head. 'You're all nuts,' he said. 'Lena, when do you need a decision?'

'By tomorrow,' she said. 'That's when I close the door on Growing Light permanently. We'll need to scout out a location in Santa Bolsas, or even in Inez, get all this stuff moved, figure out what to do with the junk hardware we're not keeping, send out notices to the poor suckers who bought the damned thing and,' she said, taking a deep breath, 'and we've gotta find another name for this company.'

Brian's eyes gleamed and he opened his mouth.

'And the first person,' Lena said, 'who suggests anything like Declining Murk is out on his New York ass.'

Brian shrugged, grinning, and Van Damme appeared at the door. 'Ms. Munro?' he said.

'Ah, jeez,' Cynthia said with disgust. 'Not again.'

To Anne's amazement, Van Damme reddened.

'Ah, no, nothing like that,' he said, and turned to Anne. 'I just, ah, thought that since you still can't drive, and I, ah, live in Santa Bolsas anyway that, ah, you might want a lift home?'

Anne's face warmed, and Lena laughed.

'Of course she would, Lieutenant,' Lena said, pushing her chair back and standing. 'We're always pleased to help the local constabulary, aren't we, Ms. Munro? Well, what are you waiting for? Out, woman! I'll see you tomorrow.'

Van Damme offered his arm. Anne glared at her colleagues' grins and allowed him to usher her out of the building and into his plain gray sedan.

Once in the car and belted, Van Damme looked at her sideways. 'I took the liberty of calling Mr. Neilsen and asking him to watch your little boy for you,' he said to the steering wheel.

Anne didn't reply.

'I thought,' Van Damme continued after a moment, 'that perhaps we could stop at Pellonari's in Inez for a bite to eat.'

Anne remained silent. Van Damme

took a deep breath.

'And, ah, discuss the case,' he finished.

Anne and her neck brace turned toward him, and she raised a finger. 'I gave up a ride in Jeremiah Hudson for this,' she said. 'If we are going to be seen together in public, you are going to have to drive something more interesting than a plain gray Ford with 'undercover' written all over it.'

Van Damme smiled. 'I've got a 1974 Dodge Custom at home,' he said. 'Blue and white two-tone, slant-six engine. Would that do?'

Anne considered this for a moment, then sat back.

'Lieutenant,' she said in her best Millie Beckson tone of voice, 'drive on.'

We do hope that you have enjoyed reading this large print book.

Did you know that all of our titles are available for purchase?

We publish a wide range of high quality large print books including:
Romances, Mysteries, Classics
General Fiction
Non Fiction and Westerns

Special interest titles available in large print are:
The Little Oxford Dictionary
Music Book, Song Book
Hymn Book, Service Book

Also available from us courtesy of Oxford University Press:
Young Readers' Dictionary
(large print edition)
Young Readers' Thesaurus
(large print edition)

For further information or a free brochure, please contact us at:
Ulverscroft Large Print Books Ltd.,
The Green, Bradgate Road, Anstey,
Leicester, LE7 7FU, England.
Tel: (00 44) **0116 236 4325**
Fax: (00 44) **0116 234 0205**

SHERLOCK HOLMES: JOURNEYS BY TRAIN

N. M. Scott

In his capacity as a consulting detective, Sherlock Holmes and his companion Dr Watson invariably find themselves travelling a good deal by train, and it is this which links the seemingly disparate events in one of the most fraught episodes in Holmes's career. A 'wheelchair mob' plans a series of daring gem heists, and ghosts are allegedly committing theft! Amid murder, poisoning and séances, someone is also threatening the faithful landlady, Mrs Hudson. Can Holmes get to the bottom of the mystery and bring the criminals to justice?